**Reviewers love *New York Times* bestselling author
SUSAN ANDERSEN**

"A hot, sexy, yet touching story."
—*Kirkus Reviews* on *Some Like It Hot*

"This warm summer contemporary melts hearts with the
simultaneous blossoming of familial and romantic love."
—*Publishers Weekly* on *That Thing Called Love*

"A smart, arousing, spirited escapade
that is graced with a gentle mystery, a vulnerable,
resilient heroine, and a worthy, wounded hero and served up
with empathy and a humorous flair."
—*Library Journal* on *Burning Up*

"This start of Andersen's new series has fun and interesting
characters, solid action and a hot and sexy romance."
—*RT Book Reviews* on *Cutting Loose*

"Snappy and sexy… Upbeat and fun, with a touch of danger
and passion, this is a great summer read."
—*RT Book Reviews* on *Coming Undone*

"Lovers of romance, passion and laughs
should go all in for this one."
—*Publishers Weekly* on *Just for Kicks*

"Andersen again injects magic into a story that would be
clichéd in another's hands, delivering warm, vulnerable
characters in a touching yet suspenseful read."
—*Publishers Weekly* on *Skintight,* starred review

"A classic plotline receives a fresh, fun treatment….
Well-developed secondary characters add depth to this zesty
novel, placing it a level beyond most of its competition."
—*Publishers Weekly* on *Hot & Bothered*

**Also available from
Susan Andersen
and Harlequin HQN**

Susan Andersen

No Strings Attached

HARLEQUIN® HQN™

Recycling programs
for this product may
not exist in your area.

ISBN-13: 978-0-373-77887-4

NO STRINGS ATTACHED

Copyright © 2014 by Susan Andersen

Printed in U.S.A.

www.Harlequin.com

This is dedicated to girls who wear glasses,
and to all the readers who've taken the time
to leave reviews and let me know you enjoy my work.
Thank you!

PROLOGUE

Seven years ago. Andros Island, Bahamas

A HOT, MOIST BREEZE, perfumed by the sea and the faintest exotic whiff of an unidentifiable flower, wafted through the hut's open window just as Tasha Riordan collapsed atop Diego. Her nose squashed into the damp curve where his neck flowed into a muscular shoulder, and as she silently breathed in his salty, slightly spicy scent, it occurred to her she hadn't once asked what his last name was during the thirtysomething hours since they'd met. Waiting for her heart to cease its thunderous reggae beat, however, she didn't dwell too closely on that just-met-yesterday thing.

Okay, you would think, given she'd spent a good part of her life keeping her chin up while living her mother's reputation down, that she'd sort of *welcome* a little soul-searching. After all, diving into bed with a virtual stranger was a big departure for her.

A big, *big* departure. Huge. And she ought to be a little concerned about it, right?

Tough-skinned fingertips ran down her naked spine, sparking back to life nerve endings that by rights should have been incinerated to cold, dead ash. "You okay, *cariño?*" Diego asked, his voice a rumbling vibration beneath the ear she had pressed to his throat.

And just like that, her half-assed inclination to whip herself into a lather of self-recrimination melted away as her lips curved into a little smile against his skin. She didn't know what it was about this guy, but one thing was for certain: he possessed an undeniable magic. In spades. From the instant he'd approached her on the beach yesterday morning, he'd kept her pretty much swept off her feet.

That was no small accomplishment. Ask anyone back home in Razor Bay, and damn few would hesitate to tell you—Tasha Riordan's feet were *always* firmly, pragmatically planted on the ground.

But she merely murmured, "Oh, yeah" and kept her heartfelt *And then some* to herself.

This was probably par for the course for him. God knew he made *her* feel things she'd never felt before, and she was usually a hard sell. She could only imagine how many women already geared up for a vacation lover had thrown their room keys at him. The fact that she'd managed to keep her undies on until today was downright brag-worthy. She'd been tempted to shed them from the instant she'd laid eyes on him.

And considering the orgasm he'd just given her, perhaps she should have. It had been the most phenomenal, amazing one of her life.

She swallowed a snort. *Like you've had so many to compare it to.* But she shrugged the thought aside as unimportant. Yeah, yeah, she hadn't experienced a plethora of non-self-induced climaxes in her twenty-two years. Still, neither was she a virgin, so she'd certainly had enough to know she'd never felt anything close to *this*. "How are *you?*" she asked softly.

He went so still she thought he'd suddenly quit breathing. She found herself doing the same. As several heartbeats passed in silence, her euphoria leaked away. *Oh, God,* she thought. *Like* you *could rock his world.* A person only had to look at Diego to understand his experience was galaxies beyond her own.

Then his hands tightened against her back, and he said in a low, gritty voice, "You wanna know how *I* am?" An exhalation of amusement, which just perhaps wasn't amusement at all, huffed out of his lungs. "I'm so blown away it's not even funny."

"No," she said on a disbelieving laugh, pushing up to look down at him. She had no illusions about herself. She was tall and skinny and had decent boobs, but hips and a booty that could belong to a twelve-year-old boy. She knew men found her reasonably attractive, but in no man's universe was she close to being in this guy's league.

Her mass of strawberry-blond curls, by now scary-crazy-frizzy from air that was still humid from an earlier, short-lived downpour—not to mention Diego's demanding hands tangling in them—fell forward to intertwine with his sleeker black curls. She looked down at her hands where they splayed against the ebony fan of hair on his deep golden-brown chest. After nine days in the tropics, her skin was the tannest it had ever been. Unfortunately, all that meant was that, instead of its usual 2-percent-milk hue, it was the color of anemic toast.

Diego brought both hands up to smooth her hair away from her face, gathering it into a fat ponytail at the base of her skull. Holding it in one fist, he looked into her eyes, and his own were free of laughter for perhaps the first time since he'd sauntered up to where she'd been dipping her toes in the surf and introduced himself. "Yes," he refuted, as the fingertips of his free hand brushed up and down the side of her throat. His thumb left a streak of fire in its wake as it briefly swept her jawline. "You blew me right out of the ballpark." His full mouth developed a wry slant, and his broad shoulders performed a minute shrug against blindingly white sheets. "I didn't see that coming."

It was probably a line, but if so, it was a good one. Lord knew it was working on her—her heart felt gooey as a chocolate truffle left out on a hot tropic night.

Diego stared up at her. "I love your mouth." His voice was rough, his dark eyes hot, and Tasha's heart pounded as he crunched up from six-pack abs with the clear intention of kissing her. Before he could, however, his cell phone rang.

He swore and glanced at the nightstand where it rested. Then swore again.

"I'm sorry," he said, turning his attention back to her. "I have to get this." He gently levered her off of him and onto the middle of the mattress. Then in one smooth, unbroken movement, he pushed to his feet, swept the phone off the stand and, thumbing the green button, brought it to his ear. "Yeah," he said. "This better be important."

Watching him, Tasha realized he didn't look charming in that moment. He looked dangerous: big and dark and unselfconsciously naked, his eyes hard and his mouth grim. Untangling the sheet from the bed, she pulled it up, covering herself and tucking it under her armpits. She glanced at her watch.

Oh, God. She needed to think about getting dressed if she wanted to catch the last plane back to Nassau.

Dragging the sheet with her, she climbed off the bed. Suddenly, what had seemed so daring and exciting several hours ago—impulsively agreeing to accompany Diego to the big island of Andros—felt reckless and so not smart. She began gathering her scattered clothing.

She slid into her panties, pulled on her sundress and was digging through her purse in search of something to pin her hair up with when warm, hard arms slid around her waist and pulled her back against a warmer, even harder chest. "Heyyyy." Diego hunched to breathe in her ear. He'd pulled on the shorts and muscle tee he'd worn earlier. "What are you doing?"

It was hard to think with his heat and scent and *feel* all around her, and she cleared her throat. "My plane leaves in an hour and a half. I need to get to the airport."

"Stay here with me another night. I'm supposed to be on vacation but my boss tracked me down and I have to go out for a bit to talk to him. But I'll only be gone an hour, tops, and then we can have the rest of the night."

"Oh." Temptation beckoned, and for a minute she thought she could give in to it. Then reason and her usual pragmatism resurfaced. She pulled her e-ticket out of her purse and wagged it in front of their faces. "I don't think so. I have a reservation."

He kissed the side of her neck. "I'd really, really like to spend the rest of the night with you," he murmured in that low, deep voice of his. "I'll get you back to Nassau tomorrow, I promise, even if I have to charter a seaplane." He moved his lips to the vulnerable hollow behind her ear.

And both Tasha's reservations and her spine melted. "Well, maaaaybe that would be okay."

"That's what I like to hear." He swung her around to face him and kissed her long and hot and deep. Her purse fell from nerveless fingers, and the next time she managed to locate two semi-functioning brain cells to rub together, Diego was pushing off of her as she once more lay flat on her back on the bed.

"I'm sorry," he said, looking down at her. "I don't like to leave either of us hanging this way, but my boss is an impatient sonuvabitch, and I told him I'd meet him in—" he looked at his watch "—shit, two minutes." He bent down and planted another fast, hard kiss on her lips before straightening again. "I'll be back just as soon as I can, okay?"

She nodded; he groaned. Then with a muttered "I will not kiss her again. I will not kiss her," he turned on his heel and strode from the hut.

She'd barely dragged herself upright, repaired her lipstick and finally located a couple of clips to deal with her hair when the pounding on the door of the little hotel hut commenced. Grinning, she whirled from the mirror and raced on bare feet to open the door. "Hah! Forgot your key, didja?"

But it wasn't Diego on the lanai. Several dark-skinned men in the light blue uniform shirts and black berets of the Royal Bahamian police pushed past her into the one-room hut. Not one of them offered her the usual friendly smiles she'd become accustomed to seeing since her arrival in the islands. These men, wrapped in Kevlar vests, were grim-eyed and grimmer-mouthed.

"What's going on?" she demanded, only to find herself herded to a chair, where all she could see was the red tuxedo stripe that ran up the leg of the officer's black slacks as he and the curve of the hut blocked her view of most of the activity going on around her.

But she could hear them dragging the mattress from the bed and opening and slamming drawers. Then suddenly the officer in front of her stepped aside, and an older man in a khaki shirt stood in his place, one hand folded at the small of his back, the other hanging loose at his side, a black dress hat with a red band and white bill tucked under his arm.

"I am Inspector Rolle of the DEU," he said in a deep, melodious voice.

"DEU?" she squeaked. "What's that?"

"Drug Enforcement Unit. Your name, please?"

"Tasha." She swallowed, wondering what the hell was going on. It couldn't have anything to do with Diego…could it? "Tasha Riordan."

"Where is your accomplice, Ms. Riordan?"

Panic punched harder. Oh, God, oh, God, this was

so not good. "Accomplice to what? I don't *have* an accomplice!"

"This is your room?"

"No. No, I'm a guest."

"A guest of whom?" he demanded sternly.

"Diego…?" She stumbled to a halt, and the austere-faced inspector raised bushy brows at her.

"I never actually got his last name," she stammered. "I know that sounds—" Then her brain finally kicked in. "It should be on the registration, though. Ask the man who checked us in."

Inspector Rolle pointed to an officer, who strode briskly from the hut. Then they sat in nerve-twanging silence, during which she could only conclude that Diego had done something horrible, criminal…unforgivable. Something he'd skated from free and clear—while leaving her holding the bag.

When the officer returned, he came straight over to the inspector, murmured something, then moved a discreet distance away. The inspector turned to her.

"The man who checked you in said the room was paid for in cash. He described you quite accurately, Ms. Riordan, but has no recollection of this Diego."

"*No!* That's not true. I didn't even go up to the counter with Diego. I stayed on the deck while he checked us in. Take fingerprints or something! I wasn't anywhere *near* the check-in desk!"

He studied her for a moment before shrugging. "That may turn out to be true—"

"It *is* true!"

"But what we have here—" he brought his hand out

from behind his back and dropped a large ziplock bag filled with what looked like powdered sugar, but which she had a sick feeling was not, on the little table next to her elbow, where it settled with a heavy thud "—is this kilo of heroin—and you. No mystery man named Diego. Just you. So, Tasha Riordan, you are under arrest for possession with intent to sell."

CHAPTER ONE

Present day

"CRAP," TASHA WHISPERED as she pulled up behind the other cars in Max's driveway. She was beyond late.

And this comes as a big surprise to you? her inner smart-ass demanded.

Well, no. But not seeing the men hanging out on the porch, grilling up a storm as usual, and knowing they likely weren't out back, either, since it had been raining off and on all day, just drove the truth of her tardiness home. Because that could mean only one thing, couldn't it? Everyone was either in the midst of dinner or—an even worse possibility—were already cleaning up.

She climbed out of the car and went around to the trunk to haul out her contributions to Harper's mom's going-away party. Dammit, not only had she not meant to be so late, she'd fully intended to get here early to help with the preparations. She certainly hadn't counted on the new man she'd hired for her pizzeria turning out to be a lush. A freaking on-the-*job* lush.

You had to appreciate the irony here. She'd thought she had it all figured out. With the drop in business now that Labor Day was behind them and most of the tourists gone, her big plan had been to hire another cook to work part-time. She really could have used help with the summer rush this year, yet with it over, they were spared the crazy thrown-in-the-deep-end, sink-or-swim pressure. Now the new hire could take his time getting up to speed, and she'd add to his hours as he progressed. Stress-free had been her aim, the end goal to be sitting pretty by the time next summer's rush began.

She snorted. In theory it was such a lovely, proactive idea and one that should eventually provide her some honest-to-God days off. And who knew, maybe it'd even give her a shot at an actual life. That was certainly something she'd had damn little of this summer. Once she got accustomed to the luxury of occasional free days, she might go totally hog wild and build her way up to treating herself to an actual vacation.

Okay, so the mere idea made her heart pound with anxiety and left a coppery taste in her mouth. But wasn't it way past time she got over that?

Not that it mattered now. At this point the question was purely rhetorical. Her new cook, who had interviewed brilliantly, had in all likelihood already been drunk when he'd shown up for work. And if he *hadn't* arrived with a good head start down Knee-walking Avenue, he'd definitely been fall-on-his-face hammered by the time she'd thrown his sorry ass out of Bella T's. On her own house wine, no less, which just added an abundance of salt to the wound.

But the final straw, what truly and royally most pissed her off, was the way the bastard had tried to blame the wine theft on Jeremy, the Cedar Village boy who'd started bussing for her just the other week. The Village was a group home outside of town that helped troubled boys get their lives together, which was precisely what Jeremy was doing. The last thing he needed was for some ass to come along and falsely accuse him of larceny.

She climbed the porch steps but stopped before she reached the door. Setting down her goodies, she did her best to brush lint off her shorts, then reached into her purse for her lipstick.

One of the first things she'd noticed about Harper when the elegant mixed-race woman had come to Razor Bay was that, no matter what the occasion, she was always dressed perfectly for it. And clearly her mad style skills were directly inherited from Gina, because that went double for Harper's sophisticated mother.

She, on the other hand, had been so rattled by the time she'd gotten the drunk cook out of Bella T's, locked up and run upstairs to change that she'd pretty much grabbed the first thing to come to hand. That had turned out to be this linty pair of black walking shorts and—more fortunately—one of her nicer tank tops in a rich blue that almost, if not quite, gave her more-gray-than-blue eyes a hint more blue. After topping it with her little black cardigan and grabbing the foodstuffs she'd put together for the party, she'd dashed back out again.

Without a speck of makeup on, aside from the mascara she'd applied this morning so people would know she really did have eyelashes—even if they were so pale one might be excused for thinking otherwise.

She swiped on some lipstick, knocked on the door and let herself in. "Hey," she called out over the laughter and voices coming from near Max's unfinished kitchen. "Sorry I'm so late. But I brought a couple bottles of red to make up for it. And some homemade guacamole and veggie-tray fixings."

She strode in sight of the long table full of people and spotted her bestie, Jenny, first, sitting next to Jake. "Hey, girlie," she said, then greeted the Damoths and Mary-Margaret, who headed the Village, and their hosts Max and Harper and Harper's mom. But she stopped dead in full-out shock as her eyes met the velvety dark gaze of a golden-skinned, chiseled-faced man. Images of a younger face flashed across her mind's screen with lightning speed even as the heat of remembered kisses, caresses, sizzled through her veins, and she blinked, certain she was seeing things.

But, no. Dear God. It wasn't, *shouldn't* be possible, but it really was Diego NoLastName, the rat bastard who'd landed her in a Bahamian jail cell back when she was younger and stupider—or at least stupidly naive—and the last person she'd ever expected to see again. Yet there he sat at Max and Harper's table, all black hair, black eyes and dark stubble, looking muscular, vital and bigger than life.

Her brain began buzzing with the staticky sound of a radio dialed half a notch off its station, and her hand went lax. The reusable cloth bag she'd stuffed full of wine and party food dropped to the floor, then tipped on its side.

She barely noticed when its contents scattered in all directions.

HOLY SHIT. THE SCENE unfolding around him went into slo-mo, and Luc Bradshaw came half out of his chair along with every other person around the table. Everyone seemed to be exclaiming and generally making a commotion in their desire to help the long-legged woman who'd stooped to gather the bottles of wine and plastic containers that rolled and skittered across the floor.

To him it was muffled white noise. He stared down at her bent head and unconsciously rubbed his diaphragm over the lower lobe of his left lung. When had all the air in here turned the consistency of Jell-O?

Jesus. It was Tasha.

Like he hadn't known that the instant she'd blown into the room. Still, how many times this week had Jenny, his newly discovered half brother Jake's fiancée, mentioned her BFF Tasha? His damn heart had seized a little every time he'd heard the name, even knowing Jenny was talking about someone other than the Tasha he'd known. It wasn't until maybe two hours ago that he'd finally reached the point where it *didn't* start up a chain reaction in his chest. So you'd have to excuse the hell out of him if for a second there he'd actually believed he was imagining things. Because what were the odds?

Damn good, it turned out. For this was *his* Tasha. Of all the women in his past he would have been perfectly content to see disappear without a trace, she had never been among their ranks.

He watched her vivid blue tank top beneath the cropped hem of a little sweater pull free from her shorts' waistband, exposing a slice of pale satiny skin as, sitting on her heels, she stretched to grab one of the runaway bottles. Then he gave her a comprehensive survey from head to toe, concentrating for a moment on her round rump. She was quite a bit more...womanly now than the barely legal girl he remembered.

He swallowed a snort. Well, big surprise; it had been seven years since he'd seen her. So, yeah, she had a little more curve to her. But she still had no hips, and by no stretch of the imagination would anyone call her voluptuous.

Those riotous curls of hers were different, too: more sleekly defined than he recalled. But her long-lidded pale blue-gray eyes and that pillowy mouth with its fuller upper lip hadn't changed a bit.

So screw the minor differences. She could have grown a mustache, sprouted a hairy mole and packed fifty pounds on her long frame, and he would still know her anywhere. He hadn't the slightest doubt in his mind that this was the girl he'd spent two days and one memorable night with in the Bahamas.

"Tash!" Jenny moved to squat alongside the tall strawberry blonde, and it was as if the speed and sound of a movie had been switched back on. "Are you okay?"

Strawberry blond. He'd discovered after his night with her that that was what people called the pale redgold color of her hair. Staring at her, he felt his entire face light up with a delighted smile.

It died an abrupt death when she suddenly raised her gaze and looked straight at him. His entire body recoiled as if a fireball were hurtling straight toward his head, and he dropped back into his seat. Because those eyes, that *expression*.

If looks could kill, he'd be sliced and diced into tiny bite-sized bits of steak tartare. *What the fuck?*

She glanced back at Jenny and apparently didn't level that scary look on her as well, because there was no recoiling on Jenny's part.

"No," Tasha said in answer to the *are you okay?* question as she handed the little brunette first one wine bottle, then another. She must have gathered the rest of the containers as well, for she rose to her feet and extended the cloth sack to Gina, an elegant, slightly darker version of her daughter, Harper, who was Luc's other half brother Max's woman.

Christ. All these relationships were making his head hurt.

"I'm so sorry," Tasha said as the older woman accepted the bag. "I hate the thought of both you going back to Winston-Salem and me missing your party, but I don't feel so hot."

"Yes, you look quite pale, dear," Gina agreed, reaching out to give Tasha's forearm a soothing rub. "You go home and go to bed. Hopefully you can sleep off whatever this bug is."

"It's not the flu, but *bug* sure seems like an appropriate word for it." Tasha shot him another lightning-fast malevolent glare, then said a touch grimly to the older woman, "I suddenly feel like a hairy, nasty spider is crawling up my spine. I haven't felt this awful in almost a decade, and what I'd *like* to do is shoot the bastard between his beady little eyes."

Twisting to set the wine on the table, Jenny narrowed a thoughtful gaze on Luc, then turned back to study Tasha for a second. "Poor baby. You want me to drive you home? Jake can bring your car back in the morning."

Luc watched a look perilously close to panic flash across Tasha's face. Or maybe he only thought that was what he'd seen, because when he blinked, she appeared perfectly calm.

Tasha patted Jenny's hand. "No, I'm fine to drive. I've just been burning my candle at both ends since tourist season started, and I guess it's finally caught up with me. I desperately need some sleep."

"Good thing you've got an extra helper in the works," Jenny said.

An edgy laugh escaped Tasha. "Ah, yeah, about that. It turns out that's not going to happen." She suddenly seemed ready to wilt as she shoveled long, pale fingers through her hair. "I'll tell you about it tomorrow." She looked away from the little brunette to the rest of the company gathered around the table.

Well, except for him. Now that she'd finished eviscerating him with her death-ray stare, she evidently had no desire to even glance his way again.

"I'm sorry for the drama," she said to the group at large, then focused her attention on Gina once more, bestowing on her the sweet, generous smile that had been branded on Luc's brain for seven long years. "Have a safe journey home," she said, giving the other woman a hug. When she pulled back, she gazed at Gina with warm-eyed affection. "I've just loved getting to know you. I really hope you'll come back soon."

"Oh, I intend to, darling," Gina said. "My favorite daughter lives here now."

"Uh, Mom?" Harper said dryly. "I'm your only daughter."

Gina gave an elegant shrug. "But you're still my one and only Baby Girl."

Harper's olive-green irises all but disappeared behind the lashes-fringed crescents her eyes became as she grinned. "That's true."

Tasha exchanged a few more pleasantries with the guests. Then between one moment and the next, she'd said her goodbyes, strode out through the kitchen and was gone.

Luc pushed back from the table and rose to his feet. "Okay if I grab myself a beer?" he asked Max.

"Help yourself," his half brother invited even as Harper said, "Here, let me get it for you" and started to rise to her feet.

No! his mind snarled. But he hadn't spent more than a decade in deep cover for the DEA for nothing. He flashed her the friendly charmer's smile that years of practice had rendered second nature and merely said, "Please, Harper, you don't need to wait on me."

"Yeah, Harper," Jake said. "He's family. Which means he can do the dishes, too."

"Or at least fetch my own drink. Anyone else want anything while I'm in there?"

No takers chimed in, and he left the room with an unhurried stride that nevertheless ate up the distance between the table and the back door. Silently letting himself out, he spotted Tasha heading toward the end of the attached garage, with the obvious intention of making a beeline for the parking apron around front. Clouds the color of a day-old bruise hung low in the sky, but for the moment at least, it was dry, and ignoring the few back steps, he dropped directly to the lawn, landing lightly on the balls of his feet.

He could move fast and silent as ground fog when the need arose, and he came up on Tasha's flank just as she rounded the end of the garage. He moved into its shadow one step behind her and reached out, his fingertips brushing her arm. "Hey, Tasha, wait—"

With a gasp, she whipped around. Wild panic flared in her clear gray eyes, and watching her suck in a breath and open her lips, Luc knew she was about one second away from screaming down the house. Snaking a hand around her nape, he clamped his free palm over her mouth to keep her from cutting loose with a screech that would bring everyone inside stampeding to her rescue.

Not that there was anything she needed rescuing from—Jesus, he would never *hurt* her. All the same, he really didn't want his deputy sheriff half brother thundering down on him. He didn't doubt for an instant that if Max heard a woman scream, he would be out here in a red-hot hurry, his big-ass service pistol drawn.

"I'm sorry," he said in the most soothing, nonthreatening voice he could summon. Her lips were soft and her skin warm beneath his hands.

He shoved the tactile sensations into a far corner of his mind where they could just wait to be examined when his concentration wasn't demanded elsewhere. "I didn't mean to scare you—I just want to talk to you for a minute. I'm going to let go of you now, okay?"

He obviously didn't follow through with the promised action quickly enough to suit her, for she narrowed her eyes at him as if to say, *Then get on with it!* Wondering if they'd be right back where they started, he gave her a hard-eyed stare back. "And you won't scream, either, am I right?" It was a command, not a question, and he stared into those crystalline eyes without blinking.

She hesitated a second, then dipped her chin in a slight nod.

Slowly, he released his light grip on the back of her neck and lifted his hand from her mouth.

Tasha promptly knocked his hand aside and scrubbed the back of hers over her lips as if they'd come into contact with hazardous waste. Pushing past him, she marched back into the rear yard before turning to face him. "If you want to talk to me, you can damn well do it out here, where people can see us," she said.

He nodded. But what the hell—why was *she* so mad? He wasn't the one who—

Being on the business end of another of her eat-shit-and-die glares chopped the thought in two, and he was still regrouping when she demanded, "So who are you pretending to be today, *Diego?*"

He kept his wince strictly internal, but...hell. She had him on the ropes with that one, since he could hardly say he hadn't been pretending to be someone else when they'd met. So he simply gave her a level look and said calmly, "My real name is Luc Bradshaw. I'm Max and Jake's half brother—"

"Oh, *please,*" she said in disgust.

He blinked, baffled by her. "What do you mean, *oh, please?* At least give Max some credit. Don't you think he had me thoroughly checked out?"

She made a rude noise, and his brows came together. "I'm not sure what your problem is. All you have to do is look at the three of us together—the general consensus here seems to be that there's a strong family resemblance. So why would you doubt that I'm—"

She got all up in his grill—and it didn't say much for him that he found it kinda hot. *"Look,"* she said, eyes narrowed to burning slits and her long, narrow nose mere centimeters from his own. "I don't know who you are, buddy, or what your game is. But you stay the hell away from me, you hear? How *dare* you come here impersonating Jake and Max's brother?" She poked him in the chest—but before he could grab her finger, she dropped her hand to her side and took a large step back.

"Tell you what," she said with a calmness that didn't match those eyes. "I'm feeling pretty generous, so if you pack your bags and get out of town—tonight—I'll let bygones be bygones." She gave him the slitty-eye-of-death look again and said, "If you're smart, you'll take that offer and go, because it runs counter to everything my gut's telling me to do."

Trying to reconcile this woman with the sweet, laughing girl he remembered—and failing miserably—he shook his head. "Say what?"

"You have trouble understanding English, Diego?"

Apparently so, because he didn't have the first idea what she was talking about. Rather than telling her that, however, and demanding to know what her problem was and exactly what it was she thought she knew, he instead heard himself say, "My name is not Diego. I know I told you it was, but I was undercover with the DEA at the time, and my continuing good health precluded telling anyone my true identity. But I am Luc Bradshaw, son of Charlie Bradshaw. Half brother to Max and Jake."

"Oh, good, you stick to that story. In fact, I really hope you do. Because if you're still around tomorrow, I'll enjoy nothing more than going to Max and telling him you're nothing but a lousy drug dealer named Diego Who-the-hell-knows-what. And then, *Dee-A-Go,* he will haul your skeevy butt off to jail."

He froze. He'd spent most of their short time together mining for every piece of her story he could get—while keeping his own to himself. He hadn't told her much more than that he was on vacation and didn't want to spend it talking about work. The one time she'd pushed for details, he'd turned on the charm and steered the subject in another direction. So how the hell had she tumbled to his cover story?

He didn't have time to figure it out before she stepped back and shook that pretty cloud of hair behind her shoulders. "And if that happens," she said in a voice edged in tungsten, "trust me, I'll have only one regret."

Shoving his hands in his pockets, he stared down at her. Taking in the flushed cheeks and electric eyes, he thought it was a damn shame that he was still so attracted to such an obvious head case.

"Okay, I'll bite," he said. "What would that regret be?"

"That unlike the tiny hundred-and-two-degree black hole of a Bahamian jail cell where I spent the two most terrifying nights of my life, thanks to you," she said flatly, "American jails are probably downright plush."

Then, before he could ask so much as one question, she whirled on sandaled feet and stalked back into the murky shadows thrown by the side of the garage.

Leaving him wondering what the *hell* had happened the night they'd spent together.

CHAPTER TWO

"TASHA RENEE RIORDAN, you've been keeping secrets from me. When the hell did you get the chance to meet Luc Bradshaw and why do you dislike him so much?"

Tasha stared at her friend openmouthed. She had barely opened her door to Jenny's knock before the question knocked her back a step as if it were an honest-to-God battering ram catching her squarely in the chest. Jenny crossed the threshold at the same time that Tasha remembered to breathe. And breathing was good, if a bit tricky around the ragged rhythm her heart was banging out. But she tried her best to sound calm and collected when she said, "What? I met him yesterday. You were right there, Jen."

"Don't kid a kidder, sweetie. You looked at him as if you knew him. So when on earth? I didn't think you'd come up for air long enough to leave Bella T's."

She tried to keep it to herself; she really did. But this was Jenny, to whom she told everything, and she simply caved. "I met him seven years ago." She shoveled her fingers through her hair and stared at her friend. "It knocked me for a loop when I walked into Max's last night and saw that Max and Jake's so-called brother is the Diego I told you about from my Bahamas trip." Admitting it out loud was both scary and a relief. There was no taking it back now, but neither was it a secret any longer, pooling its corrosive acid in her stomach.

Assuming more importance than it should warrant.

Jenny's face promptly went serious, showing why she was Tasha's best friend. "Oh, crap, Tash. How is that possible? And yet…you were too…not you, with all that bug stuff and shooting it between the eyes and the I-hope-you-die-from-a-raging-case-of-herpes looks you gave him."

"Oh, God." They reached the breakfast bar dividing the small galley kitchen from the body of her living area just as her leg muscles turned to pudding. She sagged onto one of the stools and stared at her best friend as the petite brunette climbed onto the stool next to her. "It shocked the hell out of me to see him sitting there cool as you please at Max's table. But…dammit, Jenny. I *hate* that I was so obvious."

"You weren't, sweetie. Or, okay, you were—but only to me." Jenny leaned forward to give her a quick, fierce one-armed hug, then straightened back on her stool. "And I've known you damn near half our lives." She shot her a sly smile. "And now that I know, I'm surprised I didn't figure it out for myself. Because it makes sense, doesn't it? He's the only man you've ever reacted that passionately to."

Tasha ignored that, since the last thing she wanted to talk about in conjunction with that man was passion. "I told him he had until today to get the hell out of town. But how do I break the news to the Bradshaw men that he isn't their half brother if he doesn't leave?"

"Tash. Sweetie." Jenny rubbed the back of her hand. Gave her sympathetic but firm eye contact. "You only have to look at him to see that he is."

"No," she insisted—even though the truth of it had been rattling the cage she'd locked it in from the moment Diego—*Luc*—had said the same thing. She slid her hand out from under Jenny's and used it to shove her hair out of her face. "He's not gonna just go away, is he?"

"I'm afraid not."

"Crap." She sucked in a breath. Then blew it out again in resignation. And said what she'd been thinking all night long. "What were the damn chances that the one man I never wanted to clap eyes on again as long as I lived would turn out to be Max and Jake's half brother?"

"I know, right?" Jenny agreed. "It really is a freaking small world."

LUC HAD JUST finished packing up his duffel bag when an authoritative fist pounded on his motel room door. Old habits died hard, and silently he unzipped the bag's end pocket and pulled out his SIG Pro. Pistol at his side, he kept to the wall as he approached the door and stopped just this side of it. Craning around, he peered through the peephole.

And saw his half brother Max in his khaki deputy uniform shirt.

He tucked the gun in the small of his back, covered it with his shirttail and opened the door. "What brings you to Silverdale?" he asked curiously. "And how the hell did you get my room number?" As if he didn't know.

"It's amazing what a badge can get you," Max said in his usual unsmiling, straightforward manner. "Can I come in?"

"Yeah, sure." He stepped back to allow him by. "So you came to Silverdale just to see me?"

"Yep." The bigger man gave the room a quick, comprehensive examination that Luc was damn sure took in everything there was to take. Then Max focused his attention on him. "Can you shed some light on why Harper heard Tasha say you're not Luc Bradshaw but some guy named Diego?"

Luc had been expecting the question in one variation or another, but now that it was asked, he realized he didn't know how to address it. That wasn't like him. He was the master of improvisation and deflection, killer charm his go-to line of defense. But there was something about looking into the steady, uncharmed eyes of a man who was still a virtual stranger while the knowledge that they were *brothers* punched him in the damn solar plexus the way it had every damn time he'd seen Max or his other half bro, Jake, this past week. He found he couldn't lie to those eyes.

And that sure as hell threw him off his game.

This brotherhood gig might be tougher than he'd anticipated. Having grown up an only child, once he'd located Max and Jake he'd been kind of excited at the prospect of getting to know them. But he hadn't really figured where he would fit in this new family dynamic when the other two had a lifelong history with each other. His sole excuse was he had only recently discovered that his late father, Charlie—a man he'd thought he knew inside out—had two other sons Luc had known nothing about until the day he'd cleaned out his dad's desk and come across the information.

But thinking about it wasn't getting the question answered, and he blew out a breath. "You want a cup of coffee? The story has background that might take a little time to explain."

"Sure. That would be good." Max made himself at home on the small couch in the sitting area of the narrow suite.

Luc made a cup of coffee at the amenity counter and brought it over to his sibling. "Look," he said, standing in front of Max with both hands held easy but away from his body. "I'm going to take my SIG out of the back of my jeans real slow now, okay?" It had been stupid of him not to put it away the minute he'd seen who was there.

Max's hand came to rest on his own pistol. "Wanna tell me why the hell you're packing a gun?"

"I thought you did a background check on me. Shouldn't you know I'm DEA?"

"You bet. If you really were."

"I'm gonna let that pass, since this relationship between you and me and Jake is only—what?—ten days old. I'm currently on a leave of absence, but I've been with the agency for thirteen years."

His half brother merely looked at him with watchful eyes. "I'd just as soon not pull my weapon on you, so do us both a favor and don't reach for your gun until you've shown me the ID."

"You got it." He indicated the duffel resting on the end of the bed. "It's in my bag over there."

Max climbed to his feet, his right hand still on the butt of his pistol. "On second thought, pull the gun out real slow like you said and put it on the table. Then I'll get the ID for you."

Luc felt a slight smile tugging at the corner of his lips. It was ridiculous and probably misplaced to feel proud of his half brother, but he kinda did anyhow. Because Max was clearly nobody's fool. You never, but never, let an unknown quantity paw through a bag that for all you knew could be bristling with weapons. "Good plan."

He did what the bigger man instructed and slowly retrieved his gun from the small of his back. Keeping his finger away from the trigger, he made no abrupt movements as he bent to place it on the table between them. Max swept it up.

Luc waved a help-yourself hand at the duffel. "ID's in the end pocket."

Max didn't pat him down but he clearly suspected the possibility of a backup piece, for he kept an eye on him as he crossed to the bed, then turned sideways to keep him in sight when he reached for the pocket zipper. Luc linked his hands behind his head to alleviate some of the tension in the room and watched in satisfaction as Max's wide shoulders relaxed a fraction.

His half brother felt around in the pocket for a moment, then made a little wordless sound of discovery deep in his throat. A second later, he pulled out Luc's leather badge wallet and flipped it open. He glanced down at it and the rest of the tension flowed from his big body. He took his eyes off Luc long enough to give the gold-and-black eagle-and-circle insignia a closer inspection. Slapping it shut, he turned to give him a penetrating look. "Undercover?"

"Yeah." Dropping his hands to his thighs, he sat up. "How'd you know?"

"Please," Max said. "*Diego?* Plus, I doubt most field-office agents on leave feel compelled to answer a knock on their motel room door packing a semiautomatic."

"It was a pretty aggressive knock."

The smile Max gave him was so small as to barely be present, but Luc had been around him enough by now to recognize it for what it was: his version of a big grin.

"Then there's the not showing up in my background check," Max said. "My guy does very good background checks." But he quickly sobered and pinned Luc in the beams of his hard-eyed heard-every-excuse-so-don't-even-try-to-bullshit-me cop's gaze.

"The question is, how did Tasha come to know?"

Thrusting his fingers in his hair, Luc scrubbed at his eyes with the heels of his hands. Then he blew out a breath and lowered them to his sides, tucking his fingers into the front pockets of his jeans. "She doesn't know about the DEA part—she believes I'm a drug dealer named Diego and I honest to God don't have a clue where she got that idea." He gave an impatient jerk of one hand. "Not the name part—I introduced myself as Diego. But how the hell did a twenty-two-year-old on vacation cop to my cover?"

"Maybe you had something she found?"

"No, I wouldn't live long if I was that sloppy."

Max looked at him over the lip of his coffee mug. Nodded. "Where and when did you meet?"

"In the Bahamas seven years ago. Spanish is my first language, so most of the cases I'm assigned to tend to be in South or Central America. The one I was on at the time concerned a cartel in Colombia, but I was on temporary R & R a continent away from the action, so all I told Tasha was my first name. My *cover* first name, not my real one, because you just never know when you might run into the wrong person at the wrong time, y'know? Even thousands of miles away. And before our relationship could get much deeper than that, I got called away. I thought it was just going to be a quick check-in, but that turned out not to be the case."

Christ, there was an understatement. And for a moment he was plunged back seven years to Andros Island.

"WHAT'S SO URGENT?" he demanded the minute the door to the safe house was opened by a silent agent who appeared barely old enough to have completed his training. Dammit, this was a too-rare R & R for him and he wasn't happy about being summoned by Special Agent in Charge Jeff Paulson. But he had six years in with the DEA and duty first *had been drummed into his head from day one.*

So he spared the other agent the briefest scan before looking past him to his superior, who was seated in a comfortable-looking chair situated deeper in the room. Without glancing up from the sheaf of papers he was going through, Paulson indicated the much less comfy-

looking chair across from him. "Come in and take a seat." When Luc complied, the older man set aside the papers, locked Luc in his sights and wasted no time coming to the point. "Intel gatherers have been picking up chatter about you."

"What kind of chatter?" He'd been an undercover operative for too many years to be caught flat-footed by much, but this sent a little punch of shock through his system.

"The word they're hearing is that you're gonna get yours while you're in the Bahamas." Paulson gave him a half smile. "Someone clearly doesn't like you."

And he knew exactly who. "Hector Alvarez."

Paulson sat forward. "Morales's second lieutenant Alvarez?"

"Yes, sir. He doesn't like that Morales appreciates my sense of humor, because Alvarez is the original Mr. Grim. And he really doesn't like that his girlfriend likes to flirt with me. He refuses to see that her actions have more to do with the fact that I treat her with respect while he treats her like shit than it does with any burning desire for me as a man." He'd spent the past fifteen months with the Morales cartel and ordinarily he was all about the case. Right now, however, only one thought kept intruding during his recitation of the facts. "Tasha."

The SAC frowned. "Beg pardon?"

"This trip was supposed to be a short break for me and I left a friend at my room when I came to meet with you. If Alvarez is bragging about 'getting' me while I'm

here, it's not a stretch to assume he knows where I'm staying by now."

"I thought your SOP was to bribe the desk clerk to disavow any knowledge of you checking in."

"Yes, sir, and I did that. But Alvarez could offer a bribe as well for ten minutes in my room and who's to say the guy won't double-dip in that bowl of guacamole? Shit." He surged to his feet. "I need to get Tash out of there." She had told him her best friend called her that shorter version of her name—and he'd thought at the time how much it suited her.

"Sit down," Paulson said in a voice that brooked no argument. "The only thing you have to do is board the helicopter that's going to be here in—" he glanced at his watch "—seven minutes and get your ass to D.C. for debriefing and reassignment."

"Not gonna happen until I get her out. Sir." He headed for the door, surprised at his own adamance. He loved his work, particularly the thrill of relying on his wits and the adrenaline rush of having to stay on top of his game at all times. New cases were usually right up his alley since beginnings were inherently more dangerous and exciting due to his lack of familiarity with the players' quirks. Plus, as much as he enjoyed the company of women when he had a little downtime to spend with them, once he was back on the job he pretty much forgot them. If it had been any other female, he likely would have been perfectly comfortable leaving Tasha's extraction to a DEA team.

The young agent stepped in front of him, blocking

his way out, and Luc went chest to chest, nose to nose, with him. "Get out of my way, kid."

"Sorry, sir. I can't do that."

Luc had to admit that putting his professionalism on the line for a woman—especially one he'd known for only two days—was unlike him. Yet he found himself compelled to do exactly that and he was fully prepared to go toe-to-toe with the guy in his way.

"Stand down, Bradshaw," Paulson said, coming up behind him. His voice softened. "I'll extract her myself," he promised. "But you are getting on that chopper."

He stepped back from the young agent, but his willingness to argue must have shown on his face as he turned around, for Paulson's hardened. "This is not up for discussion, Lucas. I'll call you in D.C. to let you know she's okay. But you are leaving in—" he consulted his watch again, then looked up at the sound of a helicopter coming in low "—now."

"No, sir. I'm not."

"Then turn in your badge, Bradshaw. Because I won't tolerate an agent who refuses orders from his superior officer."

He didn't have his badge with him, of course, but he opened his mouth to say Paulson could have it. Then he thought about what he was doing. His SAC had just told him he'd personally take care of Tasha himself and Luc sure as hell had no reason to doubt he'd do exactly that. "Fuck."

And the next thing he knew he was running, hunched against the strong wash of the rotor blades, toward a chopper that was lightly settling on the back lawn. Minutes after that, he was winging away from his old case, headed for a new one.

But instead of his usual anticipation over the prospect of a new case, his thoughts were back with the woman he'd left behind.

By the time Paulson called late in the evening two days later, Luc was climbing the walls. "Hey," he barked into his satellite phone when he saw his SAC's name on the readout. "What's going on with Tasha? Is she okay? Did she understand why I didn't come back when I told her I would?"

"First things first," his SAC said. "You were set up. The Bahamian DEU raided your hut not long after you left to meet with me and found a kilo of heroin."

His blood iced over as he thought of the only person besides himself who had been in his beach hut. He didn't want to believe it but— "Do you think it was Tasha?"

"No—although we thought that when we got there and found her gone."

"Gone?" He sat down hard. "As in not there?"

"Generally what that means, son. Sources reported she flew out on the last plane to Nassau that night. We ran her through all the databases, but she's not in any of them."

"So she just fucking left, *when she said—"*

Paulson's impatient voice cut him off. "You think you can focus on the case here, Bradshaw?"

He shoved aside his disappointment over Tasha's defection as well as another emotion that felt suspiciously like hurt. "Yes, sir. I'm just trying to figure out when

*the hell Alvarez had the opportunity to plant anything.
Tasha and I had just gotten there that morning." He'd
already had reservations on Andros and had talked
Tasha into going with him because he'd heard the tiny
resort was very private—and because he'd just wanted
her to come with him.*

"And you stayed in the whole day?"

*"Yes." Then he shook his head. "No. Shit. We went
snorkeling that afternoon."*

"So he had a window of opportunity."

*"Yes." Then his brain kicked in. "Jesus, he's not the
brightest star in the galaxy. If I were actually the drug
dealer he thinks I am, I'd likely give up somebody a lot
higher up the food chain than me to save my own ass. I
doubt Morales would be happy to hear Alvarez set that
scenario in motion." His adrenal glands began pumping
juice into his sytem over the thought of what he could
do with this situation. Because...* Oh, yeah. This could
work. *"Can you get your hands on a replacement kilo?"*

*"Huh?" There was a moment of silence. Then, "You
can't possibly be thinking about taking it back to Morales—can you?" The words were negative, but the
tone...*

Yeah, baby. *His SAC was considering it.*

*"I am thinking that. It's a fucking twofer, sir. Think
about it. Alvarez will be gone the minute Morales learns
what he's done." One way or the other, unfortunately,
but the guy should have thought about all the potential
consequences before he tried framing him. "More than
that, it'll likely cement my position in the cartel, which*

gives us the opportunity to close the case faster than we thought we could. We need to do this."

They disconnected a short while later after Paulson promised he'd check with the director about another kilo—with the caveat that it was by no means guaranteed they'd get one. But Luc refused to entertain the idea, because he was deadly determined to see this case through.

Unfortunately, it didn't keep him from gnawing over Tasha's defection. What had made her decide to catch the night flight back to Nassau after all, when she'd assured him she would wait?

He went around and around on it but eventually had to shelve the whole damn mess. "Get over it, chump," he said, his mood black. Chicks dumped guys—it happened all the time, even if he'd only rarely experienced it himself. There sure as hell wasn't anything he could do about it. She clearly hadn't been as into him as he had been into her.

"Well, your loss, sweetheart," he finally growled aloud. And shoving his wallet into his back pocket, he went off to find something to distract him from the pointless what-ifs pinballing around in his brain.

"SO WHAT *WAS* THE CASE?"

"What?" But he shook his head to bring himself back to the present and told his half brother a condensed version of what had gone down that day. Then he simply stared at the big deputy for a moment.

"Christ, Max," he finally said. "I was blown away to see her in your dining room last night. Then when I followed her out to the backyard, she was beyond pissed, which I don't get, 'cause like I told you, I thought she'd run out on me. Yet *she* was furious with me." Remembering her parting words, he rolled his shoulders. "And maybe with reason."

Max's eyes narrowed. "What reason?"

"Last night she said that thanks to me, she'd spent two nights in a Bahamian jail."

"So either there was a failure to communicate between the two countries' drug enforcement agencies, a clerical screwup—or somebody lied to you, Slick. I don't know the players, but I know Tasha. And I gotta tell you, if there was any lying going on, I doubt it was her."

"Yeah." Luc doubted it, too, because she knew just enough about his cover to get things wrong—and they were things she shouldn't know at all. Plus, she was crazy furious with him, which she'd have no reason to be if she had taken off.

He met Max's eyes and didn't doubt his own eyes were every bit as hard as his half brother's. "And you can take it to the bank that I will get to the bottom of this. But first," he admitted, "I have to convince Tasha that I'm not a drug dealer. Then I need to get her to talk to me long enough to learn exactly what happened that night so I can figure out where to go from there."

CHAPTER THREE

TASHA HEARD THE street door to Bella T's open while she was scrubbing down the kitchen. "We're closed," she called, which everyone and their brother should already know because—hello!—Razor Bay. Monday. Labor Day weekend now behind them.

On the other hand, it hadn't even occurred to her to lock the door while she was back here cleaning. So on the off chance it was some out-of-towner looking for a slice, she came out to give him/her the bad news. But seeing Tiffany, the young woman who had worked for her since the day she'd opened the restaurant's doors, Tasha frowned in bewilderment. "Hey, girl. What are you doing here on your day off?"

"I parked in my spot behind Bella's to run some errands," the plump, flawlessly-made-up brunette with the sunny smile, even sunnier disposition and easy way with people said. "But when I was cutting between the buildings to the street I saw…" Her words trailed away, and for a second she appeared unusually hesitant. Then she tipped her head inquisitively, gave Tasha a penetrating look and suddenly asked, "Do you and that good-looking new Bradshaw brother have something going on that I should know about?"

"What? No!" Oh, God, was it written on her forehead that she and Dieg—*Luc*—had had crazy wild sex one night a hundred years ago? "Why would you think so?"

"Because I saw him heading upstairs a minute ago," Tiffany said with a vague wave toward the end of the building where the outdoor staircase ran up to the living quarters. "And he was carrying a big duffel bag like he's moving in."

"What the hell—?" Tasha peeled off her rubber gloves, tossed them on the service counter and headed for the door. "Lock up for me, will you?"

"You got it, boss."

Her heart pounded with an emotion she didn't want to examine too closely, but she was never so rattled that she forgot to give her aqua-white-and-green-painted building a ritualistic pat as she rounded its corner. Bella T's was the realization of a dream she'd held since she was twelve years old—except better, because not only was the pizzeria a reality, but she owned the building that housed it, as well. Well, okay, she and the bank owned it, but one day it would be hers alone. And she never, but never, failed to show her appreciation when she transitioned from her work space on the street level to her home upstairs. This was likely the most well-loved inanimate object in Razor Bay.

And she intended to find out what the hell Luc Bradshaw was doing in it.

She took the solid wooden stairs up to the second floor two at a time and burst through the unlocked exterior door, but then stopped dead and stared down the narrow hallway that ran along the building's back wall as the door bounced off the inside wall. Down near the far wall, Luc stood in front of the studio apartment that her longtime renter, Will, had recently vacated, the aforementioned duffel bag at his feet. At the sound of her less-than-subtle entrance, he spun away from fitting a key in the door lock, his right hand reaching toward the small of his back before suddenly freezing.

That got her moving again. "What the hell do you think you're doing?" she demanded as she strode up to him. She thrust out a hand. "Give me that key!"

"Taking your questions in order," he said dryly, "I'm moving in, *cariño*. And no."

She stepped up until they stood nearly nose to nose. "What do you mean, *no?*"

"It's a fairly self-explanatory word, *princesa mia*. I'm not giving back the key. I signed a contract that says I'm the proud owner of this studio apartment for the next ninety days." He flashed that charming white smile of his that creased his cheeks into not-quite-dimples. Seven years ago its power had rendered her stupid.

She was neither charmed nor made stupid by it this time around, however—not by the smile *or* his damn Spanish endearments. Back in another lifetime she'd made him explain what those sweet nothings meant, but she'd long since put them out of her mind. And she assured herself firmly that hearing them now left her cold.

Luc himself, unfortunately, did not. From the moment they'd met on that long-ago dawn-cooled beach, she'd felt the heat of the sexuality he exerted with such apparent ease. And much as she might wish otherwise, she still did. He was just so damn…male. And so flipping effortlessly carnal and attractive in his plain navy T-shirt and worn Levis that she spared a second to re-gret the sullied white apron she had tied around her hips and her old, faded, shapeless T-shirt that stuck messily to her skin in the all places where she'd splashed her-self. Which, face it, in her zeal to clean the kitchen, were many. And once again she didn't have on a speck of makeup. She had to quit letting him catch her look-ing so undone all the time.

Seriously? Are you listening *to yourself?* She stepped back and stood tall. Luc Bradshaw was *nothing* to her. It didn't matter what he thought of her appearance.

Then, belatedly realizing what he'd just implied, she addressed the real issue here. "*You're* Will's college roommate?" That couldn't be right; he had to be a good five years older than her former tenant.

"Okay. Sure."

Oh! He didn't even *try* to make her believe it. "You so are not. How did you get him to tell me that you were?"

He rolled his muscular shoulders in an unrepentant shrug. "I may have flashed my badge and told him it was a matter of national security."

She gaped at him in disgust. "God. You just lie as naturally as the rest of us breathe, don't you?"

It wasn't a question, but he took a large step forward that somehow had her backing against the end wall. Propping his arm above her head, he leaned close and looked down at her, making her aware of the heat that pumped off his body, even though they weren't actu-ally touching.

"The idea, before I thought better of it, was to check

out my half brothers without them knowing who I am. And I had no idea you owned the joint—I just liked that it wasn't a hotel room and it was in Razor Bay. But as for lying," he said in a low, rough voice, "I've got a job that takes me to places where I sure as hell *better* be good at it. Being fond of staying alive and all."

She made a rude noise. "Of course—oh, silly me to have forgotten for a moment that you're a low-life drug dealer."

He blew out a breath that wafted across her face, and damn his hide, it smelled minty fresh, when by rights it ought to carry the stench of brimstone and lies. "I'm not a drug dealer, Tash," he said in the mellifluous voice she remembered, the one that was almost as deep as his half brother Max's. "I'm undercover DEA."

Cold fury pumped through her veins, and, slapping her hands to his chest, she shoved him back. "You do *not* get to call me Tash as if you and I are friends," she said through gritted teeth. "And do me a favor and skip the I'm-really-just-a-poor-misunderstood-good-guy routine, because I'm not buying it." She thrust out a hand. "Let's see that contract," she said, conveniently ignoring the fact that she had a copy filed in her own place.

He turned back to the door and manipulated the key still stuck in the dead bolt. The lock clicked softly, and Luc opened the door and waved her in.

"I'm not going in there with you," she said—and watched something in his face change that gave her another quick glimpse of the dangerous, determined man she had seen before in a faraway thatched-roof hut nestled on a white-sand beach.

"You are if you want to see the contract," he said flatly, his right biceps flexing even rounder and harder than it already was as he lifted his bag and hauled it inside. "Everything I own is in my duffel—I'm damned if I'll empty it out in the hallway."

"Fine," she said ungraciously, and, folding her arms over her breasts, she followed him into the studio.

Both apartments above Bella T's opened onto a narrow veranda that ran the width of the building and looked down on Harbor Street. They boasted sweeping views of the bay and Hood Canal, plus the Olympic Mountains that made it not a canal at all but rather a spectacular fjord. Luc struck Tasha more like a leather than a wicker kind of guy, and he looked big, dark and out of place, too tough to take up residence among the cheerful white furniture and the beachy blues, greens and beiges she'd used to decorate the compact studio.

He dropped his duffel on the end of the bed in the alcove and reached for its zipper. A moment later he pulled out the contract and carried it to her. "Have a seat," he invited, waving a lean long-fingered hand at the grouping of an overstuffed love seat and two wicker rockers.

She carried it instead over to the tiny drop-leaf table in front of the big window and took a seat on one of the two chairs tucked in on either end.

She cursed her stiff-necked pride and the impulse to follow him in here to try to make him as uncomfortable as she felt. It had been a mistake. The truth was she already knew that Washington State favored tenants in contract disputes, that basically if she as landlord tried to evict, even with a good, solid reason, the tenant could stay in her rental free of charge until the dispute was resolved—which would take a helluva lot longer than ninety days. And she didn't *have* a good reason to evict Luc. She sure wished now that she hadn't allowed Will to find his own replacement and then exacerbated the mistake by leaving him to fill in the contract. She *really* regretted barely even glancing at the thing before scrawling her signature across it. Her only excuse was that she'd been so relieved at the prospect of three months' rent money coming in while she worked to find a more permanent tenant.

Bella T's had just concluded its second summer in business, and for a new restaurant in an industry where the majority of new ventures closed before their second year, it was doing remarkably well. But the pizza parlor was in a resort town that garnered most its income in the summer months. She was fortunate that she got quite a bit of local business, which helped her to escape many of the seasonal issues. But there were still definite lull periods. So until she had a couple more successful years under her belt and was confident she'd nailed down the most efficient ways to stretch her income throughout the entire year, not just in the months that she made good money, she appreciated the added security of collecting rent.

A small brown leather folder landed on the table next to the contract, and she looked up at Luc. "What's this?"

"My DEA badge."

She made a rude noise and nudged over the top flap,

exposing a mostly gold badge of a spread-winged eagle with *Department of Justice* written in gold on a black ribbon across its torso and *Drug Enforcement Administration* and *Special Agent* circling the U.S. in the body of the badge beneath the bird of prey. It looked very official, but she shrugged and pushed it back toward him with one finger. "Big deal. People fake these things all the time."

The short gritty noise that came from deep in his throat sounded suspiciously like a dog's growl. "Jesus, you're a hard sell. It's the real deal. Here." He shoved a driver's license–sized photo ID toward her. "Here's my ID."

She yawned. "Again. Could be forged. How would I know the difference?"

He thrust his fingers through his hair and stared at her. "Look, we need to have an honest heart-to-heart about that night. There are a number of discrepancies and I'd like to figure out what the hell happ—"

"I have nothing to say to a man who lied to me about who he was." She scooted her chair back from the table and rose. "The contract is solid," she said smoothly. "But I'd like you to reconsider and find yourself another place."

"Not gonna happen."

She blew out a quiet breath. It wasn't as if she'd really believed it might. "Whatever. Just stay the hell out of my way."

"Sure," he said with the oughtta-be-patented smile that had likely left a trail of discarded undies in its wake.

And she knew *that* probably wasn't going to happen, either. "I expect first and last months' payment by 5:00 p.m. today," she said and left through his veranda slider.

Seconds later she had stalked down the decking to her own slider and let herself into her apartment. She closed it firmly behind her. Then, as an afterthought, locked it tight.

She needed a few minutes to pull herself together before she went downstairs and finished polishing up Bella's kitchen. But as she paced from room to room trying to burn off the head of steam she had going, she had a nasty feeling it was going to take her a lot longer than a few minutes to work this itchy nervous energy out of her system.

Because how on earth was she going to survive three months of having Luc Bradshaw living right next door?

"Shit," she whispered, scraping her hair away from her face as she stopped in front of the window to stare blindly out at the water and mountains. "ShitshitshitshitSHIT!"

Then she blew out a breath and tried to think. Swearing and wearing a path in her painted wooden floors weren't doing jack on the make-me-feel-better front. Only one thing could do that, and she headed for the kitchen counter, where she'd dropped her cell phone.

Screw the cleanup—she'd get it done before opening time tomorrow or, who knew, maybe even later today if she could get a handle on this awful restlessness. But that was something to worry about later.

Right now, she was in dire need of the moral support that only girlfriends could supply.

Luc heard muted sounds coming from the apartment next door. After about fifteen minutes, Tasha's front door slammed, followed seconds later by the outer door closing and the faraway clatter of footsteps growing even fainter as they progressed down the exterior staircase. He ambled out onto the veranda, leaned casually on the railing—and watched as she appeared on Harbor Street below and strolled toward his end of the building. She glanced up, and his heart gave a hard thump as their gazes clashed.

Ah, man. Scrubbing his knuckles over the sudden tightness in his chest, he stared down at her. It hadn't been enough that she'd stood in front of him in her work clothes, her gorgeous skin all flushed from her obvious exertions and her thin T-shirt clinging to her breasts and diaphragm in little peekaboo patches transparent enough for him to see that she wore a blue lace bra beneath it? The girl knocked his socks off without even trying.

She had sure as hell put some effort into her look for someone now. Her pale eyes were made up all smoky-sultry, and her mouth—God, that lush, siren mouth with its top-heavy upper lip—was painted a soft, sheer red. She had on a short flirty skirt and a next-best-thing-to-spray-paint little girlie tee that clung to her and had a neckline cut low enough for him to see the upper curves of her pale breasts.

Her eyes narrowed. Then she looked away as if he were invisible and sashayed down the block.

Luc leaned farther over the railing, possessiveness

sounding low in his throat. Who the hell was she dressing up for?

He pulled himself up short. "Jesus, get a grip." Really, it was no skin off his dick if she had a boyfriend. It had been a million years since she and *he* had—

Best not to go there, man. Anyway, it wasn't as if he weren't anxious to get back to his own life, to his work. He should probably avoid civilized company altogether. Hell, he'd nearly pulled his gun, which he likely shouldn't even be carrying here in Razor Bay, when Tasha had crashed the outer door against the wall. He was a guy who needed the buzz of living by his wits, of playing the game right up to the final rush of taking down the bad guys, of putting one more power-happy drug kingpin out of business.

Not that there didn't seem to be dozens more in the wings just waiting to take up the mantle. Still, he could only do what he could do—and he was ready to take them down, too. So whoever Tasha was or wasn't doing shouldn't matter.

Which didn't explain why he was leaning so far over the railing trying to keep her in sight that he was in imminent danger of tumbling over it and landing on his head on the street below.

"Shit." He straightened away from the balustrade and took a giant step back to drop into one of the chairs, his eyes narrowing as it creaked beneath his weight. Tasha sure did have a thing for wicker furniture.

He wasn't what you'd call an avid view guy, but he had to admit that this one was pretty damn sweet. Yesterday's rain squalls had apparently blown out to sea, for the rugged mountain range across the narrow band of water etched its craggy peaks against a cloudless blue sky. Some kid on a Sea-Doo was *rrrEAR-rrEAR-rrEARing* in relentless loops out in the canal, and Luc caught a glimpse of one corner of the local inn's float that he and Jake had rowed out to the evening that Tasha and both of his half brothers' women went skinny-dipping from it. If he'd known then that it was *his* Tasha—or okay, not *his*-his, but at least the Tasha he'd once known—he would have tried a helluva lot harder to see through the shadowy night and stygian waters. Short of X-ray vision he would've failed, but he'd have tried. Now a group of kayakers paddled past the area down toward the state park.

He felt restive. Edgy. Tired of his own company. Climbing to his feet, he slapped his jeans pocket to make sure his room key was still there. Retrieving it, he let himself out of the room, then locked up. He might as well walk down to the inn and see if Jake was around. It beat the hell out of this little memory-lane jaunt his mind kept wanting to take off on.

It didn't occur to him that he probably should have called first until he crossed the porch of The Sand Dollar, the largest of the cottages scattered around the evergreen-dotted grounds of The Brothers Inn. Then he rolled his shoulders and knocked on the front door. *Shoulda, woulda, coulda, man.* He was here now, wasn't he? He rapped out another rhythm.

"Keep your shorts on," he heard Jake's irritated voice say from the other side of the door. Footsteps approached, and the door whipped open. "There better be a fucking fire, because I'm in the middle of someth—"

He blinked at Luc. "Oh, hey, it's you." Stepping back, he opened the door wider. "C'mon in. You, I actually wanna talk to."

"Yeah?" It was stupid to feel the warm fuzzies because some guy he hadn't even known existed six months ago maybe wanted to get to know him as much as he wanted to get to know both his recently discovered half brothers. As a newly orphaned only child, he envied their obvious closeness and the way Jake had jumped to Max's defense, especially when it came to their mutual father, more than once now.

"You want a beer?" Jake asked. He glanced down at his pricey watch, which, along with his green silk T-shirt, honest-to-God pressed cargo shorts—who did that?—and razor-cut sun-streaked brown hair, screamed well-put-together-rich-guy. "It's not too early for a brew, is it?"

"Hell, no. A beer would be good." Surreptitiously checking his own plain cotton tee to make sure it was still clean, he followed his half brother into a small galley kitchen.

Jake fished a couple of Fat Tires out of the fridge and handed one to Luc. "So," he said, popping his bottle's top and snapping his fingers to send it winging toward the sink, "I hear you and Tash have a lurid past."

He started. "Where the hell did you hear that?"

"Jenny is Tasha's best friend, remember? She went over this morning to find out what was with her yesterday, because she claims Tash wasn't acting like herself."

It was small of him, but he gritted his teeth over

Jake's casual use of Tasha's nickname when she'd forbidden *him* to use it.

"I hear Tasha claims you're a drug dealer and that she got arrested for drugs you had in your vacation rental."

"Fuck." He dug in his pocket and pulled out his shield for the third time this day, flipping open its wallet and holding it out to the other man. "I was undercover, and I didn't even know she'd *been* arrested until yesterday."

Jake took the badge out of his hand and studied it. "DEA, huh? Max will be interested in this."

"He already knows—he came to see me at my hotel in Silverdale earlier."

A slight smile crooked Jake's lips. "That's our boy. Not much gets past him." He returned the shield. "Why don't you just show this to Tash?"

"I did! She said IDs could be faked."

Jake laughed. "Yeah, she was pretty hot under the collar when she called Jenny about getting together at the Anchor for some girl time."

"She's at the Anchor? With your fiancée?" It wasn't as if he was relieved or anything. He merely had a new resolve, and he took a step back. "Well, listen, I'll let you get back to that middle-of-something thing you were working on."

"So you can go to the Anchor without me?" Jake demanded. "Screw that." He disappeared into another room, but almost immediately returned. Shoving a wallet into his back pocket, he said, "You do get that she's there to trash your good name to her girls, don't you? You're not exactly gonna be welcome."

A corner of his mouth ticked up. "Yeah, why can't they be levelheaded like us?"

"I know, right? Women are a mystery, but it's some esoteric female thing, the logic of which only they understand." He sobered. "Just be prepared, bro. You're already on shaky ground." They stepped out onto the porch, and Jake locked up. "Where's your car?"

"On Harbor Street. I walked over."

Jake shrugged. "I'll drive, then." He led Luc to his SUV. Opening the doors with his remote, he paused to look at Luc over the top of the car. "You know, you really oughtta move into the inn so you don't have to do so much backing-and-forthing between the Bay and Silverdale."

"I don't need a place at the inn. I just moved into the studio above Bella T's."

"No shit?" Jake shot Luc a big-ass grin. "This just keeps getting better and better."

CHAPTER FOUR

"Aw, HELL," TASHA said morosely, "it's not like I didn't know better than to hook up with Diego/Luc/whatever-he-wants-to-call-himself in the first place." She knocked back a long swallow from her glass of the house red, then looked at Jenny and Harper seated on the other side of their booth at the Anchor. "I knew not to go there. But instead of paying attention to my instincts, I went ahead and hooked up with him anyway."

"How would you know better?" Harper asked with the near-British inflection that made her sound so boarding-school refined. "Did he have Lying Drug Dealer written all over him?" Her black ringlets shivered and swayed as she tipped her head to study Tasha. "And what, precisely, does such a person look like?"

"Beats me. I only meant that I hadn't intended to hook up with anyone on that vacation. It was just my bad luck that the one time I broke my own hard-and-fast rule, it was with a guy who landed me in a Bahamian jail."

It felt odd to have told yet another person about that time in her life. Her imprisonment in the dark, cramped cell had been the single most terrifying forty-eight hours of her life—its minutes stretching like dog years as she'd wondered if she would ever see the light of day again. When they finally did let her go, she'd wanted only to forget and had kept the incarceration a closely guarded secret, relating her experience to no one but Jenny. Now, after maintaining a stony silence for seven years, in less than twenty-four hours she had not only blurted it to Luc last night but had just told Harper, as well.

But although she may have known Harper for only a couple of months, her new friend was fast becoming important to her. And she'd deserved to hear about her prior relationship with Luc if she was ever to understand why Tasha was so furious with him now.

Raucous male laughter exploded from a table over by the window, but Harper didn't spare so much as a glance in the group's direction. She leaned into their own table. "You were on vacation," she said. "Why wouldn't you want to meet a hot-looking man?" She gave Tasha a knowing look. "And I think we must admit that Luc Bradshaw is that, yes?"

Oh, yeah. He is definitely that. Not that she intended to say so aloud. She did, however, dip her chin in the tiniest acknowledgment.

"It all stems back to her mama," Jenny said and raised a hand to hail the cocktail waitress. Catching the woman's eye, she circled an index finger over their glasses, indicating refills all around.

"Your mother wouldn't approve of you having a vacation fling?" Harper inquired. "Is she quite strict, then?"

Both she and Jenny laughed. "No," Tasha said. "Quite

the opposite, actually. My mom was known around here as the whore of Razor Bay. She moved to Olympia almost six years ago, yet there are still a few people who like to throw her reputation in my face every now and then." She shrugged. "Of course, they're morons. And don't get me wrong, I love my mom. But she and I are nothing alike."

"No fooling," Jenny said and turned to Harper. "Nola, Tash's mom, lives strictly in the moment—I don't think I've ever seen her give a microsecond's thought to what might happen tomorrow. Tash, on the other hand—she's a whole nother animal. She is the most goal-oriented person I've ever met."

Harper gave Tasha a bright olive-green-eyed gaze, then turned in her seat to study Jenny. "I know you two have been friends for a long time. But I don't believe I've ever heard exactly when or how you met."

"It was my second day at Razor Bay High School when we were sixteen," Jenny said with a fond smile at Tasha. "I was new in town, and Tash stepped in when some kids started giving me shit about my father's well-publicized incarceration for a Ponzi scheme—which we will talk about another time," she added with a little grin when she saw the light of curiosity in her biracial friend's eyes. "I just loved her from the start, because she had even less standing in that school than I did, yet instead of covering her ass and walking on by like any right-thinking individual would have done—"

Tash snorted and Jenny flashed her a grin.

"—she just jumped right into the fray. We went from that to bonding over the pizzas she made in her mama's single-wide and a mutual determination to move beyond our circumstances." Shaking her head, Jenny smiled ruefully. "I thought *I* had plans at the time. But Tash already had a full-fledged, neatly typed business plan for Bella T's in her underwear drawer."

It was true, so Tasha merely shrugged. But then she slapped a hand against the scarred wooden tabletop and straightened in her seat. "You know, I've been thinking about this off and on for a while and it seems to me that calling my mother a whore is kind of unfair." She made a waving motion as if to erase her words. "Oh, not that she hasn't slept with an astounding number of men. But I can tell you that it was never for money. I'm not even convinced it was because she loved sex all that much.

"I didn't understand for the longest time why she constantly slept around the way she did, and God knows I had to live down her reputation from the day I was old enough to understand what people meant when they said Nola Riordan was a slut. But not long before Jenny came to town, I began to realize that Mom views each new sexual encounter as a potential love match. And I'm talking *Luuuv* with a capital *L*." Her tone leaned toward the sardonic, but it couldn't be helped. "Against all evidence to the contrary, my mother sincerely, consistently and faaar too optimistically believed—"

"Believes," Jenny interrupted.

"Right, and I have no doubt always *will* believe that each new relationship is going to be the real deal. She's convinced that this time the prince will ride in on his white charger to sweep her off her feet. That *this* new lover will be The One."

Harper propped her chin in her hand and sighed. "She's a romantic."

"No kidding." Tasha made a rude noise. "Mom is definitely all about the fantasy." She had a sudden flash of Nola coming back to the trailer late at night, lipstick smeared and hair mussed, smelling of cigarette smoke and spilled beer. Her mom would wake her up and pull her out of bed to whirl her around the room. "He's going to take us away from this rattrap, baby," she'd promise. "Just you wait and see." God. How many times had she heard a riff on that tune?

Enough that she'd quit believing by the time she was nine or ten. Or younger.

"You don't believe in romantic love?" Dropping her hand, Harper sat back. "Please, tell me it isn't so."

"Okay," Tasha agreed amiably. "It isn't so. At least to the extent that I've watched you and Jenny fall in love and can see a genuine magic to your relationships with the Bradshaw boys. I just don't think it's in the cards for the Riordan women."

"Don't be silly," Jenny said. "Of course it is."

"Excuse me if I don't find it all that silly, Jen," she snapped. "But not everyone's as lucky as you." She took a deep breath, gave her best friend a grimace of apology and said in a more moderate tone, "I'm sorry. That was stupid. But how many years did I watch Mom's crazy quest for her prince and not believe? All of them, right? When I decided to unclench my grip on a bit of my hard-saved pizzeria money to take that trip to the tropics, all I was looking for were some white sand, blue sky memories of sipping mai tais in the shade of a palm tree. And, okay, maybe a few good photographs to lord over you."

"You know I was crazy jealous, too," Jenny said. "I hated that I couldn't spare the money from my college tuition to go with you."

Reaching across the table, she gave Jenny's hand a squeeze, because she did know, and she had been way too crazy defensive just now. Then she got back on subject. "So, I wasn't a believer. Then I met Diego. And for a few brief days I *got* it, you know? Finally, I understood what Mom had been chasing all those years with her perpetual search for love. From the moment we met, it was just so…effortless. He made me feel smart. Beautiful. And, God, so, so golden."

Which had simply made the crash that much more devastating. And diligently as she tried now to prevent it, she felt her expression harden as she met her friends' gazes. "It's pretty clear I have my mother's crappy taste in men. So, no, I'm not looking for love. Ever." Seeing her friends' distress, she tried to lighten the mood. "I wouldn't mind having hot sex once in a while, though. My brushes with *that* have been pitifully few and far between."

"Guys find you hot, and you know it," her best friend disagreed mildly. "So I'm thinking that if you really wanted to, you could have sex a lot more often than you do."

"Okay," she conceded slowly, "maybe."

"Men do seem to stare at you as if you're a *Playboy* foldout," Harper said.

"I know. It's weird, right? I don't get it." She grinned

at Harper. "My ego's quite healthy, so I'm not saying that because I consider myself a dog. Heck, at times like this afternoon when I've put a little effort into it, *I* think I look pretty damn hot, too. But except for my boobs, which are *very* nice, if I do say so myself, my body is a long way from sexpot-curvy. Plus, I've got this head of crazy-ass hair." She grasped a couple of handfuls and gave them a tug, then gave Harper's equally curly mop a rueful smile. "Well, I hardly need to tell you about that. And thank God I've finally found some great products for it. But then there's my damn upper lip."

"Which men seem to find fascinating," Harper said.

I love your mouth, Luc's voice whispered in her head. She shut it down fast. And sighed. "Yeah, a lot of them do. And I've made my peace with it. I took a lot of grief for my lips when I was a kid, so it took me a long time to realize they aren't actually freakish."

Harper opened her mouth as if to protest, but Jenny suddenly straightened on the bench seat beside her.

"Uh-oh," she said. "Don't look now, but Jake and Luc just walked in."

Tasha's heart gave a solid thump against the wall of her chest. For a good half hour after she and her friends had settled into their booth at the Anchor, she had half expected Luc to show up hot on her trail. Which was ridiculous when she actually thought about it, but she had seen the look in his carbon-dark eyes when he'd stared down at her from the veranda above Bella T's, and the seed had been planted. Away from his presence, however, her tension had relinquished its grip on her shoulders.

Each new bit of her story that she'd related to Harper had also helped her to unwind. Growing up in a town the size of Razor Bay, it was a given that everybody knew everybody else. It had been kind of nice to share a little of herself with someone who didn't already know nearly every blessed thing about her.

Now, curse Luc Bradshaw's hide, she was tense all over again. "Dammit, why did he have to come in here and ruin everything? Are they coming over?"

"Maybe. I think so." Jenny exhaled sharply. "No. I know they saw us, or at least Jake did. But they're headed toward the back."

Since they'd just passed into her line of vision, she nodded. "I can see that. Oh. Looks like they're going to play some darts."

She didn't want to watch Luc, and she didn't *mean* to. But she was facing that end of the tavern, and as Harper had said, it was hard to deny he was one hot-looking man.

She couldn't seem to look away.

"For God's sake, what is this, the official Bradshaw family rendezvous or something?" Jenny suddenly demanded, and her tone had Tasha finally tearing her gaze away from Luc, who was flashing those soft creases in his lean cheeks at the cocktail waitress serving him and Jake their beers. Pig.

Not that she gave a great big rip if he flirted with someone else or anything.

Preferring not to examine the validity of that claim too closely, she craned around in time to see Max pausing a few steps inside the Anchor, no doubt to let his vision adjust to the change in lighting. He looked around, and it was obvious when he spotted the guys. Then he located the three of them in their booth.

And, weaving his way through the half-filled tables, he strode over to them. "Ladies," he said to Tasha and Jenny, giving them each a nod. Then he turned his attention to Harper. "Hey there, sweetheart." Bracing his knuckles on the tabletop, he gave her a tender smile, then leaned down and kissed her. Straightening back up, he glanced over at Tasha. "I have some information on Luc for you," he said. "You want to step outside with me?"

She considered it for maybe two seconds, then shook her head. "You can say what you have to say here. I'll just tell them anyway." Her voice was cool, but her pulse was tripping like Timothy Leary at the height of the psychedelic Sixties. Curious, she studied him. "How would you even know I wanted information on him?"

"I noticed last night that you were upset with him," he said. "And Harper mentioned that you said something about him not being Luc at all but someone named Diego. It set off my spidey senses." Faint color washed across his sharp cheekbones when they all looked at him, and he hitched his massive shoulders. "I'm a cop," he said with what for Max was near-defensiveness. "My suspicions tend to be raised when somebody I know says a newly discovered relative isn't who he's told me he is. So I paid Luc a visit in his hotel room this morning to find out what was going on."

"At last," she said. "Someone who doesn't simply take him at face value."

"Yeah, well, you might not be as happy about this. Or, hell, maybe you will. I don't know. But he's not a drug dealer. He's with the Drug Enforcement Administration."

"Oh, please," she said dismissively. "Did he show you his badge, too? I'm kind of disappointed in you. You must realize that anyone can buy anything on the internet these days." But her stomach had begun to roil. Because if Max thought it was genuine—

It probably was.

"Anyone can maybe buy a knockoff that fools the general public," he agreed easily, but in that deep, no-nonsense voice that just seemed to carry more authority. "But I've seen my share of badges in both the Marines and my time in the sheriff's department and his looks legit. Besides, I called an old Marine buddy who's now with the DOJ. He ran Luc and confirmed it. Guy's DEA, Tash."

"Thank you for letting me know. You're a good friend." She climbed out of the booth with stiff gracelessness. "I've gotta go."

"No," Jenny protested, but something in Tasha's face when she turned her head to stare at her best friend must have warned Jenny off, for the petite brunette merely said quietly, "Must you?"

She couldn't help herself; she glanced down the room to where the other two Bradshaw brothers were. Luc stood with his back to the dartboard and, even as she watched, sent a dart flying over his shoulder. It stuck in the fat above the double ring. She couldn't hear Jake, but she was fairly sure he'd informed Luc of his score from the way Luc laughed.

Then he suddenly looked at her.

She started and jerked her attention back to Jenny. "Yes, I really must. When I found out that Luc was the one who'd rented Will's apartment, I left the kitchen at Bella's half cleaned. It needs to be finished before I open tomorrow."

"I'll help you." Jenny started to slide out of the booth.

"No." Tasha took an abrupt step back. "No. I love you for offering, but stay. Have a glass of wine with your fiancé."

She was so happy that her best friend had found happiness with Jake. Glad for Max and Harper, as well. But she didn't think she could bear to be around all that happiness right now. Not when she was so steeped in misery.

Her gaze glanced off Jenny's, and she hoped her smile didn't look as frozen as it felt. "I'll talk to you soon," she whispered. Then she whirled on her heel and made her getaway.

Luc GRABBED Max by the arm as the other man made his way to the bar. "What the hell did you say to her?"

Max glanced down at the hand on his biceps, then transferred his gaze to Luc's face. The you-don't-wanna-be-doing-that cop look in his eye, coupled with the size and heft of his half brother's muscle beneath his fingers, made Luc reconsider, and he dropped his hand to his side.

"Good to see you, too, bro," Max rumbled, then met

his gaze with the straight-shooter directness it hadn't taken Luc long to figure out was Max's default mode. "I told her I was damn near a hundred percent certain your DEA badge was real."

"But…isn't that a good thing?"

"You'd think so, right? But I guess not, because she looked like she'd just been kicked in the stomach. Maybe you being legit makes it somehow worse in her eyes. Because if you were the supposed good guy, how did she end up in jail—and why didn't you lift a finger to help her?"

"I didn't *know* about it! I gotta go talk to her." He started to push past his half brother, but Max stepped more fully into his path. The guy was big and solid, so Luc had no option but to stop. That didn't mean he had to be happy about it. *"What?"*

"You need to take a big step back here. Just think about this for a minute—and try to look at it through Tash's eyes. Something damn traumatic happened to her seven years ago, but she's had time to put it behind her and move on."

Realizing he'd been doing more reacting than thinking, which wasn't his usual M.O. at all, Luc shook out his hands. "Then I show up."

"Not only show up but are related to her best friends' men. Which means there's going to be no avoiding you. And Tasha just said something about you moving into her studio apartment? How the hell did you swing that?"

"I didn't have a clue about Tasha when I sublet it from Will—I actually arranged it last month when I discovered you lived in Razor Bay. From the time I found out I had brothers, I'd been looking for you and Jake. I didn't know when I found you, though, that Jake lived here, too.

"My original plan was to take some time to scope you out. I wasn't sure how that was gonna work, but I figured if you didn't want anything to do with me, I'd have a more private place than a motel room to kick back in while I looked for Jake. I put in for a sabbatical when I learned Dad died while I was on a job and figured I'd have a while before I was assigned to a new one. Worst-case scenario seemed to be that I'd be forced to relax for a while."

Max shrugged. "But you can see how Tasha might be overwhelmed by all these surprises, right?"

He gave a terse nod.

"Then take my advice and back off a little. You can't fix everything in twenty-four hours. Give her some space and yourself a little maneuvering room."

He slipped on his Laid-Back Luc persona, doing everything except calling Max "Dude" as he agreed that was a good idea. And in all honesty it was.

Everything Max said rang true for him. He did need to give Tasha some breathing space.

But he realized he had another truth, as well. He intended to spend time with his half brothers. And that meant spending time with their women.

Which meant spending time with Tasha.

So, for however long he ended up being here, he needed to put some serious thought into figuring out how to get back into her good graces.

For everyone's sake.

CHAPTER FIVE

"I'M REALLY SORRY, TASHA," Tiffany said as they walked out of Bella T's kitchen the following Friday afternoon. "I hate that I'm letting you down." Her normally cheerful face was etched in misery, causing Tasha to stop in her tracks to stare at her waitress.

Then she reached out and grasped Tiffany's plump shoulders, giving them a squeeze as she bent her head to pin the younger woman with a no-nonsense look. "Tiff. Honey. *No.* You have nothing to be sorry about, and you haven't let me down at all. I didn't really think you'd be happy in the kitchen. But you've been with me since I opened this joint, and I thought I should at least give you the right of first refusal before I go outside again for help." She grinned at the plump brunette. "Just in case you've been harboring a secret hankering all these years to be a cook."

"Gawd, no." Tiffany shivered. "Even with it half-open to the dining room, I'd go nuts in the kitchen all day. Not to mention mess up my mani. I like being around people."

"And that's where you shine, so don't give it another thought." Dropping a hand, she slid her other around Tiffany's shoulders and pulled her in for a quick one-armed hug. Then she stepped back and automatically gave the dining room a swift perusal. "Looks like the after-school rush is kicking in, so get your tush out there and hustle some orders."

"Aye, aye, boss."

Tasha took up her customary station behind the counter, where she could keep an eye on the growing crowd until the orders started coming in. She watched Tiffany sashay from table to table, laughing and joking with the students as she wrote down their orders, then turned her attention to Jeremy, the Cedar Village boy who bussed dishes for her.

She'd originally hired him as a favor to Max and Harper, who were both very involved in the boarding school for troubled boys. Yet it turned out they had done her the favor, because Jeremy was working out great. He was a tall, built, good-looking eighteen-year-old, and when she'd first agreed to take him on she had half feared that he'd spend his entire time flirting with the high school girls. But no matter how many of those girls tried to get him to do exactly that, he refused to be sucked in. He wasn't a social creature like Tiff. He did his work but kept to himself. She could only assume the loner trait made him even more attractive to the young females, because God knew they didn't let up in their attempts to get his attention.

And when they weren't trying to flirt with him, they watched him.

She saw Peyton Vanderkamp doing exactly that right now. The pretty fair-skinned, black-haired girl shared a table with Davis Cokely, but she kept shooting covert glances Jeremy's way as he cleared a table a short distance away. Davis was a handsome kid himself, but as far as Tash was concerned, his smug air of entitlement took the shine off his nice looks.

Peyton, she didn't know that much about. The Vanderkamps were relatively new in Razor Bay, but they were immensely wealthy, from all accounts, and the girl ran with Davis's posse, so Tasha didn't expect a lot from her in the way of character. She knew that prejudices born of her own high school experiences likely colored her opinion, and she freely admitted that wasn't very grown-up of her. But since she doubted she'd ever have an intimate relationship with the girl, she didn't see the point of spending a lot of time worrying over her lack of maturity.

She was about to turn away when Davis turned so he was facing her more fully. The calculating look that crossed his face caught her notice, so she was watching when he, oh, so casually stretched out a foot just as Jeremy passed his table.

Her employee stumbled over it and went down like a felled tree. The bus tub in his hands bounced on the floor before tipping onto its side and spilling half its load of crockery out onto the floor with a resounding clatter.

Like field crickets at a predator's approach, all the kids went stone silent. Davis laughed.

Incensed, Tasha reached for her Ping-Pong ball gun under the counter. Bringing it up, she fired off a shot. The ball bounced off Davis's temple and stopped that annoying guffawing.

He spun to face her. "What the *hell?*"

She came out from behind the counter and strode over to his table. Planting her knuckles on the tabletop, she leaned down until she was nearly nose to nose with him. "*No*body messes with my people in my restaurant," she said flatly. "You wanna be a lowlife, kid, go home and trip your dog."

"Not the dog!" one of the girls from a nearby table protested. "Go home and trip yourself," she suggested alternatively and her friend nodded in earnest agreement.

Tasha stooped to scoop up a pizza pan whose lazy elliptical spin on the floor was rapidly losing steam. She put it back in the tub. "You okay?" she asked Jeremy in a low voice.

Muscles jumped in his jaw, and his pale blue eyes burned with outraged pride. She thought he was going to come up swinging, thus starting a bare-knuckles brawl with Davis—and wondered what it said about her that she intended to let him get a shot in before she intervened.

But Jeremy merely nodded in answer to her question and pushed back to sit on his heels. Silently, he helped her gather the other plates and glasses that had escaped.

She couldn't help but impressed. Not many eighteen-year-old males would have reined themselves in the way he was doing.

A sudden idea made her pause mid-stretch for the plastic soda glass she'd intended to nab before it rolled out of reach. Letting it go, she sat back on her heels and contemplated him for several heartbeats while she silently debated the merit of her brainstorm.

Then leaving him to deal with the tub, she rose and turned her attention to Davis. "As the sign on the wall clearly states, I reserve the right to refuse service to anyone. I'm exercising that right. If you want to come back and play nice another time, you're welcome to do so. But you've lost your pizza privileges today."

"Big deal," he said, shoving back his chair and standing. "Your pizza's only so-so."

Jeremy surged to his feet as if *that,* of all things, was the final straw.

But before he could say anything, a football player named Sage from a few tables down demanded, "Have you and me been eating the same pizza, Cokely? 'Cause Bella T's makes the best damn slices in the county." He gave Tasha a guilty look and held up his hands. "Sorry, Miz Riordan—don't shoot. Best *darn* slices, I meant to say."

She merely grinned, and red crept up Davis's neck at the reprimand from one of his teammates. Ignoring everyone else in the restaurant, however, he gave Peyton an imperious jerk of his chin. "Let's go."

She didn't budge from her chair. "You go ahead," she said coolly, making Tasha wonder if she ought to re-evaluate her original impression of the girl. "I'm going to stay. I *like* the pizza here."

He swore under his breath and stomped over to the door. A moment later it slammed closed behind him.

"We've got a number of orders stacking up, boss," Tiffany called, and Tash nodded.

"You might want to take the meat lover's slice off

mine," Peyton said in her I'm-much-too-cool-to-ever-get-rattled way.

"Will do," Tiffany said, then grimaced apologetically. "I'm afraid you're stuck paying the tab for the two pops."

With a haughty lack of concern, Peyton hitched a slender shoulder. "Not a problem."

"Then I guess I'd better get back to the kitchen so no one has to wait too long for their pizza," Tasha said and turned toward the kitchen.

Only to find herself looking straight at Luc's amused face.

Her heart gave a hard thump. *Oh, perfect.* He'd been in here at least once a day every day this week to grab himself something to eat. Sometimes he tried to talk to her, and other times he didn't. But always, she caught him watching, watching, *watching* her. He'd already been in earlier for a cup of coffee to go, so she'd mistakenly thought she could relax for the rest of the day.

More fool she, clearly, for here he was once again, this time lounging bonelessly at one of the tables, his long jeans-encased legs stretched out and one elbow hooked over his chair back—watching her once more. She'd chew her tongue off before admitting this out loud…but his constant scrutiny was disconcerting.

When their gazes met, he gave her a one-sided smile and a thumbs-up—the latter presumably for her handling of the tripping altercation. Without acknowledging either, she looked away and turned back to Jeremy. And acknowledged the decision she'd come to several minutes ago as a really good idea. "Bring the tub to the kitchen," she said a bit more brusquely than she'd meant to. "I'd like a word with you."

JEREMY FOLLOWED SO CLOSELY behind Tasha he came within centimeters of tromping on her heels. *Crap.* He should have known the past few weeks were too good to be true. Now she was probably going to fire his ass for losing her Richie Rich's business. He wasn't stupid; he knew the after-school crowd was a big part of her low-season profits—and growing bigger all the time, from what he'd heard Tiffany say.

He liked working here. It was…cheerful. Except for Cedar Village in a lesser way, that wasn't an environment he'd had much experience with. Which didn't mean he couldn't recognize it when he was surrounded by it. People tended to laugh and smile in Bella T's. It made for some nice working conditions.

Even nicer was the way Tasha had stood up for him just now. *My people,* she'd said, as if she considered him a part of her team. But not only wasn't he a Razor Bay native, he was from the Village, which probably already put a black mark next to his name. Tasha ran a tight ship around here. She didn't tolerate even mild swearing in Bella T's, though he had heard her swear like a sailor— but never when clients were in the restaurant. Even after having been here only a short while, he could point out several kids who'd testify to her lack of tolerance, having seen them run afoul of Tasha's Ping-Pong ball gun the same way Cokely had. He was surprised she'd let the football player get away with saying *damn,* even if it had been in defense of her kick-ass pizza.

If he lost this job, he didn't know what he would do. Right now he still had a roof over his head, but he was graduating the Village's program on the thirtieth, so he knew he was on borrowed time being able to live there. He sure as hell didn't want to go back to his White Center neighborhood on the southern outskirts of Seattle. Not when he couldn't say with any certainty—even given all the coping skills he'd learned from his counselors—that he wouldn't go back to his old bad habits. If he took up again with his old friends—and face it, they were the only people he knew outside of the few friends he'd made at the Village—it was pretty much guaranteed that he'd fall back into the same old pattern.

A pattern that spelled *L-O-S-E-R*.

He was so engrossed in the What Ifs that he didn't realize Tasha had stopped until he bumped up against her back. Rattled, knowing he was probably gonna get it for not watching where he was going, he jumped back. "I'm sorry," he mumbled. Then, clearing his throat, he added, "I'm sorry about out there, too. I didn't—"

"Don't you apologize for something that was not your fault," Tasha said fiercely. "You have *zip* to be sorry about in the Cokely incident—that one is all on Davis. Actually, watching the mature way you handled yourself when I'm sure you would've preferred smacking him silly made me want to talk to you about something else."

He wasn't in trouble? His counselor Jim had *said* he had to stop blaming himself for everything that went wrong in people's lives, but when you grew up the way he had, it was a hard habit to break. But he took a breath, crossed his arms over his chest and gave her a jerky nod. "Okay."

She pulled the orders from the wheel Tiffany had clipped them to and went over to the industrial-sized fridge to get out two round dough balls and several triangular ones. Swiftly, she began rolling out the full pizza crusts atop pizza stones. She glanced at him over her shoulder. "You want a Coke?"

He nodded. His throat was drier than Mr. Mitchell's math class back at his old school.

"Go pour yourself a nice tall one, then, and come back here. I have a proposition for you."

He didn't have a clue what that might be, but it sounded a helluva lot more positive than, oh, say, being fired. He strode out into the restaurant, loaded up a tall cup with ice at the machine, then filled it with Mountain Dew from the fountain. He drank down half of it in one long gulp, then topped it off again. After a brief hesitation, he filled another one with a different beverage. He took both back to the kitchen and offered Tasha the second cup. "I've noticed you sometimes like a Diet Dr Pepper in the afternoon."

She took it, gulped down a large sip, then grinned at him as she lowered the container. "You see, this is exactly what I like about you. You're a hard worker and you pay attention to the details." She studied him for a moment. "You're graduating at the end of the month with a high school diploma, right?"

He nodded.

"Do you have plans to go to college?"

He wished. But he merely shrugged, as if he couldn't

care less. Yet he found himself answering honestly. "I'd like to go, but I can't afford it. I'm not even sure where I'm gonna live after graduation."

"Do you plan to stay in Razor Bay or are you chomping at the bit to go home?"

"I'd totally like to stay. I like it here."

He'd noticed before that she possessed the same kind of genuine interest in people that Harper Summerville did when she interacted with him and the other guys at the Village. Except for during his interview, however, Tasha had never focused it on him quite the way she did now. Her gray-blue eyes seemed to bore straight into his mind. "What, exactly, do you like about it?"

"It's so…clean here. And quieter than anywhere I've ever been. Every time I look at the mountains and water, they just—I don't know—give me this…still feeling. Like they're smoothing my insides all out or something."

She simply stared at him for a moment, and he wanted to kick himself. Where had *that* crap come from? Now she was going to think he was a complete ass.

"Oh," she finally said, and he was shocked to see tears rise in her eyes. She dashed them away. "Good answer."

His heart lightened, and a rare smile tugged at his lips. "Yeah?"

"Definitely. Drink," she said, nodding to the mostly untouched cup in his hand. She took a sip of her own soda. "Is there a particular thing you'd take in college if you could?"

"Nah." He shrugged. "I don't really have a clue what I wanna do with my life—but I'd like to get my AA while I'm figuring it out. No one in my family has ever gone to college. It'd be beyond dope to be the first." His mom wouldn't give a shit, but his dad would sure be proud.

"Okay." She set aside her drink and, with quick, efficient movements, used her fingers on the triangular dough to shape the slices. "This is my proposition. You know I tried to hire a cook." Grimacing, she waved a flour-covered hand before saying dryly, "Forget I asked that—it's a stupid question, considering he tried to blame you for all that house wine he knocked back. Of course you remember."

"Yeah, kind of hard to forget that." He'd thought for sure his ass would have been out the door that day, too, but Tasha had looked the hammered cook in the eye, said that he was a stone liar in the hardest voice Jeremy had ever heard out of her and told the man to get the hell out of her restaurant. Then she'd turned to *him* and apologized that the lying sack of slime had dragged Jeremy into his lies. As if that were somehow *her* fault.

He would have done anything for her that day.

But he gave himself a mental shake now and tried to concentrate on this conversation, not the one almost a week ago. "What does a drunk cook have to do with your mystery proposition?"

"I'd like to make you my new cook."

He froze. "Huh?" His hand made a totally spastic movement, and he shoved his fingers into his back pocket to keep from looking like an oversized puppet being jerked around by a three-year-old. "I mean, I heard you, I just…" He shook his head. "Why me?"

"Because you're smart, you're levelheaded and, as I said before, you pay attention to details. I have a feeling you'd be good at it. I admire the way you're not easily shaken—admire more that even when you are, you control your temper. That's a rare quality in anyone of any age. In an eighteen-year-old guy it's downright golden."

He no doubt looked as stunned as he felt because she stepped closer and gave his forearm a comforting *there-there* pat as if she were an old Italian auntie.

"I'm not asking you to commit to it as your life's work," she said softly, as if maybe she was worried he felt trapped or something. "But it could be a bridge to get you through the next few years. I can help you find a place to live and pay you a livable wage." Her lips developed an ironic slant. "Well, livable by Razor Bay standards, anyhow. And Jenny and I—and I bet Mary-Margaret, as well—can help you find funding for a community college to get your AA. Jenny, in particular, is brilliant at finding tuition money. She put herself through school without help from anyone and got her bachelor's in hotel management in large part by hunting down a number of scholarships that were offered by Rotaries, clubs and other organizations. None of them tend to be huge, but if you put the work into getting enough of them, they can really add up.

"Which is all a long way of saying I can work around a school schedule if you're up for both working and studying." She tipped her head to thoroughly inspect his expression. "Are you interested? Don't be afraid to say no if you're not. It won't affect your current job, and I know cooking isn't for everyone."

He finally shook off his shock and regained his power of speech. "No. Are you kidding me? That would be *great*." He laughed out loud and didn't even notice when most of the teen girls on the other side of the service counter turned to stare. "You wanna pay me to play with knives and fire." He looked at the red wood-fired pizza oven with its brick-arched opening, at the gleaming stainless-steel and butcher-block work spaces, industrial appliances and the black-and-white tiled floor.

Then he looked at Tasha again. "I get to learn the secret of making the best pizza in the county—and maybe even the world," he said in amazement, then smiled at her and shook his head. "Man. I can't believe it. It doesn't get much better than that."

CHAPTER SIX

THE SUN WAS a spectacular flaming ball minutes shy of sinking behind the rugged peaks of the Olympic Mountains Sunday evening when Luc let himself into his studio. Tossing his keys into the wooden bowl on the coffee table as he passed by, he strode over to admire the panoramic scenery through the slider. Before he could lock on to it, however, a movement from the corner of his eye caught his attention, and turning his head, he spotted Tasha out on their shared terrace.

Or more accurately, he spotted her feet. Within hours of his move-in, she had thrown up a screen of live plants to divide the veranda, lining them up to march from the wall that connected their two units to within three feet of the balcony railing. Even with a little space between each one, it made a surprisingly effective barrier between her part of the deck and his.

So all he could see now was the end of a white wicker chaise lounge and its cushion in the same cheery blue-and-green patterned fabric she'd used to furnish a good part of his studio. Atop the cushion, he caught a glimpse of the long pale-skinned bare feet he still remembered as clearly as if seven years hadn't passed since he'd last seen them.

He stared in bemusement, for they appeared to be performing a complicated seated dance, clearly the movement that had grabbed his attention in the first place. Her feet heel-toed across the cushion, bopping from one side to the other. Her toes pointed toward the fabric one moment, then arced back toward her shins the next as she segued into differing rhythms. Within the ever-changing patterns he caught here-and-gone glimpses of the candy-bright polish decorating her toenails, the color of which he couldn't determine from inside his studio.

Suddenly it seemed important that he learn what that color was, and he opened the sliding door.

Laughter and voices floated up from the street. In the bay, several boat engines rumbled softly while boaters followed the five-miles-an-hour restriction in the protected inlet as they steered toward the marina to put up for the night. This town had a laid-back, feel-good vibe that Luc could appreciate after all the cartel hot spots he'd lived in.

The terrace ran the width of the building, but wasn't very deep, and since Tasha's apartment was larger than his studio, so was her share of the outdoor space. It didn't take Luc more than a few long strides to reach the improvised plant divider, and he rounded the end of it, only to stop dead at his first full-on sight of her. For a moment he simply stood there and stared.

Decked out in a Forties-style halter top and short-shorts, a glass of wine on the table next to her, she lounged against the not-quite-upright back of the chaise. He couldn't see her eyes behind the lenses of her sunglasses, but her face was expressive as she sang in heart-felt, off-tune synchronization with the song playing through her earbuds. Firm arms raised overhead and shapely shoulders added sinuous moves as she undulated her upper torso side to side in counterpart to the rhythms of her head and feet.

Her toes, he took note, were painted a pretty orangey-pink.

Watching her in all her unselfconscious glory was like a slingshot straight back to the woman he'd met on that long-ago beach; she hadn't had a shy bone in her body then, either. Now he couldn't have stopped himself from grinning his appreciation if his eternal soul hung in the balance.

The temptation was sugar-sweet to stroll right up and say something suggestive in hopes that it might re-ignite the explosive chemistry they'd once shared. He managed to catch himself before following the impulse, because doing so would undoubtedly be the next best thing to shooting himself in the foot.

He'd found a dozen excuses and opportunities this week to show up wherever he knew she'd be. And if the dangerously-close-to-stalking-her thing lacked a certain subtlety, he'd tried real hard to make up for that by *not* pushing the our-attraction-is-off-the-charts button any and every opportunity he found.

But he had to admit the current enticement wasn't an easy one to resist. He had only to look at her for the sexuality she radiated to start buzzing like static electricity along every neural pathway departing his brain. It triggered an all-consuming urge to reach for her.

Dammit, she *had* to be feeling the attraction, too, but it was pretty clear she'd rather swallow bleach than admit as much. So while he'd deliberately been putting himself in her path, he'd also been working overtime to tamp down his natural inclination to crowd her, trying real hard not to pull out every speck of sexual wizardry he could muster the way his instincts urged him to do. God knew he had enough trouble getting near her without pissing her off even more by coming on too strong.

If the way she kept her eyes averted now was anything to go by, she was still firmly entrenched in ignore-him-to-death/silent-treatment mode. So instead of moving in on her to try to charm a slow dance out of her, he managed to say quietly instead, "Listen, Tasha, can we talk?"

Her entire body jerked and, tearing the iPod buds from her ears, she cut loose a short, sharp shriek.

Jesus! Breath exploding from his lungs, it took everything he had not to clutch his heart to make sure it hadn't seized like a blown engine. Machismo bred to the bone by his *abuelo*'s early cultural influence would never allow him to admit this aloud, but only years of conditioning—gained by surviving more situations than he could count where displaying a reaction could court a bullet to the back of the head—kept him from letting her see that her scream had damn near given him heart failure.

Some big fucking operative he was.

Stepping closer, he carefully dragged replenishing oxygen back into his lungs. And after softly exhaling, he started over. "I'm sorry," he said soothingly. "I didn't mean to startle you."

Hot color splashed her cheekbones. The orangey curls gathered atop her head quivered as she pushed more upright on the chaise, and it didn't take a genius to see that she was all but vibrating with anger. "You come sneaking up on me and think I *won't* be startled?" she demanded incredulously.

"That's the thing, though, Tash—"

"Tasha! To you I'm Tasha! Or Ms. Riordan, if my first name is just too difficult for you to remember."

Part of him admired the hell out of her in-your-face attitude. Another part, however, had to work overtime to fool himself into believing that her determination he no longer call her Tash didn't royally hack him off. Shoving everything else aside, he said with careful neutrality, "The thing is…Tasha, I didn't think I was sneaking. When I came around your plants and saw you chair dancing, I thought you had seen me as well but were just ignoring me as usual."

"And had that actually been the case," she retorted coolly, "a man would probably be smart to take the hint."

"I'm a smart man," he said with dogged good humor. "But more importantly, I'm a determined one." He crossed over and sat uninvited on the lounge next to her hip. Her thigh was bare where her shorts hem ended, and blistering awareness pumped through his bloodstream at the warmth that promptly sank through his jeans at the feel of the shapely leg and hip pressed against him. Gritting his teeth, he shoved down the sensations it evoked—knowing damn well he'd be dragging them back up again once he was alone. He cleared his throat. "Determined that you're finally going to listen to me."

"Oh, you are, are you?" She scooted sideways, putting some daylight between them.

Now close enough to make out her eyes through the rosy-brown lenses of her sunglasses, he saw they were dangerously narrowed. He merely nodded, however, as if he'd encountered an expression all sunny and welcoming. "I am. I'm not trying to anger you or step all over your rights. But we need to clear the air. I am not a drug dealer, and frankly, I'm getting kind of tired of being called one."

"Oh, well, then. We certainly wouldn't want my pesky feelings to *weary* you." The sun chose that moment to sink behind the mountains, and Tasha plucked off her sunglasses and shoved them atop her head, burying the temple tips in the riotous mass of curls. "How silly of me to think that if the Bahamian police said you were a drug dealer and a very large bag of heroin was found in your place, for which I was *ARRESTED,* that…hmm… you might indeed be a drug dealer."

"I have explained, several times, that I'm an undercover DEA agent. And before you bring up my badge again, it is neither stolen nor a forgery."

"Okay, fine. I accept that."

The way her arms crossed militantly over her breasts suggested otherwise, and studying her warily, he looked for the catch. "You do?"

"Yes. Max said he checked with a friend in the DOJ, and he verified that you are an agent with the Drug Enforcement Administration."

He leaned into her. "Then we can be friends again?" And more? Much, much more?

"No."

He reared back. "Why the hell not?"

"Don't you use that tone with me, Diego," she commanded, staring at him all slitty-eyed.

"My name is Luc," he said stonily.

"Fine. Don't give me that tone, *Luc*." She sat even straighter yet, drawing her legs up and wrapping her arms around her shins. "You think because it turns out you're not a crook, it makes it somehow easier that your job got me thrown in a foreign jail? Where the hell were you when I needed you? When I was rotting away in that black hole?"

"How many times do I have to say this—I didn't know, I didn't know, I didn't fucking *know!*" Shit. Was that him shouting and swearing? He never raised his voice. To the contrary, he was trained to suck it up and compartmentalize his emotions.

Drawing a calming breath, he held it deep for a moment, then slowly exhaled. "I'm sorry. I didn't mean to yell. And I guess I told Max, not you, about the not-knowing-they'd-put-you-in-jail thing. But here's the story, Tasha, and I swear on my *madrecita*'s grave that it's true. When I was called away that night, I was told I was being relocated ASAP, because the people who monitor that sort of thing were hearing chatter about a second lieutenant in the drug cartel I'd infiltrated saying he was gonna take care of me once and for all."

She gave him a shot to the biceps with the heel of her hand. "You put me in danger by taking up with me at the same time you were infiltrating a *drug* cartel? What kind of careless creep are you?"

"Dammit, that's not the way it was!"

"Really? You sure as hell had that gargantuan bag of heroin hidden in the same room where you and I—" Cutting herself off, she avoided his gaze for probably the first time ever.

He reached out and stroked a fingertip along the heat that bloomed in her cheek, smiling sardonically when she promptly smacked it aside. "The case I was working on then was in South America. I was on a break—taking a much-needed R & R—when I met you."

"Do you always drag heroin with you on R & R?"

"Man, you are just determined to see the worst in me, aren't you?" He dug for patience. "The heroin wasn't mine, Tasha. It was planted. The call I got that night? That was the special agent in charge of the cases I covered, saying he needed to see me. I thought it was for a quick update, but discovered when I got there that not only were they pulling me off the job, they were shipping me off to D.C. right away. I don't know how Alvarez—the thug whose threats they'd picked up—found out I was in the Bahamas, but word was out that I was gonna get mine while I was there.

"I fought like hell to go back for you, Tasha, but my SAC had an agent on the door to make sure that didn't happen. He promised he'd extract you himself, though, or I never would have let them hustle me onto the helicopter. As it was, I was going crazy in D.C. by the time I finally heard from him a couple days later. He told me I was set up, that the Bahamian DEU raided my place and found a kilo of heroin."

"Which is not exactly news to me," she said impatiently, "considering I know way more about that raid than I care to remember."

"Did you also know the DEA thought at first that you were the one who planted it?" Being nobody's fool, he kept his own early suspicions to himself.

"What?" She surged up off the far side of the chaise and turned to look down at him, her hands planted militantly on her hips, her face a study in righteous indignation.

"As far as they knew, you were the only other person besides myself in that hut. So when they found you gone—" He shrugged. "They ran your prints and your name through all the databases. When that didn't garner any hits, they concluded you were just in the wrong place at the wrong time. Then when a woman answering to your general description left for the States a few days later, they didn't pursue it any further." Something that he'd just said niggled at him, but the disgusted look Tasha gave him drove it underground.

"Yeah, heaven forbid anyone should take time to find out I was being detained in a Bahamian jail and spring me," she said bitterly.

"I'm not sure how my people could have known you were in jail if the DEU didn't bother to mention they'd arrested you. That doesn't mean that I'm not sincerely sorry about the hell you went through." He looked at her. "Or that I'm not gonna find out what happened."

He didn't mention that he'd been pretty damn mad at her himself. He might not have been falsely arrested, but she'd told him she'd wait for him, and he'd believed all these years that she'd instead turned right around and bailed on him mere minutes after he'd left.

But he was just marginally smart enough not to say that out loud. He didn't doubt for an instant that as someone who'd been arrested because of heroin *she'd* believed all these years was his, she wasn't ready to give a great big rip for his emotional pain.

He rubbed a hand over his jaw, then dropped it to his side and merely said quietly, "Despite what you think, that night mattered to me and so did you. I'm sorrier than I can say it all turned to shit."

Tasha rubbed polish-free fingertips at the furrow between her brows. She blew out a sigh and simply looked at him for an instant. "Look," she finally said, dropping her hand to her side. "Intellectually I appreciate your apology, because it sounds as if you didn't have much more control over your destiny that night than I did."

Heartened by her first civil words to him since he'd come to Razor Bay, he rose to his feet and stepped over the chaise to face her. "No, I didn't. And I found myself thinking a *lot* about—"

"The thing is, though," she interrupted, taking a sizable step back that made him realize he'd moved in maybe a little too close, "while my imprisonment is obviously all new to you, I've been doing my damnedest to shake my memories of it. That was hands down the worst forty-eight hours in my life. And it might not be fair, Luc, but I don't want to be friends with you. How can I forget that awful time if you're always around? You're just too strongly linked to that night."

"Part of which was killer good."

"Yeah." A corner of those do-me-daddy lips quirked up. Then the tiny smile dropped away. "Unfortunately, the arrest part overshadows it, and that was so horrendous I can barely remember what came before."

Irritation that the memories he'd never quite been able to shake meant less than nothing to her made him crowd her and slide his palms around her cool nape. He tipped her head up. "Then let me remind you."

And even as her gray-blue eyes went from wary to don't-*even*-go-there-buster, he lowered his head and rocked his mouth over hers.

Anger—and maybe a bit of hurt pride, too—made his kiss rough. But the way Tasha's back stiffened and the sweetness of the soft, cushiony lips he hadn't tasted in over seven years promptly drove him to lighten up. Loosening his grip on the back of her neck, he cupped her head with an easy touch, his thumbs tenderly framing her face and stroking little circles into the supple skin just below her cheekbones. He dialed back on his too-aggressive demand for entrance to her mouth and instead gently sipped at her lips, first catching her luscious top-heavy upper one between his own, then letting it slide free to do the same to its almost-but-not-quite-as-full counterpart. Finally he opened his mouth over hers, then dragged it slowly closed with soft suction.

And groaned when her lips parted.

Stepping in closer to align their bodies until they pressed from chest to breast, belly to belly and thigh to thigh, he eased his tongue into her mouth and absorbed flavors that were both brand-new and yet more familiar than he might've expected from somebody with whom he'd spent only a couple of days years ago. He slid his tongue over hers, and she made a soft murmur of surrender and slicked her own along his in return.

Something about that sound accessed the Latin pride with which his grandfather had indoctrinated him the first seven years of his life, and he raised his head. Took a step back. It mattered a little too much that a woman who wanted nothing to do with him was every bit as turned on as he was. Possessiveness and satisfaction rolled through him, but he had just enough sense not to let on.

He merely brushed a curl out of her eyes and said gently, "I hope that when all is said and done, *mi reina,* you'll remember this. Because you and me? We were— no, we *are*—really good together."

Stepping back, he admired her flushed skin and kiss-swollen lips for an instant. Then he turned on his heel and strode around the end of the plant barrier to head back to his apartment.

CHAPTER SEVEN

IT IRKED TASHA no end that she couldn't get Luc's kiss out of her head. Not Sunday night and not yesterday, either. Even today—all right, this very minute if she were to be honest—as she and Jenny and Harper began looking through racks of dresses at La Belle Michelle's Bridal Shoppe, a montage of resurrected sensations kept popping up to distract her. She knew she ought to be paying more attention to their search for the perfect bridesmaids' dresses and a lot less to reliving a stupid kiss that never should have happened in the first place. Jenny had only a little over four months to pull her wedding together, a goal with which Tasha fully intended to help her. The very last thing she needed yanking her focus from the job at hand was…*that*.

That damn hot, wet, *thigh*-clenching—

"Oh, Tasha, look!" Jenny's sudden exclamation made her start in the midst of remembering that moment she'd parted her lips to Luc's insistent tongue and the feel of it sliding across them to enter her mouth. "I do believe I've found the perfect maid-of-honor dress for you."

Blinking, still lost in the kiss that would not go away, she glanced at the dress her best friend held against her petite frame—and didn't absorb a single detail. "Uh-huh," she murmured with agreeable vacancy.

Then the near-pea-green color that the garment turned Jenny's complexion belatedly sank in and she truly focused on the gown. Her eyes widened.

The thing was a revolting more-baby-puke-green than the shade it turned Jenny's face, and it was all gathers, ruffles and balloon sleeves, trimmed to within an inch of its life in stiff, itchy-looking black lace and droopy black satin bows.

"There's a stunning little hair ornament that goes with it," her BFF said and held an explosion of color-coordinated netting and black bows to the side of her head.

"Omigawd, that *is* me." Tasha grinned and reached for the gown. "Lemme see that." When Jenny relinquished it, she held it up to herself and watched in the triple mirror as her own complexion promptly turned green. "Let's buy it. It'll go with Jake's eyes."

Jenny snorted.

"Where's La Belle Michelle?" Tasha asked, glancing around guiltily. The shop owner was an easygoing, no-pressure saleswoman, and Tasha would truly hate if her words hurt the woman's feelings.

"She went to sign for some deliveries." Harper reached out for the dress. "My turn."

Tasha handed it over, then shook her head in faux disgust when Harper held it up to herself. "Oh, for pity's sake. Is there a color you *don't* look good in?" Her friend's creamy brown skin merely glowed creamier. "God, that thing is hideous."

"Yeah, like you even saw that when you first looked at it," Jenny said. "You've been distracted all morning, and I gotta tell you, it's not helping my fight to not start panicking a little here. I've got my own dress and the cake ordered, and that's about it. And my wedding is only a hundred and sixteen days away."

"I know, sweetie. I was just thinking that I should be concentrating on helping you instead of thinking about Luc kissing me—"

Oh.

Crap.

Useless as that old horse-and-the-barn-door adage, her hand slapped to her mouth too late to help a blessed thing. All she could do was mentally kick herself as Harper stared at her, the ugly dress sliding unnoticed from her hands. Jenny gaped at her, as well.

The latter didn't last long, unfortunately, since Tasha's best friend almost immediately drew herself up to her full barely five foot three inches and sternly said, "Tasha Renee Riordan. You've been holding out on us. You *know* that violates every code of BFFdom."

Making a rude noise, she dropped her ineffectual hand to her side. "Please. Like you told me everything when you and Jake were carrying on."

Clearly considering that neither here nor there, Jenny waved the rebuke aside. "Luc *kissed* you? And you've been holding out on us? When did that happen?"

There was no use trying to dodge the question. She knew Jennifer Salazar far too well to ever believe her friend would let her get away with it. "Sunday night. And it wasn't much of a kiss." She shifted uncomfortably, because really: *liar, liar.* "Well, it wasn't a very long kiss, anyhow."

"Did you kiss him back?"

"No!" The friend who knew her better than anyone merely looked at her, and she amended, "Okay, fine, I might've started to. But it ended before I actually did much more than lift my tongue off the floor of my mouth, so I'm gonna go with no."

"I'm voting yes," Harper murmured, and Jenny nodded her agreement.

"Yeah, well, you two weren't there. It wasn't a lovey-dovey-type kiss. He was P-Oed because I'd agreed he probably was the DEA agent he said he was, but I still didn't want to be friends."

"He got *rough?*" Jenny demanded, her expression going all commando. "Did he hurt you? I'll have Jake beat the crap out of him if he hurt you!"

"No, no," she said in alarm. "No Jake, no beating! For a second it was all hard hands, hard mouth, but I have to admit he gentled pretty quickly. And I swear, Jen, he never hurt me. You know me better than to think I'd put up with that."

Her friend's combative posture relaxed, and she gave her a puzzled look. "But if he didn't get all rough with you, what's the harm in at least being friends?"

"Omigawd," the shop owner, Michelle, said as she sailed up, pulling a rolling rack full of dresses in both cocktail and gown lengths. She gave them a dazzling smile and bent to pick up the dress Harper had dropped on the floor. "Where on earth did you find this?"

"It was in with the gowns on the hanging rod across the back wall," Jenny said.

"Of course. Now I remember. I had it out the day a huge wedding party came in looking for attendants' dresses. They tried on a lot of styles and I must have racked it with all the dresses I put away after they left." She gave them all a big grin. "I've been searching for it to enter in the Top Ten Ugliest Bridesmaids' Dresses contest that the Bridal Association holds every year."

"Oh, thank goodness—you do know it's hideous," Tasha said, then could have smacked herself. Because, *seriously?* She'd had more social finesse when she was thirteen.

The attractive sixtysomething woman's immaculately groomed eyebrows disappeared beneath her feathered salt-and-pepper bangs. "Have you looked at my inventory, dear? I know taste differs, and not all gowns are going to appeal to everyone. But, honey, none of them approach this level of awful."

Tasha grinned. "You're absolutely right, and I sincerely apologize for inferring otherwise. I have no idea where that question even came from. Jenny got me all riled up while you were away, so I think we should blame it on her."

"Oh, now, we never blame the bride." She turned to Jenny. "You said you were leaning toward the richer blues, greens and purples, but weren't yet wedded to any particular color, right?"

"Yes. I can't seem to make up my mind. Tash looks best in the stronger colors, and we've determined that Harper looks good in just about everything."

"Okay, good. I brought a range of colors. Now, there are several options when it comes to picking your party's gowns. You can select a color and let your attendants pick whatever style they want within that shade. You can pick a style and either select identical gowns or mix and match the colors within the style. Or you can just plain have eclectic colors and styles. It all comes down to what suits you best, as you can always pull everything together with your flowers." Turning back to the rack, she pulled two full-length gowns off it. "Going with the same style but different colors, I picked these two to start. I thought the deep grape would look good with your maid of honor's coloring and the orange sherbet with your bridesmaid's, while the style should suit both their body types."

She displayed them side by side, two strapless gowns with finely gathered chiffon that crisscrossed the empire bodice and wrapped around the ribs to the back. "What do you think?"

"I like them—and I actually like that orange. It never would have occurred to me to select it, but it looks wonderful next to the deep purple." She looked at Tasha and Harper and raised her eyebrows inquiringly.

"They're lovely," Harper said, admiring the heart-shaped cut of the strapless neckline.

"They are," Tasha agreed. "I like the style. It's killer attractive without being fussy." She nudged Harper. "Let's try them on."

They came out of the dressing rooms a moment later and crossed to stand side by side in front of the triple mirror. "Whoa," Tasha said, turning side to side, checking her image from all angles. "How elegant are we?

You're already a classy woman," she informed Harper cheerfully. "But for the first time, I look like one."

Jenny grinned at her. "You do. I love the contrasts, not only between the dress colors but between you two, as well."

Tasha had to agree. She and Harper were both tall but very different in build from the waist down. Harper had more hourglass curves to her lower half. Then, of course, there was their coloring.

As if reading her mind, Jenny said, "The gray undertone in that deep purple makes your skin look really creamy."

"I know!" She laughed in delight. "And isn't that a nice change from my usual skimmed-milk look? That pale orange does the same thing for Harper." She butted her friend's bare shoulder with her own. "Of course, your skin always looks gorgeous. I so envy that."

They tried on several other options from Michelle's rack, but in the end all three agreed that the first choice was the one they loved best. "You're good," Tasha said to the shop owner. "You knew exactly which ones we'd pick, didn't you?"

"Oh, dear, no, I never know for sure. But I have been in this business for a long time. Long enough to have an instinctual feel for what looks good on whom." She essayed an elegant shrug. "It didn't hurt that Jenny walked in here without a hard-and-fast palette in mind. Sometimes a bride's preferred colors and styles aren't particularly bridesmaid-friendly." She gathered the gowns. "You two don't even need alterations, except for hemming. And if you bring your shoes in sometime this month we can get that done handily."

Michelle left them to tag the dresses and start the paperwork, and Jenny turned to her and Harper. "Speaking of hemming, could I ask you both a favor?" she said. "Would you consider wearing flats or a really small heel with your dresses?"

"Sure," Tasha promptly agreed.

Harper gave her an earnest smile. "Of course."

"Aw, you guys are the best. There's no getting around the fact that any way we cut it, I'm going to look like the Tacoma Dome between two skyscrapers. But if I put on my tallest heels and you two wear sandals, I'll be a little less dwarfed."

"Please," Tasha scoffed. "There's a big ole hole in your metaphor or whatever. Number one—you're more in that gorgeous Seattle green-glass-domed building's league than the Aroma Dome's. Green-Glass might be smaller than its neighbors, but it more than holds its own among the surrounding skyscrapers. And two, you've got nothing, but nothing, to worry about." Tasha pulled Jenny in for a quick hug. "You, my friend, are going to be the silky-haired beauty in the gorgeous wedding dress. Harper and I will be lucky if we're spared so much as a glance on your wedding day. I bet if you ask Jake what Harper and I are wearing that day, he'll be hard-pressed to tell you. And you know Jake knows his clothing."

Jenny tilted her head against Tasha's jaw. "Aw, this is one of the many reasons you're my bestie." Then she gave her a stern look. "But don't think for a minute that

I've forgotten what we were talking about before Michelle showed up with the gowns. Why don't you want to be friends with Luc?"

Tasha pulled back and blew out a put-upon sigh. "Really?"

"Yeah, really," Jenny said firmly even as Harper said, "Yes."

"Okay, fine. I don't want to be his friend because even though I believed him when he said he didn't know about my arrest, he's still linked to it, which makes him a constant reminder of those awful days in jail."

"That was a long time ago," Harper said.

She looked at the other woman. "Yes. It was. But have you ever spent time in a four-by-six dark-as-death room, with only a narrow cot and a bucket for a toilet?"

Eyes wide, Harper shook her head.

"Those hours felt like a *decade* because I had no way of knowing if I'd be released or if that was going to *be* my life from that point on. I try very hard not to think about it because I never want to feel that helpless, that *hopeless,* again. I understand now that Dieg—*Luc* wasn't responsible for what happened to me that night. But it doesn't make him any less a trigger for those emotions. And in truth? Even if he wasn't, I can't see being friends with him—at least not 'just' friends, you know? Much as I wish it wasn't true, we've got a chemistry that's off the grid, and I only have to be around him to find him really, really hard to resist."

"So why do it?" Harper asked. "I'm not trying to be argumentative, Tasha—I'm merely attempting to understand. If you could get beyond the linked-to-your-imprisonment part, if you could accept that he truly has no connection to what happened to you after he left that night, could you see yourself going for it?"

She shook her head. "No. Even if I did want more with him, what would be the point? I'm not sure I could be casual about a relationship with him. It was incredibly intense just during the two days we spent together in the Bahamas, and God knows I don't want to be my mother, convinced I'm getting true love when in truth what I'm getting is only short shelf-life sex. Luc is in a dangerous business that takes him to foreign countries for months—maybe even years—at a time. I'm certainly not signing up for something like that. Plus, the last time he and I got together, it took me two years before I even dated again—and three before I had sex with another guy. You think I'm anxious to ever re-open the door for *that* crap?" Not bloody likely—not when, much to her disgust, he was already the damn gold standard against which she measured other men.

She squared her shoulders. "No," she repeated firmly. "I know, between renting my studio and his relationship with Jake and Max, that I'll be running into him a lot while he's here. And I promise you right now that I won't do anything to make you all uncomfortable— I'll play nice when I'm thrown in his company. But the best thing for everyone concerned is for me to keep as much distance between the two of us as I can."

She picked up her purse. Slinging it across her torso by its long strap, she looked solemnly at Jenny and

Harper. "And that, my most excellent friends, is precisely what I intend to do.

"I'm going to stay as far the hell away from Luc Bradshaw as I possibly can."

CHAPTER EIGHT

LUC KNEW HE should leave Tasha the hell alone. It was what she obviously desired, and he'd never been one to push himself where he wasn't wanted. Clearly, while she might want him physically, he sure as hell wasn't *wanted* wanted. Not in the whole-package way she once had. She'd all but ripped the welcome mat out from under his feet making that clear.

But even knowing it, he'd managed to hold out for only a few stinkin' days. He didn't know what it was about her. In any other situation, with any other chick, he was the damn king of control. Yet when it came to this particular ginger-haired woman...

Friday night he found himself back at Bella T's ordering a slice—and not to-go this time. Instead he scored the last available table, and luck was clearly on his side, because when he took his seat, he had a direct line of sight into the kitchen.

After the charmingly friendly waitress, Tiffany, walked away, Luc sat back to watch Tasha as she supervised the boy who used to buss—the same teenager she'd stood up for when that other, full-of-himself teen had tripped him up. Jeremy, she'd called him. Apparently she'd promoted him, because the kid was concentrating for all he was worth as he tried to assemble a full-sized pizza and several slices at the same time.

After the first glance, Luc barely spared him another. When it came to commanding his attention, Tasha had more pull than the moon on the tide. And not just this evening, either; she tugged at his awareness anytime she was within sight.

As usual when she worked, she had her hair pulled back, this time in a loose braid. Nothing, however, could quite control that incredible strawberry-blond mass; several of the shorter tendrils had worked their way free to curl around her face and spiral down her neck, and the ones that stayed secured lent wave, texture and size to her plait. Moving around the kitchen like a dancer, she spun from one chore to the next.

Damn. Luc blew out a soft breath, because the woman was just always so...herself. It didn't matter what she wore, whether it was a T-shirt and jeans, with her narrow hips wrapped in one of her ubiquitous white work aprons like today, or a skimpy little summer dress and killer heels. It didn't matter what she was doing, either. At the moment, for instance, even as she multitasked her way through her own chores, she talked Jeremy through his training. And a guy didn't have to actually hear what she was saying to tell she was all easy and low-key and smiling. The teen giving her his earnest attention looked half dazzled.

Luc could sympathize; even after all this time, he remembered how it had felt to be the recipient of all her attention, remembered the way he'd basked in her conversation and her friendly, warm laughter. He, a guy about as far removed from a poetry lover as a man could get, had thought the latter sounded as if it were saturated in sunshine.

Okay, that was beyond embarrassing. Luckily, no one but himself would ever know of it.

Luc's focus on Tasha abruptly fractured as he became aware of a soft hum of irritability filling the air around him. It reverberated like a beehive that had been disturbed, and he realized the sound had been tugging at his subconscious for a couple of minutes now—even if it was only at this moment, as the buzz grew louder, that it truly sank in. He twisted in his chair to see what was up.

People were stacked up waiting for a table. It wasn't, he saw as he glanced around, because there weren't any available. The problem was that there weren't any clean ones. Spotting Tiffany, who looked a lot less amiable and more frazzled than he'd ever seen her as she delivered an order to someone in the take-out line, he rose from his table and strode over to the short stack of tubs that sat on a small stainless-steel cart at the end of the counter. He picked one up and headed for the nearest table to start clearing up.

From the corner of his eye he saw the girl who'd refused to leave with the little shit who'd tripped up Jeremy when he'd stormed out after Tasha's set down. She, too, got up from her table and grabbed a tub and began clearing some of the other tables. It surprised him, because she looked like everyone else in that group of affluent kids who came in here. They all had in common soft-skinned hands that looked as if they'd never attended to a chore in their lives.

Then he shrugged, because it just went to show that appearances really could be deceiving.

Tiffany raced up with a sponge seconds later and went to work wiping down the tables they'd cleared. "Thank you, both of you!" she said fervently, and Luc finally figured out what it was, besides the uncharacteristic dip in her sunny personality, that was so different about her. He had never seen her without flawlessly-made-up eyes and perfectly applied lipstick. But at the moment, the former was smudged and the latter was entirely chewed off, a result no doubt of trying to keep up with everything in the front portion of the restaurant by herself.

"Bella is busier than it was the same time last year," she said. "And, of course, Friday night." She hitched a plump shoulder as if that last were a no-brainer. "There's a big void now that Jeremy's moved into the kitchen." From one of the pockets in her apron she pulled out flatware that had been rolled in paper napkins. She efficiently laid one out in front of each chair on the now-clean tabletop.

Then she looked up at them again, her expression devoid of its usual effervescence. "You ask me, the sooner we put an ad in the paper for a new busboy, the better."

PEYTON VANDERKAMP BLEW out a breath, shook out her hands, then elevated her chin, because that was the only way she got through the hours these days—by making it look as if she was just too cool to care what people thought of her. She poked her head into the kitchen, which was now deserted except for Bella T's proprietor. "Excuse me, Ms. Riordan?"

Of course, her assumed haughtiness often meant people thought she was a bitch, a belief given teeth by the fleeting annoyance that flashed across Tasha Riordan's face. Peyton's chin ratcheted a notch higher. Better the other woman thought her a bitch than looked at her as if she was someone who was perpetually terrified that her life was spiraling out of control.

Even if that was a lot closer to the truth.

Then the redhead's pale eyes warmed. "Peyton Vanderkamp, right?"

Peyton nodded. She'd lived in Razor Bay just over three years, yet still she was occasionally taken by surprise by the way everyone knew at least the minimum about everyone else.

"Tiffany tells me you stepped in to buss the tables when they started stacking up on her."

"Me and the new Mr. Bradshaw guy." She shrugged. "That's what I want to talk to you about."

Tasha's eyes cooled considerably. "You want to talk about Luc Bradshaw?"

"No!" *Too vehement.* She drew in a silent breath and tried to infuse some sophisticated boredom into her expression. "No, not a *man*." She attempted a careless laugh but wasn't at all certain she pulled it off. "*God* no. The job."

"What job?"

"Tiffany said you all need to hire a new busboy to

pick up the slack for Jeremy's promotion. I'd like to apply."

Auburn eyebrows quirked skyward. "You want to be my busboy?"

"Yes. Well, busgirl, I guess." She squared her shoulders. Looked the other woman in the eye. "I'd like to be your busser, whatever title you give it."

Tasha considered her for a nerve-racking moment, before she said with soft-voiced finality, "I try to hire kids who need the money."

She almost walked away then. Almost. But the truth was… "I need the money."

She'd said it as quietly as she dared, hoping that the few people still in the pizzeria wouldn't hear. Tasha must have heard her just fine, however, because she said in an equally low voice, "Word around town is the Vanderkamps are— How can I put this delicately?" One shoulder hitched, and her mouth quirked as if to say, *Who am I kidding?* "Richer than God."

"And my stepfather is," she admitted. "But he and my mom are divorcing, and I guess he's divorcing me, too, because he says I can figure out how to pay for my own college tuition." She had practice willing back tears, and if she had to swallow the lump in her throat that rose every time she remembered him telling her that—well, that was her secret.

"Oh, sweetie, I'm sorry." Suddenly the woman every teen in Razor Bay thought was so hip and too cool for school went all soft-eyed. "That stinks."

She had no idea just how much, and Peyton tilted her chin so far up she hoped to hell the fire sprinklers in the ceiling didn't go off, because she'd drown in seconds flat. "I don't need your *pity!*"

"Oh, trust me," Tasha said flatly, all softness erased. "With your attitude, nobody's going to pity you."

And just like that, any possibility of getting the job disappeared. Peyton knew she should have dialed back on her pigheaded pride, but these days it was the only thing she had going for her. "Well, thanks for your time," she said with stiff politeness. Then, before turning away, she met Tasha's gaze. "For now, my mom and da—" The word stuck in her throat and she coughed. Cleared her throat. "For now, they're keeping their problems on the down-low." She detested the very idea of begging, but God— "I'd appreciate it if word of them didn't get around."

"No one will hear about it from me."

"Okay, then. Thank you." She turned to go.

"I pay minimum wage, but you get a small cut of Tiff's tips on top of that, which, trust me, given that she's probably the best waitress in the known universe, is not small spuds."

Peyton froze in shock, then slowly twisted around to stare at Tasha over her shoulder. "What?"

The other woman's brows lifted. "You have a hearing problem to go with that attitude?"

"No. *No!*" Turning the rest of the way, she smiled— heck, maybe even grinned—for what felt like the first time in months. "Minimum wage, small percentage of the tips. Oh, man." Remembering the persona she'd built so no one would know how messed up her life had become and dare to feel sorry for her, she reined herself in. Gave the other woman a cool look. "When would you like me to start?"

Tasha just shook her head as if Peyton couldn't fool a toddler. But all she said was, "You started tonight—figure out how much time you put in and fill it in on your time card tomorrow. We need you more on the dinner shift then, but if you want more hours, you can fill in the lunch shift, as well."

Two shifts would give her more money and more time to avoid home. Lord knew she tried to do that as much as possible. "I'll take both."

"Shift starts at noon, but you should get here a little early. You'll have paperwork to fill out." Tasha gave her a sober-eyed once-over. "You strike me as a girl who's put thought into all your contingencies, so have you considered what that crowd you run with will say when they find you working here?"

Oh, yeah. She knew perfectly well what they were going to say, considering most of the kids who made up her clique, especially the girls, could be snobs to the nth degree. Well, not Marni; Marni was sweet and thought the best of everyone. But peer pressure was tough, so who knew whether her friend would follow the herd? "Yes. Maybe not my working here so much because everyone thinks you're pretty hot stuff, so that could go either way. They might think bussing is beneath me or they might find it too kitschy for words and start hounding you to give them jobs they can play at."

She shoveled her fingers through her hair and blew out a breath. "It's the minute they find out I'm no longer a part of their income bracket that's gonna kill me with that crowd. I don't have real high hopes in that regard." Or any, truly. She shrugged, as if pretending she didn't give a great big rip would actually make it true. "Not much I can do about it, either way."

"True," Tasha agreed. "And if you don't listen to any other advice I ever give you, listen to this." The exotic-looking woman stared her in the eye. "Screw 'em if they don't support you. When times are tough, you find out very quickly who your real friends are. I know this probably doesn't help, because you no doubt think I don't remember the way it was in school—but I promise you, I can summon up those days like that!" She snapped long fingers. "I only had a few friends then and only one real honest-to-God through-thick-and-thin-type friend. If you have your one bestie, then, girl, nurture that friendship. Don't lie to her and don't do that pretending-everything-is-cool thing you do, if in fact it's not. Because if you're real with your friend, she'll likely be the same with you. And real friends do make the assholes not matter so much."

Peyton stared at her. How could Tasha read her so easily? Looking at the tall strawberry blonde, she couldn't wrap her head around the fact that there was a time when this woman, so assured, so *together* and easy in her own skin, had to struggle through shit in school. "I find it hard to believe you didn't have many friends."

"Please. This town is peanut-sized—you can't tell me you haven't heard stories of my mother."

She had, of course, but wanted desperately to say, "No, ma'am. Can't say that I have." But thinking of her instructions not to pretend, she nodded. "It's true—I have. So I guess if high school when you went was anything like it is now, there were probably a lotta people who reminded you of her reputation every day."

"Yeah, there were—and the hierarchy was the same, so a lot of them were from a group like yours that thought status was the be-all and end-all. And I won't lie to you. It wasn't easy being made fun of or reviled for something I had no control over. But when Jenny Salazar came to town in our sophomore year, we just clicked, and it changed everything. It was amazing how much easier it made putting up with crap like that. Do you have anybody you can lean on?"

"Maybe. I won't know for sure until I see what she does when the other girls in the clique I hang with turn their backs on me." Marni was already on the fringes of the group, so Peyton supposed she couldn't really blame her friend if she turned away with the rest of them. She'd hate it, but she'd try not to blame her for it.

Because truth was, she couldn't say with 100 percent certainty what she would have done before her own life crumbled around her. She'd like to think she'd have had empathy if their positions were reversed.

But maybe she was just fooling herself. Maybe she would have been the biggest bitch of all.

Leaving Bella T's minutes later, she decided to do the rip-the-Band-Aid-off thing and find out where she stood sooner rather than later. She'd tell Marni the truth and see where it led her.

She knew she was taking a chance, because if Marni spread her parents' troubles around, Peyton would lose her standing even sooner than she anticipated. But she was going to take a page out of the Tasha Riordan play-book and go with the truth. It was probably better to know one way or the other anyway instead of waiting around for the other shoe to drop.

As she climbed into her car, a sudden awful thought hit her. What if her dad—?

Pain shot through her. Matt, she meant—she had to get it through her head once and for all that he didn't want to *be* her dad anymore. But as she drove over to Marni's, she wondered if Matt would take her car back. It had been her sixteenth-birthday present, but the way everything else was upside down these days, who knew? She sure hoped not, though, because now more than ever she was going to need it to get to work.

To her surprise, those two simple words were like an analgesic balm to the open wound that was the past several months. *To work.* She had a job. She doubted it would turn out to be her life's work, but she was ex-cited about it. Bella T's was a popular place staffed with interesting people.

Not the least of which was Jeremy Newhall.

It was probably best not to think about Jeremy, but, oh, God. It was hard not to. There was just something about him. He couldn't be more than a year older than she, but he had a quiet reserve and a way of carrying himself that made him seem older than any of the senior boys in her class. Maybe it was the fact that he'd spent time in Cedar Village outside of town. Everyone knew that place was designed to reform bad boys.

Ooh. *Bad boys.* Just the words gave her a little shiver.

"For God's sake, girl, get a grip!" As if she'd have

the first idea what to do with one of those anyhow, even given the opportunity.

She pulled into the driveway to Marni's house and parked behind Mrs. Dreesen's Buick Enclave. Turning off the engine, she sat for a moment, staring at the back of the house.

When Peyton had moved here midterm in the eighth grade, Marni had been the first kid on the school bus to and from the school in Silverdale to talk to her. The Dreesens had welcomed her into their home as if she were one of their own. If she counted up all the hours, she wouldn't be surprised to find she'd spent more time at their house since moving here than she had in her own. She definitely felt better here than anywhere else.

She unbuckled her seat belt and exited the car, admiring the stars hanging low and bright in the sky as she crossed the brick-paved back patio to the kitchen door.

Expelling the air in her lungs, she drew in a final calming breath and peeked in through the door window. The room was dimly lit and empty of Dreesens. She pressed the doorbell.

Pandemonium broke out inside. She heard Marni's mom yell "Somebody get that!" from the depth of the house while Beckett and Castle, a dog small enough to hold in two cupped hands and a motorcycle-sized mutt, skidded around the corner on the hardwood floor, barking their heads off. Marni's Tutu, a ginger-striped tabby who must have been sleeping somewhere in the kitchen, barreled out through the cat door, making Peyton leap to one side to avoid being run over. She'd run afoul of

Tutu's claws in the past, and it was an experience she'd as soon not repeat.

Marni appeared in the same archway the dogs had come through, and she was dressed in a stretched-out black leotard and pink toe shoes. She reached the door in two long *grand jetés*. Landing lightly in front of the door, she opened it and gave Peyton a happy-to-see-you smile. "Hey."

Something about Marni always made Peyton smile. Her dishwater-blonde friend had the sweet friendliness of a young Drew Barrymore, with the same kind of girl-next-door prettiness. "Hey, yourself. Am I mixed up? Is this dance-class day?" But, no, that couldn't be—it was Friday night.

"Nah, I was just practicing." She went over to pull the fridge open and leaned in. Her leotard cut up over a J-Lo-full butt to her invisible hip bones. Marni didn't have the usual dancer's body; she was a far cry from anorexic stick-straight, instead possessing full breasts, a small waist and round hips and thighs. But her aunt Stace had a dance studio in Silverdale, and Marni had been taking classes there since she was four. She was a kick-ass dancer.

One who glanced over her shoulder now at Peyton. "Want an ICE on ice?"

"Yeah."

Marni pulled out a bottle of the black cherry flavor and grabbed two glasses, filling them with cubes out of the fridge-door dispenser. She divided the tall, skinny bottle of carbonated water between the glasses, rinsed out the now-empty bottle, tossed it in the recycle bin and handed Peyton her drink.

"Who's there?" her mother called from another room.

"Peyton!"

"Hey, darlin'! There's cookies in the jar. Be sure to grab a couple."

Marni made cutting motions at her throat and mouthed, "No! No!"

Peyton grinned. Mrs. Dreesen cooked like an angel but was a notoriously bad baker. "Thanks, Mrs. D.!" She made a production of opening the glass jar, then rattling it noisily closed again without withdrawing any of its contents.

She loved coming here. Marni's family was what Peyton always thought families should be: close, loud and loving. There was always something going on, it was always chaotic and it was such a contrast to the silent mansion on the bluff where she lived. The Dreesens didn't give a flying flick about climbing any social ladders. They owned this million-dollar house, but it was lived-in comfy, full of clutter and only minimally stylish.

Behind Marni's back, several of the other girls in their crowd made fun of her home and often of her figure as well, because it wasn't a size six. If you asked Peyton, they were stone blind. Marni radiated happiness—and that was sure as hell nothing to sneeze at. Plus, this was the most comfortable house in the world.

Even if it sometimes made her ache a little for what she lacked herself.

Marni grabbed a bag of pita chips out of the cupboard. "Let's go to my room."

"Yeah, I have something I want to talk to you about."

When Marni opened the door to her bedroom, it was to find her twelve-year-old sister, Bree, snooping through the baskets on Marni's shelves. "Get out of here, you little shit!" Marni snapped, then raised her voice to yell, "Mom! Tell Bree-the-Brat to quit coming into my room uninvited and pawing through my stuff!"

Bree's nose went in the air. "Like you have anything worth looking at," she sneered and strolled toward the door slowly enough to make the point that no one was running her out of the room. She slammed the door behind her.

"God!" Marni flopped on her back on the bed. She looked up at Peyton. "You're so lucky to be an only child."

A snort escaped Peyton as she dropped down next to her friend. "That's one way of looking at it," she said, rolling onto her side and bracing her cheek upon a drawn-up arm to better see Marni's face. "My house is quiet as a morgue half the time."

"Like I said." Marni sighed. "Lucky."

"Maybe not so much. My parents are getting a divorce."

"What?" Marni, too, turned onto her side and propped her head in her palm. "Aw, Peyton, I'm sorry. That really sucks."

She nodded. "And that's only part of the problem." Sharing the things that had led up to the dissolution of her parents' relationship with her friend, then admitting that her stepfather was cutting her off financially as well, she found that, rather than feeling mortified the way she'd expected when someone else knew how dicked up her life was, she actually felt better to have shared some of the crap that had been bottled up inside of her for so long.

"What are you going to do?"

"The good news is my grades should qualify me for some pretty decent scholarships. The bad news is I doubt I'll qualify for a full ride. But I guess there's always student loans. Plus, I got myself a job tonight and I'm going to start putting away as much money as I can."

"You got a *job?* Where? How?"

"Bella T's." She shared the events of the night with her friend and held her breath, waiting to see how Marni would react.

"Are you *serious?* You're gonna work with *Jeremy Newhall?* Omigawd." Marni laughed deep in her throat. "That is so awesome."

"I know, right?" She grinned at her blonde friend. "I hope I don't say something incredibly stupid."

"Nah, that would be me. You always seem to know just what to say."

She sobered, because in truth, so much of her personality was a great big act. She heard Tasha in her head telling her not to pretend. "I...don't really. I'm scared a lot of the time and just do my best to make sure no one can tell." *And, please, oh, please, don't spread that around.* It was the most vulnerable she'd ever allowed herself to be in front of another girl, and she didn't know what she would do if it turned around and bit her on the butt.

"Well, it doesn't show."

"Nobody knows about my parents' divorce yet."

"Then I won't say a word."

That simple. Peyton blinked back tears. "Thanks, Mar. You're the best."

"I know what a lot of our group say about me, you know," Marni said with sudden fierceness. "About my figure and about my family, too. It's funny how as individuals, they'll make a point of telling me so-and-so said such-and-such—as if they're so righteous for not saying it themselves, even as they rush to make sure I hear about it. I also know that you haven't joined in to bash me."

She snorted. "As if. You and I both know you're probably fitter than the rest of us combined. And I wish I *had* your family."

"Well, that works out pretty handy, then. Because as far as the Dreesens are concerned, you do."

CHAPTER NINE

TASHA HADN'T HAD a day off since the end of May. The summer rush was becoming an ever-shrinking speck in her rearview, however, and while she hadn't quite weaned herself from the pizzeria's seven-days-a-week schedule, she was quickly developing a particular fondness for Mondays. That was the day the pizzeria didn't open until three o'clock in the afternoon, when the after-school rush began.

Bella T's had become the unexpected favorite in-town teen hangout, making the post–school day income a lucrative part of her business. And when it came to Monday's schedule, it didn't hurt that she'd applied her own logic and made up for the late opening by closing early. People in Razor Bay had learned all there was to know about the new hours pretty damn quickly once word got out that you'd better pick up or consume your pizzas by seven-thirty Monday nights, because Tasha was serious about her closing time. She shut down Bella T's on the dot.

This particular Monday found her still lounging in bed at almost ten in the morning. It was a beyond-rare activity, or non-activity as the case might be, but she'd crawled out of bed this morning only long enough to make herself a mocha and now sat propped against a pile of pillows, sipping her drink and reading book two in a Virginia Kantra trilogy—a luxury she rarely had time for these days. She had errands and chores that had been steadily piling up, but they could just cool their jets a

little

bit

longer.

She was feeling so mellow that when her phone rang she reached out a languorous hand, swept it off her nightstand and brought it to her ear without taking her gaze off her book. Things were just beginning to heat up between the woman who'd been fired from her job in the big city and come home to the Carolina island town that as a teenager she couldn't wait to escape and the guy she'd tried to forget.

She pushed the talk button and murmured, "Good morning."

"Good morning, baby doll," her mother's voice sang at the other end of the line. "Guess what? No, no, don't bother. You'll never guess!"

With a regretful sigh, she shoved a strip of paper into her book to mark her place, then set it on the nightstand. Throwing back the comforter, she swung her legs over the side of the mattress. "Oh, let me try anyhow, Mom. Hmm. Could it be…you're in love?"

"Yes!" Her mother laughed in delight. "I guess you have heard that before."

"Maybe a few times." *Try a few hundred.*

"Ah, but this time it's different!"

"I'm sure it is," she murmured, not sure at all. "So, tell me all about him. What's his name? What does he do for a living?"

"His name is George. Oh, honey, I wish you could see him—he's so tall and handsome."

Tasha waited, but it soon became apparent her mother didn't intend to say anything else. "And he does what?"

"He's, uh, sort of between jobs at the moment. Employers can be a little judgmental when they find out he has a record."

"Yeah, go figure." Okay, so she'd been arrested herself, which one might think would make her reserve judgment. She thought she'd hold off on bonding with the guy over their respective arrest records, though. Because going by experience, she gave her mom's new relationship two months.

Tops.

As Nola sang George's praises, Tasha attended to the conversation with only half her attention. The other half began prioritizing that list of chores and errands.

Yet the minute she said goodbye, she changed into a bikini, topped it with a cover-up and donned a pair of water socks. Grabbing a beach towel out of the bathroom closet, she shoved it into a tote. After adding her keys, phone, SPF and lip balm, she slung it over her shoulder and let herself out of her apartment.

Screw the errands and chores; she was gifting herself an hour to play. The weather was gorgeous, and that probably wouldn't last much longer. The tide was closer to high than low, which she preferred for what she had in mind, and she could be at a spot she liked between the bay and the inn in ten minutes. That left her fifty for one of her favorite things: swimming.

She'd worked like a dog for months. It meant she was growing her business, so she didn't begrudge the sweat equity that required. But it also meant she'd missed out on most of the highlights of summer. She could spare an hour to give herself a taste, at least, of one of the delights of that season in Razor Bay.

She'd love to talk Jenny into joining her, but being general manager at the inn meant working with the public. *That* meant dressing up and, face it, swimming was notoriously tough on the 'do. She supposed Jenny could try keeping her hair out of the water, but where was the fun in that? Preserving your 'do wasn't swimming. At least not the way they did it.

Come to think of it, preserving the 'do was actually more her thing than Jen's, since unlike her own, Jenny's hair was enviably stick-straight. All *she* usually had to do to have it dry as sleek and shiny as a model's was run a comb through it when it was wet. It would be quite irritating, really, if she didn't love her friend so much.

Tasha pulled her Droid out of the towel bag as she strode along the boardwalk and gave her best friend a call. It went straight to voice mail, which meant Jen was tied up.

"Hey, girlie-girl," she said after the beep. "I'm gonna grab a swim off the boardwalk at our usual town-side spot and was calling to see if you could join me. Guess not, though, huh? Your loss—I'll wave as I go by." Laughing, she hit the End button, then threw the phone back in the tote.

Moments later, closer to the inn than to town, she climbed over the boardwalk railing on the high-bank side and dropped to the beach. Grateful for the protection of her aqua socks, she picked her way over small smooth rocks to a sun-bleached log up near the bluff.

After spreading out her towel in the patch of sand in the log's lee that made this one of their preferred swimming spots, she shucked out of her cover-up and dropped it atop her bag, then headed back the way she'd come. She had to climb over the boardwalk again, but the only other place to score a patch of sand was quite a distance past the inn, and she didn't intend to spend her free hour doing more hiking than swimming.

The pebbles gave way to rocks in a mix of sizes. They were interspersed with the sand-and-water polished detritus of oyster, muscle and clam shells, and she employed care to avoid their razor-sharp edges. Old-timers who'd lived in Razor Bay since mid-last-century told stories of how the beach had once been all sand. None of them could agree on what had caused it to change, only that the change had been gradual. And it was true that Tasha remembered a lot more pockets of sand when she was a kid than you found these days.

But she shrugged as she approached the water, because, really, it was what it was. Besides, a moment later she reached a long narrow mostly shell-and-rock-free spot and, whooping, she raced across the last few feet of gently sloping beach and entered the water. Resistance against her legs slowed her down as it rose around her thighs, and she dived beneath the surface.

"Damn!" she yelled as she surfaced, flinging her hair to get it out of her eyes. "That's *cold.*"

She loved the canal. It was salty and chilly and buoyant, and there was no other place like it—at least not that she'd ever been. She struck out several more feet from shore, then turned to swim parallel to the beach, lazily propelling her forward momentum with a freestyle stroke that cut through the calm water.

She stopped to get her bearings a while later, but as she trod water, she found she'd picked a particularly cold spot for pinpointing her exact location. Peering down through the crystalline water, she noticed she was over what was a large sand flat at low tide and sidestroked until she floated above a rockier patch. When the tide was out, the rocks and shells on the beach collected the heat of the sun. Those in turn warmed the water above them once the tide turned to come back in. Sand flats just didn't possess the same thermal absorbing properties.

Hearing voices from the shore, she realized she was nearing the inn, and as she swam past the float, she did as she'd promised in her message to Jenny and waved. She grinned to herself when she turned her head to breathe—because, please. Like anyone she knew would see. But a promise was a promise.

A while later, seeing a landmark that made her realize how far she'd swum, she decided it was probably time to turn for home. Executing a flip turn, she headed back the way she'd come. She wanted a little time to lie on her towel in the sand and soak up the day's lazy heat. Given her pale skin, she couldn't afford much sun exposure, but ten minutes this early in the day and late in the season would give her all of the joy of sunbathing and none of the damage.

She was maybe three-quarters of the way back to her spot when something sleek brushed up against her right side. It startled her so much she almost breathed in water, but lifting her head in time, she saw a dark-haired, deeply-golden-skinned man swim past.

Her heartbeat, already beating like a bongo drum, went crazier than an orangutan on crack. Because, dammit, she knew that hair, that skin.

What she didn't know was what the hell Luc Bradshaw was doing horning in on her swim time.

REALIZING TASHA WAS no longer swimming alongside him, Luc stopped as well and turned to face her, lazily treading water. "Hi."

She gently bobbed in the buoyant surf three feet away, all her wild curly hair as flattened to her skull as that much texture and mass could be and looking more red than its usual ginger-orange soaking wet. She regarded him through narrowed water-spiked lashes, her pale eyes flashing fire. "What the hell are *you* doing here?"

Good question. But before he could muster an answer that would satisfy both of them, she demanded, "Omigawd, are you *following* me?"

"*No,* hey. I was with—"

"Because I already told you I appreciated the way you stepped in and bussed tables Friday night."

"Yes, you did," he murmured. "You even comped my tab, beer and all."

"Yeah," she agreed dryly. "I thought it showed a more immediate appreciation than cutting you a check for the requisite hours of minimum wage that I pay my bus-kids. And I am grateful—I should never have allowed Tiff to get so overworked. But that doesn't mean you can follow me like some creepy stalker guy."

"Really? A stalker? Conceited much?" He regarded her levelly. "I was with Jenny and Jake when she listened to your voice mail, and it brought us down to the beach to see you wave like you said you would when you went by."

"Oh."

Okay, embarrassing her wouldn't win him any points. Besides, her cheeks held a faint wash of pink and the sun shone in her eyes, making the gray-blue irises look fathoms deep and highlighting the little striations of gold he'd forgotten she had around her pupils. He swam in close, but was careful not to touch. "I'm sorry about nudging you when I swam past. I can see how that might seem kinda stalkerish when you think you're in the canal alone. But it wasn't deliberate, *angelita*. I was trying to catch up and thought I was farther away than I was." He wisely kept to himself that he *had* leaped at the opportunity to be where she was. That was a long way from stalking anyway.

"Okay, so maybe I jumped to conclusions," she admitted with a self-deprecating twist of her lips. Her wry humor was one of the many Tasha things that grabbed him by the short hairs—and had done so since their very first encounter on that long-ago island. "I know it bothers Jenny that I swim by myself."

"She says you can easily swim a mile and a half, and it scares her that you do it without a spotter." He moved in closer yet, and this time didn't sweat it when one of his legs momentarily tangled with hers as they trod water. He lowered his voice. "Think of me as your spotter."

She snorted and started swimming again. He admired her form for a moment, then followed in her wake.

She swam steadily for a while, then began pausing every hundred feet or so, clearly searching for something. He knew she'd found it when she turned and commenced a serious push toward the beach. Moments later he found himself hanging back to watch in appreciation as she strode out of the surf, admiring the long, fit torso bisected by her colorful T-back bikini top. As for the bottoms…

Well.

Her butt constantly caught him by surprise. It was seriously nice, amazingly round, considering her near-total lack of hips.

His hands itched to shape both. Made uneasy by the urge, he shoved his fingers into the pockets of his shorts to keep from following her and doing just that. Since he needed his hands free for balance as he picked his way barefoot over the rocks and shells, however, *that* lasted about two seconds. But, man, what was he thinking?

Oh, not so much in regard to the lusting—he was a guy, and she was so damn desirable that he really had no choice but to lust. This compulsion to pursue her, though…that was a whole nother matter.

Hell, it was nuts, was what it was. His life's work was taking down cartels, and no doubt sooner rather than later he'd be heading back to a new assignment in the dark world of the Latin American drug trade. So it wasn't as if anything between them had a snowball's chance of actually going anywhere.

For a moment, he remembered the exhaustion of always living on the edge rather than the compensating adrenaline rush. He did purely love that rush.

But sometimes constantly living a lie was just…tiring.

He shook off the traitorous thought. Hell, it was a momentary dissatisfaction; he'd felt it before, and it always went away as soon as he was back in the game. The point here was his persistent pursuit of Tasha. If he just wanted to scratch an itch with a desirable woman, then the smart thing would be starting fresh with someone he didn't share a history with. His chemistry with Tasha was every bit as combustive as it had ever been, but she was pissed with him six ways from Sunday, and convincing her not to be would take a helluva lot of work. For minimal returns.

A vision of her as she'd been in the midst of an orgasm in the Bahamas blasted through his mind, and he had to bite back a groan. Okay, not so minimal. But still…

He laughed at himself and picked up his pace to catch up. Because, face it, he knew damn well he was gonna go for it. Hell, *Jake and Jenny* knew he was gonna go for it after the way he'd yanked his shirt off over his head in the wake of Jenny's *no spotter* remark and thrust it, his wallet, Tevas and cell phone at her with a muttered "She's got one."

He caught up with Tasha at the boardwalk and gave her a boost over the railing with a hand to that siren butt. It was sweetly firm through the saltwater-and-sun-faded spandex and cotton.

Without so much as a glance behind her, she slapped him away. "Hands off the goods, bud."

He grinned, because, *damn,* he loved her take-no-shit attitude. He had from the beginning. "Just trying to be helpful."

"Yeah, well, help your own self up. And then keep on going until you reach town." She moved toward the far railing.

"Okay." Before she could clamber over the other side, he swung himself onto the boardwalk and took the giant step necessary to snag her wrist. Pulling her back around to face him, he looked down at her non-encouraging expression. "But before I do—" He bent his head and kissed her.

The shock of discovery that hit him every time his mouth connected with hers constantly seemed brand-new. Yet at the same time it felt as if her taste, her textures, had been imprinted on his brain at birth. Like her personality, Tasha was both sweet and tart, and the need to just lick her up was so damn imperative that a rusty groan sounded deep in his chest. Moving to bracket her between his body and the railing at her back, he raised both hands to frame her face as he stepped in closer.

He loved the softness of her lips, especially that plush

upper one. Loved, too, the helpless way she kissed him back. She might not want to want him, but she was every bit as powerless to resist the electricity they generated as he. Her arms wrapped around his neck, and she pressed her water-stippled body to his, her skin cool from the water and her little suit damply chilly. But the incendiary inferno of her mouth was all he truly zoned in on.

He pulled his mouth from hers with a final gentle suck and bent his knees to get a taste of the fragile skin beneath the angle of her jaw, licking the salty droplets that dripped from the ringlets beginning to reclaim their shape. Dragging openmouthed kisses down her throat, her chest, he arrived at the swells of her breasts rising out of the cups of her bikini top. After several long moments enjoying the pliant give of her pale cleavage, he lifted his head. Had to clench his jaw to disentangle himself from her.

He stepped back. "That should get me back to town," he murmured, running a knuckle down her cheek. Dropping his hand to his side, he met her slumberous gaze. "Maybe you could remember this the next time you do the auto-push-away." Then he turned toward town and started walking.

The instant his head cleared he wanted to smack himself for not shutting the hell up after his kiss-getting-him-back-to-town remark. Because he knew the way Tasha's mind worked. If he had just walked away, then she might have given the ain't-going-away reality of their sexual chemistry some genuine consideration. But he'd had to go rub her nose in her response—and now it would be an icy day in hell before she admitted to anything, let alone her own enthusiastic participation.

Well, damned if he intended to stew over it. He had better things to do with his time.

Unfortunately, he blanked on what those things might be because his head was reeling, swamped with memories of his short time with Tasha on Andros Island, memories he had long ago determinedly and deliberately bricked up in a far, dark corner of his mind. The walls had started exhibiting cracks the minute he learned she lived here and now had well and truly imploded. He felt as if he'd been bombarded by percussion bombs.

Then he remembered the call he'd made to his SAC's office.

He'd been so fucking worried about her that night when he couldn't get back to the fancy little beach hut they'd shared, afraid she would think he'd abandoned her, that he hadn't cared enough to send people for her to make sure she was safe. His concern had rapidly turned to furious betrayal when Paulson informed him she'd left only moments after him.

Except she hadn't. And ever since talking with Tash on the veranda the other day, he'd been wondering just how the hell his team had missed the fact that she had been arrested by the Bahamians. They'd clearly talked to them enough to learn of the bust—but they missed the arrest attached to it? What kind of intel was that?

Every time he thought about it, he got a little bit angrier. Somebody on the ground that night had really dropped the ball. Their job was to gather all the facts on a mission, particularly if it was one that had turned out to be as FUBAR—fucked up beyond all recognition—as that night.

Someone had failed to do their job, and Tasha was the one who'd paid for it. So Friday morning he'd called SAC Paulson to find out who the hell had headed that detail. When it turned out that the special agent in charge was on vacation, he'd requested a copy of the report. He planned to go over it with a fine-tooth comb to find out who had let Tasha fall through the cracks.

It was possible it was a bureaucratic mistake, that some secretary somewhere had passed on bad information or read an agent's piss-poor handwriting and interpreted the data incorrectly. It happened. Except that didn't explain how they'd missed the fact that *she'd sat in a fucking jail cell for two nights*.

Either way, Luc wanted to both check the report and speak to Paulson when he got back to the office. If he was lucky, the report would be in his mailbox when he got back to the apartment. He sure as hell hoped so.

He needed something to focus on besides gun-shy Tasha Riordan and her wickedly addictive lips.

CHAPTER TEN

GOOD THING THIS is a short day. Tasha chopped veggies in Bella T's kitchen and watched Jeremy build pizzas. But she was hard-pressed to get her mind off that kiss. Damn Luc Bradshaw! Something had to be done about him—he had a way of sucking her into his agendas far too easily.

First order was to quit thinking about him. After watching Jeremy an additional few minutes, she gave him an approving nod. "You're doing a great job."

He shot her a pleased smile. "You think so?"

"Definitely. You're a fast learner—and you're neat. I really like that. I have a problem with messy kitchens—they make my teeth tight."

"Yeah, I don't like them, either. I hate having to dig through stuff to find the things I need."

She liked that he was growing more comfortable with her. It showed in the way he occasionally offered opinions now. Before, his conversation had been mostly about the things that needed doing and how he could improve on the way he did them.

But when Peyton waltzed into the kitchen hauling her tub of dirty crockery and glasses, he went abruptly silent, his easy smile erased like a mystic writing pad whose top sheet had been ripped upward to clear the slate. Tasha watched him as he covertly observed the pretty teen through lowered lashes while the girl deftly emptied dirty dishes into the washing machine.

And smiling ruefully, she was positive it wasn't to make sure Peyton loaded it to his satisfaction. It looked as if she wasn't the only one with romantic longings.

Her shoulders stiffened. Where the hell had *that* come from? She didn't long for Luc Bradshaw—and God knew all this sexual awareness between them didn't constitute a freaking *romance*.

But since he'd come to town she'd found herself bombarded out of the blue more than once by memories of the way it had been during those few short days they had spent together before everything went wrong. And she couldn't lie—she did kind of yearn for that.

"Well, get over it," she muttered beneath her breath. Noticing that Tiff was trying to simultaneously deliver orders to tables, take new ones and stay ahead of the kids lining up to pay, she went out to give her employee a hand by taking over the cash register.

She finished ringing up seven cheerleaders—you had to love teenagers and their separate checks—and was deliberating whether to crack another roll of quarters for the till when a man cleared his throat. She looked up and saw Axel Nordrum.

And smiled because, at last, here was a man who didn't pose a problem. She'd known him since the first grade.

Axel was tall, blond and good-looking. But rather than breeze by on his trifecta in the gene pool, he tended to be self-effacing, a little bit shy and a lot sweet. He was just a really nice guy.

And he'd had a crush on her for a long time. Somehow, though, it was low-key enough to be flattering without pressuring her to reciprocate. "Hey, Axel. I haven't seen you in a while. Been out of town on another trip?" He traveled quite a bit for his engineering job.

"Yeah, I've been up in the Aleutians doing some fieldwork."

"Well, good timing coming back. You're just in time to catch a little Indian summer while it's still around. I can't believe it's going to be October first on Wednesday."

"No fooling. Where did September go?"

She gave a rueful shrug. "Beats me, but I doubt this weather is going to last much longer."

"Hey, we've been known to have it last into October." His smile was slow and rueful. "Although, okay, I'll admit not often." He shifted in place, and faint color swept his cheekbones. "I ate a lot of fish up in Alaska and spent the last couple of weeks fantasizing about steak." He cleared his throat. "I, uh, wondered if you'd like to go into Silverdale with me one of these nights and have a nice dinner."

"Oh, I don't—"

"I'm just talking about a meal between friends," he assured her.

Her refusal had been knee-jerk, and her first thought—much to her disgust—had been that accepting his invitation would be disloyal to Luc. Which was crazy.

To make amends, she shot him her biggest and best

smile. "You know what? That would be nice. The trick, of course, is figuring out which night. Let me check my schedule and ask my new cook if he feels comfortable being left on his own or if I should close early. Can I give you a call when I hammer out the details?"

"You bet." He grinned at her and dug his wallet out of his back pocket. A second later he thrust out a business card. "Here—both my office and my cell numbers are on it. Thanks, Tash. I look forward to it."

She did, too. But she had a feeling maybe not in quite the same way.

AT ONE MINUTE past closing that night, she banged through the door of her apartment and headed straight for her bedroom. She pulled the fastener from her hair, quickly unbraided its unruly length and shook it out. Leaving it down, she kicked out of her work clothes and changed into an old favorite, her comfy gold-embroidered, faded turquoise nightshirt. She was on her way to the kitchen when a commanding knock sounded on her door.

Her mind shot straighter than an arrow to its target as pictures of Luc exploded across her mental screen. Visuals of his muscular shoulders, hair-furred chest. Of his big gentle hands and stupid kisses.

No! She was tired of being emotionally jerked around by him, and after stalking over to the door, she reached out and yanked it open, ready to rip him a new one.

She had to adjust her sights significantly downward. "Jenny!" She gawked at her petite BFF, who stood clutching a bag in her arms. "What are you doing here?"

She stepped back and waved her in. "That is, good to see ya. But what brings you?"

"Girls' night in, just you and me." She reached into the paper bag and withdrew a cylindrical object wrapped in butcher paper. She tossed it to Tasha, and then her hand immediately dived back into the bag.

Tasha snatched the offering out of the air. It was warm through its white paper wrapper, and she brought it up to her nose and inhaled the aromas of French rolls, pork, cilantro and marinated veggies. "Yum, Vietnamese sandwiches."

"Yep. I stopped by Saigon Boat." Jenny gave her a little one-sided smile. "Thought you might appreciate a break from Italian food."

"Good idea. It smells wonderful." She tilted her head toward the slider. "You wanna take them out on the deck?"

"Nah. I'm in the mood for a glass of red and your comfy couch. I call dibs on the chaise end!"

"Damn. You always were better at that dibs thing than me." She set her sandwich on the table next to the non-chaise end of the couch and walked around the breakfast bar to fish a wineglass and an old Starbucks insulated cup out of the cupboard. She poured Jenny's wine, then reached in the fridge for a Coke for herself. After emptying it into the cup, she grabbed a couple of ice cubes from the freezer, plopped them in and carried both beverages over to the couch.

They ate in silence, the only conversation Tasha's moaned "I *love* these things" before she took another bite and Jenny's wry "I know, right?"

Then they sat back, replete. Tasha rolled her head against the back of the couch to look at her friend. "You want some more wine?"

Jenny shook her head. "No. Thanks. I'm stuffed."

"Good. I don't think I have the energy to get up and get it anyway."

"You don't have to move a muscle." Jenny turned her head to look at her, as well. "You just sit there and tell me what the deal is with you and Luc."

Several of those muscles Tasha didn't have to move contracted beneath her skin. "Oh, ambush! Is that what bringing me dinner's all about? Softening me up for the kill?"

"Well, *yeah*." Jenny's tone said *duh*. "I know you saw him today because he was with Jake and me when I got your message. We all walked down to the beach to watch you go by, and I said, as I do *every* time I know you're swimming alone, that it bothers me that you do it a lot."

"Yeah, he mentioned that."

Her friend's lips quirked up. "I must say I've never seen a guy so anxious to lend a hand. He seemed pretty damn intent on playing lifeguard with you."

Tasha made a disparaging noise deep in her throat. "Oh, yes, he's a regular Samaritan."

"And quick with the mouth-to-mouth, I bet."

"What the hell?" She jumped. "What, you have X-ray vision now? How do you *know* these things? And how come *I* never got that girlie gene?"

"Oh, please. It's hardly master sleuthing. Girlie gene, my butt." Shaking her head, Jenny wiggled the tip of her index finger at Tasha's face. "You've got a little patch of whisker burn beneath your bottom lip."

Her fingertips flew to the spot indicated, and she felt the small abrasion. "Well, that's just stinkin' wonderful." She blew out a disgusted breath. "Practically every high schooler—not to mention the good-sized more parental-controlled dinner crowd—was in and out of Bella's today. And all the while I sashayed around the joint with a *damn kiss rash* on my face!"

She turned to face her friend. "He keeps *doing* this shit, Jenny," she complained. "He knows that I have a tough time resisting him, so he just keeps laying 'em on me."

She sighed. "It doesn't help that everywhere I turn these days, he's there. I can't escape him. And it *really* doesn't help that the chemistry between us seems even hotter and fiercer than it was in the Bahamas." *Oh, please, Riordan. Bitch, whine, complain.* She sat up a little taller. "Still, it *is* only chemistry, and I can hold strong."

"Damn straight you can."

"Which is why I accepted a dinner date with Axel Nordrum."

"You're going out to dinner with Axel?"

The question didn't even register. *"Orrr..."*

"What? No *or*," Jenny protested. "*Or*'s not a good idea."

Tasha stared straight ahead but didn't truly notice the scenery that usually filled her with delight because she was too busy thinking about the idea that had popped to mind. "Actually, it is. Because the attraction goes both ways. And two can play this game."

Alarm flashed across Jenny's face. "Um, I'm not sure that's a—"

She looked at her friend. "Why does Luc get to dictate all the terms, Jen? If he wants to play games—well, I'm a competitive woman, and I can sure as hell play every bit as well as he can." She'd turn his strategy right back at him. Get a little of her own back.

It would be nice to be proactive for a change.

She turned determined eyes on her BFF. "Why get mad when I can get even? It'll be a cold day in the tropics before I'll ever let Luc hit another home run with me, but why not let him get to first base, second base, hell, maybe even third if I'm in the mood? God knows it's been a long dry spell for me."

"And you don't worry that cock-teasing might be a bit Joanie-junior-high?"

She shot her friend an evil smile. "Oh, I'm sure it is, and if that makes me cheap and tawdry...well, I can live with it."

"I don't know about this plan, Tash—"

"That's okay, sweetie, because I do." She reached over and patted Jenny's hand. The dratted man had haunted her dreams for years, had *ruined* her for other men. It was only fair that she do her best to return the favor.

Let *his* damn dreams be haunted for a change.

THE FOLLOWING THURSDAY EVENING, in the relatively-quiet-for-once Anchor, Luc sipped his beer and waited for Max to throw his dart. He'd learned that the big guy liked to study every angle.

"Jesus, would you take your shot already," Jake finally demanded. "It's like playing with my grandpa."

"Eat me," Max said mildly without removing his serious gaze from the board. "And like *you'd* know anything more about having grandparents than I do." He glanced over at Luc. "Do you have grandmas and grandpas?"

"My *abuelo* Cesar on my mom's side is still alive. My *abuela* died when I was in middle school. There was no one from my—our—dad's side."

"That gives you a leg up on Jake and me." Max let the dart fly, and it hit just to the left of the bull's-eye.

You would have thought the thing had bounced off the board and fallen to the floor instead of sticking *this close* to center, if Jake's long-suffering sigh was anything to go by. "Okay, you gotta be some embarrassed over that pitiful throw," he said, muscling Max aside. "Move over and let a pro show you how it's done."

But Luc saw the fond smile he bent on his brother and had to tamp down an unworthy covetousness.

Dammit, he enjoyed these get-togethers with his half brothers. Yet for someone who never broke a sweat traversing the drug world, where his real identity could be discovered at any time and get him killed, he was learning that they were kind of stressful, as well.

He'd never been a man given to envy, yet he was discovering that the more time he spent around Jake and Max, the more he felt a little jealous of the relationship they shared.

He hadn't spent his entire life in the same town as his half brothers, and he lacked the easy relationship they shared. Instead he felt as if he had to prove himself to them.

Christ. He was thirty-five years old. He would have said he'd outgrown the need for approval a long time ago. But apparently not, at least not when it came to his family.

Maybe that was the thing, though. His job tended to preclude close relationships of any kind, and he'd long since lost touch with his friends from high school and college.

But—*family,* for God's sake. With Max and Jake that wasn't all gone. He just sort of longed for the deeper connection they had.

He still had a hard time coming to grips with the fact that his father—*their* father—who had been the best of dads to him, had just walked away from these two decent guys as if they didn't matter. Worse, as if they didn't even exist. And he couldn't wrap his head around Charlie never having said a word to him about the two half brothers he had living in another state.

Maybe if the old man had, if he'd manned up to his responsibilities, Luc, too, might have had a relationship with them that had a history of its own.

They wrapped up the game a little while later, and he knocked back the remainder of his beer and set the empty on the table that they'd been using as their home base. "Well, I gotta get going." He was still getting accustomed to this family shit and felt a sudden itch to get a little distance from it.

"Put Saturday on your calendar," Max said. "Harper and I want to have a barbecue at our place. We thought we'd make it earlyish so Tash can come between her rush hours. You can bring the chips."

"Sounds good." He swept his wallet off the table and shoved it in his back pocket. "See ya, what? One? Two?"

Max's massive shoulder hitched. "Beats the hell outta me. I'll check with the boss and let you know."

Jake gave him a pitying look and quirked a brow at Luc. "He's so whipped."

"Yeah," Luc agreed dryly. "Good thing you aren't."

His half bro merely shot him a hey-I'm-the-luckiest-guy-in-the-universe grin. With a shrug and a wry smile of his own, he bid them goodbye and headed back to Harbor Street.

When he got home, he stood awhile at the slider of his studio apartment, staring out at the water. The protected bay was flat as a mirror, but the canal beyond it was choppy and laced with whitecaps. A roil of clouds moved across a partially blue sky. He watched them for a bit and wondered what his big hurry had been to leave the Anchor, since he didn't have a clue what he was going to do with the rest of the evening. Jesus, he'd been back in his room only ten minutes and already he was itch-under-the-skin restless.

He heard music coming from next door and the occasional clatter of Tasha moving around her place. He tried to figure out what she was doing by the sounds she made, but they were too indistinct to pinpoint. Finally, tired of straining his ears like a high school geek trying to get a bead on the cheerleader, he pulled open the slider and stepped out on the veranda. Her sliding door was closed against the brisk breeze, which further muffled the noises coming from her apartment.

He strode over to the balustrade and, bracing his forearms against its solid ledge, watched two boats enter the harbor and jockey for space at the marina.

The weather had changed yesterday. It was still mostly sunny, but there was an influx of clouds that had begun moving in, blowing away, then building up again. A new briskness gave the air a bite that hinted at the approaching fall. Which he supposed was hardly surprising, considering it was the second of October.

But he regretted the fact that he likely wouldn't see Tasha in her bathing suit again anytime soon.

Or ever, in all probability, since he'd be long gone before next summer rolled around. By then he'd no doubt be ass-deep in some South American cartel.

He waited for the rush that a new case—or even the thought of one—always gave him. It didn't come, however, and he wondered why the idea of getting back to work didn't fill him with quite the same anticipation he usually got.

He rolled his shoulders. It probably had to do with the fact he still had some unfinished business here in Razor Bay. With Max and Jake. With Tasha, too, whether she wanted to admit it or not. Hell, he—

A knock on his front door interrupted his thoughts, and happy for an excuse to shelve them for now, he went inside and crossed to the entrance. He opened the door—then froze. And stared.

Tasha stood on the other side, but this wasn't everyday Tasha. This version wore a short greeny/bluey dress with a sweetheart neckline and little sleeves. The color no doubt had some froufrou name, but he was more interested in the tall strappy sandals she wore that easily brought her up past the six-foot mark. "Whoa."

She had smoky eyes, her crazy-sexy mouth was painted a glossy rose color and her hair was an untamed riot of long curls. She was a fucking vision.

"Don't just stand there gawking," the vision said, pushing her way past him, and then she turned her back on him when he faced her. Scooping the long curls from her neck and back, she pulled them around to tumble down her left breast. "Zip me up."

That was when he saw that the dress, with its darted-and-seamed formfitting top and short flowing skirt, had a wide, rounded V in the back as well, the top of which gaped from the highest point that she had managed to zip it. He stepped up behind her and reached for the zipper tab. It felt about the size of a sewing needle in his big fingers.

Standing this close to her, he detected an elusive musky sandalwood scent with a hint of—caramel?—and bending his head close to the side of her bared neck, he inhaled it as he unhurriedly fastened the dress the rest of the way. The skin on her neck, her exposed nape, was pale and fine-grained, and he wanted to lick it from the curve of her shoulder to her ear.

She slowly turned her head to look at him over her shoulder. "Are you *sniffing* me?"

"Hell, yeah. It's why you put perfume on, isn't it?" Okay, not so suave.

But she merely hitched a shoulder. "I suppose you're right. I did apply it...for my date."

Everything inside him stilled. "You're going on a date?" *No.*

"Yep." She turned the rest of the way, and it left her close. Very close. "Thanks for the zip job," she said cheerfully and, placing a long-fingered hand on his chest, rose on her toes. She pressed a quick here-and-gone kiss on his lips, then dropped back onto her tall heels. "I'm sure Axel appreciates it, as well."

Then with a small one-sided, knowing smile, she turned on those needle-thin high heels and went out the way she'd come in, closing the door behind her with a quiet click.

Leaving Luc pent-up and edgy and wondering what the hell had just happened here.

CHAPTER ELEVEN

"HELLO AGAIN."

Jeremy looked up from his work as frigging perfect Peyton Vanderkamp breezed past him on her way to the pizzeria's dishwasher. He grunted a begrudging response.

When she'd first started working here, she hadn't said word one to him, yet *now* she thought she had to greet him whenever she came into his domain? She made his mouth go dry every time he saw her, and this was her third damn trip through the kitchen tonight.

The shift wasn't even half over yet, and it was shaping up to be a long night.

Okay, so it was her job, and she was merely doing what she'd been hired to do—bussing dirty dishes from table to tub to the kitchen—where she unloaded her haul into the dishwasher. Nothing he could do to change that. Trouble was, she merely had to breathe to pull his focus, and without Tasha here to act as a buffer, Peyton was even more of a disruption to his peace of mind than usual.

As if it wasn't stressful enough being completely on his own tonight—even if he had told Tasha that flying solo wouldn't be a problem.

And it wasn't. He could—and would—do his job. But he wouldn't mind doing it without the distraction.

Peyton was sure as hell that. She was so damn pretty, with her baby-fine skin, golden-brown eyes and her short black hair that made her look like some kick-ass Disney animation pixie. But that body was all too real.

Oh, not that it was all gargantuan tits and traffic-stopping boo-tay. Unfortunately, it didn't have to be. At the moment her inverted heart-shape of a butt was pointed right at him as she bent to fill the soap dispenser, and it definitely had his attention. He wouldn't complain if she gave it a little shake.

Instead she straightened and closed the dishwasher door. She jabbed a button, and the hum of the appliance permeated the kitchen. He blinked to clear away the vision that felt burned into his retinas.

And got real in a hurry.

Jesus, the chick was one of the rich girls who ran with that whole money's-no-object group that came in here and acted like they owned the joint. Well, not all of them, but it was a sure bet that more of that clique did than didn't. And the worst of the lot was Peyton's boyfriend, that tool Cokely, who'd tripped him up and thought it so frigging hilarious.

Okay, to be fair, Peyton had refused to leave with the guy that day. And Jeremy couldn't honestly say he'd seen them together since then. But he was still way out of his league here.

That sentiment, however, just pissed him off. He'd worked hard on his self-esteem with the counselors at Cedar Village, and as a rule these days he felt pretty damn good about himself. No girl was gonna make him double-clutch that progress into reverse. No way, no how—he didn't care how hot she was.

He glared at her back as she gathered her tub. He had to keep his cool for only five more seconds, and she'd be out of here. Ten, tops. Just ten lousy seconds.

He could put up with anything for that long.

Which gave him one serious I-don't-*believe*-this moment when he heard himself demand, "Why are you working here, anyway? You sure as hell don't need the money."

She slowly turned to face him, her expression closed. Haughty. "So everyone keeps telling me." Her tone was cool, and she strolled up to him as if she didn't have a care in the world.

But when she tilted her head back to look up at him, she returned his glare with interest, her eyes a bare glint of bourbon-brown behind furiously narrowed black lashes. Holding the tub balanced against her hip, she poked him in the chest with the slender index finger of her free hand. "How the hell do *you* know what I need?"

God, she was a peanut. Oh, she might hit close to the mid-mark in the five-foot range, but she was still a good half-foot-plus shorter and a whole helluva lot slighter than he was.

Which—Jeezus, Newhall—is hardly the point. Straightening to his full height, he stepped back from that drilling finger. "I know you live up on the bluff with the rest of the fat cats."

"So you think *I* pay the mortgage on the house?

Sorry to disillusion you, pal, but that's all on my da—"
She cleared her throat. "My stepfather."

"And—what?—he doesn't give you a big enough
allowance?"

She looked at him as if he were something that
needed scraping off the bottom of her fancy red san-
dal. "I'm not sure what makes you think this is any of
your business, but he doesn't give me an allowance, period. He and Mom are getting a divorce, and as far as
he's concerned, I no longer exist."

"Aw, shit." His ire deflated like yesterday's helium-
filled latex balloon, and he reached out without thinking—then dropped his hand to his side before touching
her when he saw her stiffen. "I'm sorry," he said. "That's
rough. My mom has…issues, so I know what it's like to
have a parent just check out on you."

She shook her head. "I can't believe I even told you
that. Not that the news won't get around and probably
sooner rather than later. But until it does, I'd planned
to keep it under wraps." She hitched a shoulder. "Of
course, knowing Mom, she probably intends to drag me
out of Razor Bay the minute the ink dries on the decree,
so I don't know why I'm working so hard to keep it all
a deep, dark secret. I don't suppose it'll make a big difference who knows what about it if I'm not here for the
fallout. And despite wanting to keep it on the down-
low, I've already told Tasha and my friend Marni." She
narrowed her eyes at him. "And now you."

"Hey, your secret's safe with me." He gave her a swift
once-over, then cocked an eyebrow. "You, on the other
hand, pretty much suck at keeping it."

That startled a little laugh out of her. "I do not!"

"Me." A finger ticked up. "Marni." A second finger joined the first. "Tasha." He wiggled all three at her.

"Well, okay, I guess I do. In *this* instance. Ordinarily, though, I'm a sphinx. You can't *pryyyy* a secret from my lips."

"Yeah, right."

She slugged his arm. "It's true!" Then she studied him for a moment before asking, "So, how did you handle your mom's issues?"

He grimaced. "I didn't, at least not in any constructive way—that was kinda what landed me at Cedar Village. Which in the end turned out to be the best place for me, so I can't say that was such a bad thing." *Dude. She's not the only one who's suddenly chatty. What's up with that?*

He waved the mental reservation away. She had no agenda as far as he could tell and apparently was genuinely interested in what he had to say. So he blew out a quiet breath and added, "They helped me learn how to deal."

"Hey," Tiffany suddenly called from the counter separating the kitchen from the dining area, and he started, so focused had he been on Peyton. "We have tables that need clearing out here."

"Whoops." Peyton gave him a smile that was surprisingly sweet for someone who nine times out of ten came off as a chick far above all the crap that the rest of them slogged through on a daily basis. Then she turned away. And raising her voice as she headed back out into the restaurant, she called, "Sorry, Tiff. I'm on my way."

As Jeremy turned back to assembling pizzas, he wondered what he was thinking getting so relaxed with her. As a general rule he kept to himself, *particularly* when it came to the town kids. And yet…

By the end of the week, he supposed he could be considered a town kid himself. And he already worked here. He wasn't just a Cedar Village boy anymore—this Sunday he was moving out of his room at the Village and into a tiny rental on Henderson Road.

He was a little nervous about it. He'd have to look around for a cheap bike to buy, because his new house was a couple of miles from work. And except for a fairly decent bed and a few shabby pieces of furniture in the postage-stamp-sized living room, plus a pot or pan or two in the kitchen, he needed…well, everything.

But for the most part, he was pumped, because, *dude,* this would be the first place that was his alone. And once he had his very own address…well. He, too, would be an official Razor Bay citizen.

Maybe then he'd feel on more equal footing with Peyton, who, it appeared, was a whole lot more than just some rich girl from the bluff.

He never would have guessed it, but her I'm-above-the-mess-the-rest-of-you-call-life exterior was apparently a front, because the girl he'd thought she was, the one who observed everyone through shuttered, amused eyes and said little, turned out to be a chatterer. Hell, a chatterbox squared. She started talking the minute she hit the entry her next trip through the kitchen.

"This is your first time being in charge of the kitchen

on your own, right?" she asked as she started unloading the dishwasher and shelving its contents.

"Yep."

"Does it make you nervous to be totally responsible for everything?"

He wanted to be cool and deny it. Somehow, though, the truth just sort of jumped out of his mouth. "A little."

She shot him a smile over her shoulder. "Yeah, it'd make me nervous, too. You're doing great, though, so that's pretty sweet, right?"

His mouth quirked up. "Yeah. It is. Damn sweet."

She gave the last plate she'd stacked on the shelf a little pat, then reached for her tub and started unloading it into the now-empty washing racks. "Tiffany says Tasha went on a date tonight."

It took him a second to catch up with the change of subject. Then he nodded, because he actually knew something about it. "Yeah, she mentioned that. With some dude named Axel Someone-or-another."

Peyton turned to face him, the dirty glass she held clearly forgotten as she stared at him. "You're kidding me. She didn't go out with the new Bradshaw guy? The way those two look at each other, I thought for sure—"

"Nope. Axel. You don't forget a name like that."

She laughed. "No, I guess not." She fell quiet for a whole minute while she finished transferring the contents of her tub into the machine.

Tiffany came by with two new orders and a large Mountain Dew in a cup of ice, which she carried into the kitchen. Impeccably made up as usual, she handed him the drink. "Thought you might be getting thirsty."

"Thanks," he said, surprised and gratified that she'd thought about him. He guessed they really were starting to work as a team.

"Not a problem." She flipped him an acknowledging wave over her shoulder as she strode back into the dining room.

"She's nice," Peyton said and closed the appliance door. "And the girl knows makeup. Even the biggest snobs in school ask her advice on cosmetics. She can take one look at a girl and tell her exactly what color lipstick or eye shadow will do the most for her complexion—right down to the brand." She turned to him. "It's a—" Breaking off midsentence, she simply stared, apparently struck by the way he chugged down half his drink in one long gulp. Then she gave her head a shake. "—um, gift."

"Sorry," he said, using the side of his hand to blot the drip he felt on his bottom lip. "Is knocking it back bad manners? Sorry 'bout that, but Tiff was right. I was thirsty."

"I don't blame you. It's hot work." She shook herself. "Speaking of which, I better get back to mine. It seems busier than usual for a Thursday night."

"Tell me about it."

She laughed and strode back out into the restaurant.

Jeremy returned to work, as well. But as he assembled the new orders Tiff delivered, he found himself with a big—and he was pretty sure goofy-ass—grin on his face.

ARRIVING AT HER front door, Tasha turned to her date. "Thanks for dinner, Axel. I had a great time." The Good

Night ritual was upon her, that awkward moment she had…well, not dreaded, exactly, but had not been looking forward to. Would he try to kiss her? Would she let him? They'd agreed they were having dinner as friends, but she knew he'd like more.

And sure enough, he braced one hand on the lintel next to her head and leaned down. She didn't protest but merely looked up at him. And he kissed her.

It was nice. *Very* nice, actually. He was a…really excellent kisser. But no matter how good he was—

The door to the studio apartment next door suddenly opened. Axel took his time raising his head, and both of them slowly turned their heads to look down the hallway at Luc, who had stepped out and was locking up behind him.

His jaw was tight, and although he held a garbage bag in one hand, he seemed to forget it as he looked back at them. "Getting back kind of late from dinner, aren'tcha?"

She stiffened. "What are you, the dating police? We had a nice time and got to talking." Which was all true enough, but perhaps she sounded just the *slight*est bit defensive.

"Just saying," he said easily. "When I helped you into your clothes before your friend there picked you up, I—"

"Oh!" She pushed Axel back, stalked down the few yards that separated her apartment from Luc's and gave him a shot to the chest that didn't budge him an inch. "Helped me into my clothes, my ass. You are so full of it!"

Belatedly, it hit her that she'd left her date standing by her door, and, silently cursing herself, she turned on her heel and hurried back to him.

"I'm sorry, Axel. That was inexcusably rude of me." She appealed to him with her sincerest look—and she truly was sorry that she'd allowed Luc to draw her attention away from where it belonged—on her date. "It's just—I hate that he's trying to make it sound as if something happened between us that most certainly didn't." Or mostly hadn't, anyway. She had gone to his apartment to have him fasten a dress she could have zipped herself into with a modicum of contortion because she was tired of having him mess with her emotions.

Thinking about how effective his messing tended to be made her glance away from Axel again to glare at Luc. Truth was, she *still* thought he could stand a little of his own medicine. "Don't you have a bag to take out to the Dumpster?" she demanded, and, okay, that was weak.

But then she really looked at the drawstring kitchen sack hanging limply from his hand—and gave him a knowing little smile. The thing wasn't even half-full. "After all," she said smoothly, "it would be a shame if you missed next *Monday's* pickup. Not when you're so weighed down with. All. That. Garbage."

A satisfying hint of color washed his cheekbones, and he stalked past them and banged through the exterior door. It slammed closed behind him, and Tasha could hear the heavy thud of his feet pounding down the wooden treads of the exterior staircase.

For a second she felt exultant—until she turned back

to Axel, who regarded her with blank-faced neutrality. That was when it sank in that her rudeness had been beyond inexcusable. She'd said she was sorry, then just turned right around and gone back to one-upping Luc, making her apology little more than lip service.

"Oh, crap," she said miserably. "I really, truly *am* sorry. I know better than to get into it with Luc, but I can never seem to help myself." Axel's expression didn't change, and she offered tentatively, "Would you like to come in for a cup of coffee? Or I have some wine if you prefer. I promise to be better company."

He simply looked at her for a silence-filled moment. Then one big hand abruptly slashed to indicate first her and then himself. "You and me," he said slowly. "There's not even a spark of chemistry for you, is there?" His tone wasn't accusatory, but she felt abjectly guilty all the same. Because—

"No," she admitted. "I'm afraid there isn't. I like you immensely, Axel. I— Just not in that way."

"I've kind of known that since the sixth grade," he said gravely. "I suppose I thought that if I didn't admit it, things might change." He drilled her with Nordic blue eyes. "But that's never going to happen, is it?"

She shook her head. "No. I'm sorry. I really wish I could say otherwise." Lord, did she!

"So do I. But it is what it is." He bent and pressed a kiss to her forehead, then straightened once more to his full height and gave her a long unsmiling inspection. It ended with a terse nod. "Good night, Tash."

"'Bye, Axel." She longed to apologize once more but doubted he was interested in hearing her abject regret yet again. The last thing he needed was to be forced to make conversation to make *her* feel better.

She watched him walk away, knowing that for all she prided herself on being a decent person, she hadn't been in this instance. Now she had to live with the knowledge that she had treated a really good guy very poorly.

Dammit, she was more like her mother than she cared to admit. Because like Nola, she'd rejected someone perfectly nice to play stupid unproductive games with a man whose time in town was limited to say the least.

The Riordan women really did suck when it came to romance.

CHAPTER TWELVE

"THROW IT TO ME, Uncle Luc!"

Luc grinned and winged the Frisbee in a low, fast arc to Jake's son, Austin. He watched the kid catch it and snap it off to Max. He was unaccountably tickled when Max then sent it diagonally back to him instead of tossing it to Jake.

The four of them had been throwing the disc around Max's backyard while they waited for the briquettes to reach their optimum cooking temperature. Max didn't believe in gas grills—according to him, only a pussy would use one. Luc's two half siblings had trash-talked each other's choice in barbecues for a good ten minutes. No quarter was given on either side, but the bottom line today was Max's house, Max's rules. He had a plate stacked with truly excellent-looking steaks, and he was grilling them old school.

Luc rolled his shoulders. The barbecue his half brothers preferred wasn't the real issue here—although you had to appreciate how invested they could get in the subject. The real issue was how blown away *he* still felt knowing he was somebody's uncle. He had a *nephew,* for crissake. And not just any nephew, either, but this dark-haired, pale green–eyed awesome kid.

He had seen Austin on other occasions since he'd been in town, of course, but when Luc first came to Razor Bay it had been the tag end of the kid's summer vacation. He was fourteen, and as with teenagers everywhere, his waning vacation equated to hanging with friends and trying to cram in every last entertainment he could before school started up again.

Now that it was back in session, Austin stayed a bit closer to home, although he still spent as much time as Jake and Jenny allowed with his girl, Bailey, and best friend, Nolan. Little by little, however, he and Luc were getting to know one another.

"Wait!" the kid called now. "You gotta see this one!" He flung the Frisbee at an angle that flew parallel to the back of the house, before moving close enough to actually touch its wall. It skimmed along the cedar shingles for a few feet, then skipped away to sail within a foot of Luc, who snatched it out of the air.

All three Bradshaw brothers whooped their enthusiasm over the successful trick shot and Austin grinned in delight.

"How did you *do* that?" Luc demanded. Because, truly, it was brilliant. And looked damned difficult.

"I've watched the Brodie Smith YouTube videos, like, a million times," his nephew said. "And I've been practicing." Then he smiled sheepishly and admitted, "I only get it right about every third or fourth time."

"Which is a hundred times better than I'd ever get it." Having children of his own had never even been a blip on Luc's radar, but he could see why Jake was crazy proud of Austin. He really was a great kid.

"Tasha!" Harper exclaimed at the same time that Jenny said, "You made it!"

It jerked Luc's attention away from Austin, and after winging the disc he still held to Max, he stopped to watch Tasha as she strolled around the corner of the garage into the backyard.

"I did," she replied with a grin. "And unlike the last time I was here, I even remembered to slap on a little makeup."

The weather had dropped a good fifteen degrees since Thursday, and she had on skinny jeans and ankle boots. She'd topped them with a patterned blouse in autumn colors that was almost entirely covered by the rust-colored tunic-length sweater fastened over it with oversized bone buttons. Her hair was loose, the long mass of curls shifting with every movement.

He vaguely heard Jake's murmured, "Heads up, bro." But it was Austin's "Look out, dude!" that caught his attention. He was just turning his head to see what had put the alarm in his nephew's voice when the Frisbee caught him in the chest. It stung, but refusing to let it show, he slapped a hand to the plastic disc to keep it from bouncing off.

He felt stupid enough getting caught gawking at Tasha without the ignominy of having it smack him, then roll away to flop at her feet.

"Good reflexes," Max said. "You must've got 'em from my part of the family. Jake never would've caught it."

"Dude," Austin said without heat. "That's my father you're dissin'."

"Sorry, kid. But better you accept now that your old man's got certain failings that can't be worked around. If you don't expect much from him in the way of physical prowess, you won't be constantly disappointed. You clearly got yours from your uncle Luc and me."

Austin laughed. "Don't listen to him, Dad," he said, patting Jake on the arm. Then, in the way of teenage boys, his thought processes immediately skipped on to the next thing that popped into his mind. "I'm hungry— I'm gonna go check the coals." He raced off.

Luc turned to Jake with a grin. "You sure raised a great kid. You must be really proud."

His brother nodded. "I am proud. But I can't take credit for raising him. That was all on Jenny."

"Huh? I thought Jenny was your girlfriend. Is she Austin's mother?"

"No," Jake said. He hesitated for an instant, then shook his head. "Look, I need a beer if I'm going to tell this story." Covering ground with long-legged strides, he led the way to the cooler by the back stairs. He pulled three bottles out of the ice, opened them on the opener affixed to the side of the cooler and passed Luc and Max theirs. He took a long pull from his own, then lowered the bottle and met Luc's gaze.

"When I was in high school," he said, "I earned a full scholarship to Columbia University. I'd barely stopped whooping over my acceptance letter when I learned I'd knocked up my girlfriend." He blew out a quiet breath. "Man, I'd *dreamed* about leaving town, had worked toward that goal for years." He gave his head a little shake as if reliving the shock all over again. "Instead Kari and

I got married and I took a job at the inn. Like so many kids who get caught like that, I was miserable and so was she. Our marriage was pretty much in shambles by the time Austin was born." Looking off into the distance, he drank down more beer.

Then he looked back at Luc. "Insurance companies dictate that hospitals release people way too early these days, and shortly after Kari got home, she started hemorrhaging. The long and the short of it is, she died."

"Jesus." Luc didn't know what to say. "I'm sorry."

"Yeah. I was a mess. Emmett and Kathy, her parents, said I should take the scholarship, that they'd take care of Austin. I jumped at the chance—but I'm pretty sure they didn't intend that I wouldn't look back until this past spring."

"Dude." He couldn't wrap his head around that in conjunction with the man he'd been getting to know. "Seriously?"

"Unfortunately, yes. I have no excuse—I was young and selfish, and because of it I missed out on most of Austin's life."

Luc glanced at the women, who were lounging in chairs across the yard, laughing raucously over something. He got hung up as usual on Tasha, but pulling his attention from her, he looked back at the youngest of the Bradshaw brothers. "So where does Jenny come in?"

"Jenny came to town when she was sixteen," Max answered for his brother. "The reasons why make for a long story, and I'll let her share those details with you if she wants to. The upshot here is that she started working at the inn after school and on weekends maybe two days after moving here. She was a hard worker and got close to the Pierces." He seemed to realize that Luc didn't know who they were, for he added, "Kari's folks."

"Wait. They own the inn?"

"Yeah. Or owned—they're both gone now. Anyhow, when Jenny's mother died a year or so after they came here, Emmett and Kathy invited her to move in with them."

"She's the closest thing to a sister Austin has," Jake said. "Hell, the closest thing to a parent, really. She's the one who made sure his grandparents didn't spoil him rotten, which was their inclination with their only child dead and me deadbeating my responsibilities."

"Coals are ready," Austin yelled from the porch.

"Thanks, buddy," Max called back, then lowered his voice and gave Jake a level look. "Let it go, bro. You've paid for your mistakes, and you're doing everything you can to make up for your absence."

His ready defense touched Luc. At the same time it gave him the by-now-familiar pinch of envy over his half brothers' closeness. He was still trying to figure out what his place in this family was going to be.

He didn't have time to dwell on it, however, because Max yelled out Harper's name. When she twisted in her chair, raising her elegant eyebrows at him, he gave her quelling look the minimalist smile that anyone who'd spent any time with him knew was his version of a big shit-eating grin. "We're ready to throw the meat on," he said. "Is everything else ready?"

"Of course," she said regally. Then she grinned back, and hers was wide and showed white teeth and pink gums. Her olive-green eyes morphed from big and round to narrow little crescents, and she raised her beer bottle to him in a silent toast.

"Excellent!" He shot her a warm, private look, then turned back to the men. "Let's go grill us some steaks."

Luc took his turn manning the barbecue but didn't mind when he was shouldered aside by one half brother or another. Most of his attention was focused on Tasha anyway. She appeared to be ignoring his very existence, but he watched her as she and the other women went in and out of the kitchen to bring out the tableware, side dishes and drinks. Right up until they decided it was growing too cold and carried the items they'd brought out back inside.

He'd kept an eagle eye on Harbor Street the other night as he'd waited on the veranda for her to come home from her date. When he'd seen the tall blond walking her home, he'd gone into his studio and waited to hear them enter through the outside door—then manufactured that fucking flimsy excuse, which had been the first thing he thought of to put him out in the hallway with them.

That sure as hell hadn't been a well-thought-out idea. She'd seen right through his weak pretext and hadn't hesitated to call him on it, making him look like an idiot. Of course, he'd *been* an idiot, but what guy wanted to look like one in front of the woman he wanted?

Worse than that, however—much, much worse—had been having to witness her kiss another man.

He'd been totally unprepared for the hot wash of outrage that had roared through his veins. In truth, he hadn't even been able to stomach actually looking longer than that initial glimpse. But the damage had been done—the sight had burned itself into his brain.

Damn. No other woman provoked the kind of feelings in him that she did.

Undercover drug agents didn't have relationships. They had superficial encounters. Hookups. It was simply the nature of the job. It wasn't as if he could tell anyone the truth about what he did for a living. He couldn't use his real name. Lying through your teeth at every turn made it hard to lay any kind of foundation on which to build a sustainable relationship.

Back when he'd worked cases in the States, he'd spent his down hours hanging out with other undercover agents. They were the only ones who understood the pressures of the job they did—and it made the life easier because at least you had a few real friends. In South America, where, due to his fluency in Spanish, he'd spent the majority of his career, he hung out with drug exporters and killers.

And that had been okay with him, because the trade-off was the constant rush of staying one step ahead of a violent death. But seven years ago when he'd taken off for R & R, he'd wanted something different. He'd wanted to talk to somebody who was real. Someone not constantly playing an angle.

And he'd gotten that. In spades. He'd gotten Tasha.

Everything had been different with her—especially the way she'd made him feel. She had been so unselfconsciously, electrically *genuine,* and she'd made him feel alive in a way that hadn't had a damn thing to do with dodging death. He'd wanted to just spend hours talking to her. Had wanted to learn everything about her and to tell her things about himself. For two days he'd felt as if he were real, too. Just another regular guy.

Then that night had happened, and now everything had turned to shit. She no longer looked at him and laughed and said whatever came into her head.

And it was just as well, really. There was no way in hell he and she could have any kind of relationship when he spent months, sometimes even years, out of the country. His work was dirty and dangerous, and he had to have his head in the game 100 percent. An agent couldn't afford to worry about his family or his girl back home.

The few agents he knew who'd tried had ended up either dead because their focus was fractured or had lost that family back home because their wives had grown tired of being alone all the time.

So he had to quit crowding Tasha. Had to quit saying "But first" or "Before I go," and kissing her every time she rightly tried to ward off his attentions. He had to *not* be so gut-destroyingly jealous when another man kissed her.

Yeah, well, fuck.

He doubted that last thing was gonna happen anytime soon. The only reason he hadn't gone ape-shit after he'd stormed off Thursday night was because he'd seen the blond guy leaving the building just minutes after he had. If he'd had to come back and listen to the headboard banging the wall, he couldn't say what he might have done.

If it weren't for his brothers, he'd take off and re-move himself from temptation. Find out where the DEA needed him next and head there. Maybe see if he couldn't get a stateside case for a change.

But he did have two new half brothers, and he felt a real need to cement a lasting relationship with them. He wanted to forge a bond between them so he could come back here between jobs and not have them look at him and say, "Luc who?"

It knocked him sideways to know that Jake had been absent from Razor Bay for so many years. He and Max had probably kept in touch during his absence, but Luc had imagined them hanging out together the entirety of their lives, and clearly that hadn't happened.

"Steaks are done!"

Under Max's direction, he grabbed another beer for each of them and followed his brothers into the house.

He chose a chair at the opposite end but same side of the table as Tasha so it would be harder to see her. As a consequence, he enjoyed his meal without having to worry that he'd be outed at any moment for staring at her. God knew neither of his half brothers would shy away from calling him on it.

They feasted on perfectly grilled meat—porterhouse steaks for the men and Austin and filet mignons for the women. Harper had made a huge casserole dish of something called party potatoes that was kick-ass, plus a green salad, hot crusty bread and a platter of fresh pears, apples and grapes.

When everyone had finished up, Max looked around the table, meeting their gazes one by one. "You all probably already know that Sheriff Neward is retiring the first of the year," he said and hesitated. Then he gave a little dip of his chin. "Harper and I have talked about it—and have decided I'll run for his office."

The response was immediate and enthusiastic. "Good plan!" Jenny said.

Jake nodded. "Everyone knows you're the clear choice for sheriff. I've heard some of your ideas for improving the office, and they're well thought out."

Thinking of some of the measures his half brother had told him he'd like to put in place to improve efficiency, Luc, too, nodded. "You're definitely the guy to bring your department into the new millennium."

Tasha grinned at the big deputy across the table. "Oh, Max! As Harper would say, 'Good-oh on you.'"

Max flashed them a wry smile. "I'm glad you guys approve, because I'm gonna need your help. The downside to this running-for-office crap is that I'll have to stump for it. You may not have noticed," he said dryly, "but I'm not the chattiest guy in the world."

Eyes rolled toward the ceiling, Tasha whistled.

Jenny gave him a look of faux shock. "No!" she exclaimed. "You?"

"Yeah, smart-ass. I have no idea at this point who I might be up against, but you know they'll be more personable than me. I'm not sure I can kiss babies and glad-hand a thousand people and come off as credible."

"Your only real job is to show people you're the best man for the job," Luc said. "And since you are, tell them the same thing you've told us. Share all your ideas on how you'd improve the office and save the taxpayers money. That and your record as a longtime deputy in Razor Bay will sell you."

Max gave him a pleased smile. "That makes sense. *Thanks,* bro. That is exactly what I'll concentrate on. I have a lot of ideas on how to make our department the best damn sheriff's office of its size. Silverdale's is easily twice our size, and I bet I could make ours even better than that."

It felt good to have said the right thing to his brother, and he realized that was the way he was beginning to think of both Max and Jake, as his brothers—full stop, period, no half designation needed. He had dropped in on them out of the blue, yet from the beginning they had been nothing but great about including him in all their functions and get-togethers. And he appreciated it. Emotion abruptly swamped him, and he swallowed a lump in his throat. *Really* appreciated it.

Feeling a little sheepish for the rush of maudlin sentimentality, he took refuge in action and reached for the party potatoes to help himself to another serving. He didn't want them all to grab hands and break into a chorus of "Kumbaya," for crissake.

"Did Tasha tell you about tomorrow?"

He froze, the big serving spoon he'd just emptied onto his plate suspended in midair as he looked from it to Max. "Huh?"

"She found Jeremy a little house out on Henderson Road, and he's moving into it tomorrow. He was one of our Cedar Village boys before he started working for Tash, so we're pretty pumped. In fact, Harper hooked them up."

"And that was a gold-star day for Bella T's," Tasha agreed. "He was one of my damn-girl-you-lucked-out hires." She actually, voluntarily looked at Luc. "He's moving out of the Village tomorrow. It's kind of a big deal for him, and we're going to lend him a hand." She subjected him to a comprehensive look-over. "You can come—we can always use another strong back. Not that Jeremy has much, but we're scrounging some things together—furniture, linens, well, anything, really, a person can use in a house."

"I only brought a duffel to Razor Bay, so I don't have any of that kinda stuff. But I can kick in some cash for the things you aren't able to scrounge."

She gave him the first truly friendly smile he'd seen from her in quite a while. "That would work. We're going to caravan to his place at nine tomorrow morning. Be in front of Bella's if you're coming with—or one of us can give you the address if you can't make it that early."

"I don't have anything going," he said honestly. "Count me in."

CHAPTER THIRTEEN

A BRISK RAP on the lintel accompanied Mary-Margaret as she stuck her head through the open door to Jeremy's room. "Hello, dear. Harper called to say she'll be here in about five minutes. Are you almost ready to go?"

He looked over from the final inspection he'd been conducting to make sure he hadn't missed anything and nodded at the Cedar Village director. "Yeah. I think I've got everything."

"And if not, you're only a mile and a half away," she said with a smile. "If you ever need help or a refresher session with the counselor, you know you only have to call."

"Thanks, Mary-Margaret. That means a lot." Every Village resident he knew had had the same reaction to Mary-Margaret as he had the first time he'd met her—they'd all been pretty damn sure she was gonna be their personal Nurse Ratched. When she wasn't actively smiling, she had naturally downturned lips that gave her a more-than-sour look—you got the impression she'd just as soon kick kittens as look at one.

The truth was, though, she smiled most of the time, and anyone who got to know her could plainly see what a sweetheart she was. God knew it didn't take long to get to know her, either. With the exception of the confidential counseling sessions, Mary-Margaret had her fingers in every corner of Cedar Village life.

"Are you nervous?" she inquired gently, stepping into the room.

He opened his mouth to say *Hell, no,* but then shut it again, the words left unspoken. If today was to be the start of his independence, of his life as a grown-up, then he'd better be honest. That was the cornerstone of what his counselor, Ryan, had taught him: that truth was the primary ingredient he could bring to every aspect of his life. *If you want the right to be called a man,* Ryan was fond of saying, *then you have to own your actions.* And your feelings as well, although the counselor had acknowledged wryly that *that* tended to be a lot harder for most men.

He hitched a shoulder now. "A little bit. I'm mostly excited, though." And he was. He was nervous that he didn't have all the basic necessities he was going to need, but he thought that was probably more a matter of logistics than an inability on his part to get them. Harper had found him the house and wrangled a contract that didn't make him pay the last month's rent up front. She'd cheerfully cosigned the lease to get the concession, and he would *not* let her down. The fact that he didn't have to come up with an additional big chunk of cash along with the first month's rent and the damage deposit had really helped his campaign to put away as much of his paychecks as possible. So he had the means to outfit his place if he was really frugal and kept an eye out for some good deals. The problem was how to get stuff home once he bought it. Because while finding it was doable, it was likely to take a lot of trips to transport everything he needed.

It would sure be great if Razor Bay had better bus service than the twice-daily round-trip to Silverdale, since he didn't yet have the secondhand bike he planned to purchase, never mind a mode of transportation that included a trunk. But he had feet that would get him where he needed to go until he could afford something that got him there faster.

Another knock on his open door interrupted his thoughts, and Harper breezed in. "Hullo, you! Are you ready to make the big move?" She looked beyond him. "Hi, Mary-Margaret."

"Hello, dear. I'll leave you two to your work." She turned to him. "Congratulations, Jeremy. We're so proud of you—and if you need anything at all, you let us know and we'll do our best to see if we can get it for you."

"I wouldn't mind a subscription to *Maxim*."

Seriously, asshat? He could have kicked himself for blurting *that,* of all things, to a woman who could've been his grandmother if he'd been luckier in the gene pool.

But Mary-Margaret merely laughed. "Anything except that," she said dryly, and she pulled him in for a quick, hard hug, then turned him loose. "You be good," she said fiercely. "And come back to visit me." Then she strode from the room.

He thunked himself on the forehead. "I can't believe I *said* that."

"Don't beat yourself up," Harper said. "Mary-Margaret's

heard it all, and I imagine that wasn't even close to being the worst." She laughed. "Inappropriate, certainly, but not the worst." She indicated the belongings he'd piled on the stripped bed. "Is this everything?"

"Yeah." He didn't have that much, so it shouldn't take them long to carry it to the car. He suddenly realized who was missing from this equation and had to swallow his disappointment. "Did Max have to go to work?" he inquired nonchalantly. The big quiet deputy was one of his all-time favorite people. Max spent a lot of time at the Village, and all the guys liked him because it was as if he knew exactly what it was to *be* them. He'd been open with everyone on how he'd screwed up at their age and what it had taken to turn his life around. They could all see that he was a successful adult. And the beauty was, he didn't seem to doubt for an instant that every one of them would turn themselves around, as well.

It made you want to do just that—if only to keep from disappointing him and people like Mary-Margaret and Ryan.

Harper shook her head. "He had a few things he had to do, but he'll meet us at your place."

Sidetracked by that last phrase, he grinned. "*My* place," he murmured and savored the sound of it as if it was rocky-road ice cream.

"I know." She flashed him that huge smile that narrowed her eyes to cheerful little crescents. "*Brilliant,* right?"

"No shit."

She raised her eyebrows at him, and he added hastily, "Kidding, I meant. No kidding."

They put his stuff in the backseat of her car, and as Harper drove them away, Jeremy craned around until Cedar Village disappeared from sight. It seemed as if he'd barely settled back in his seat when she turned into a short driveway and pulled up in front of a little beige house. "Welcome to your new home."

He broke out in a sudden sweat. Jeezus. What was he *thinking*—he'd never lived alone in his life. Oh, he'd dreamed about it often enough when his mom was on one of her erratic tears. Faced now with the reality of actually doing it, however, he had an overwhelming urge to beat feet back to Cedar Village.

His misgivings must have shown because Harper reached across the console and squeezed his hand. "It's going to be all right," she said softly, but then shook her head. "No. It's going to be much more than that. It's going to be *good*. You're going to be brilliant at this the same way Tasha tells me you are at your job."

"She says that?"

"Yes. She thinks you're amazing, Jeremy. As do Mary-Margaret and Max and I."

The praise from his boss and the other adults he most admired shored him up, and, sitting taller, he released his seat belt. "Let's take my stuff in."

"Can you grab that? I have some things for you in the back." She climbed out of the SUV and went around to open the hatch.

He bypassed the backseat where he'd put his stuff and followed in her wake. When he looked over her shoulder, he saw the compartment was filled nearly to the top of the backseat with boxes and bags. "Oh, *wow*—all that's for me?"

"It is. It's mostly secondhand, mind, but when we told people you needed everything for your new place, they were very generous about contributing to the cause."

"This is—" He broke off, overwhelmed. Then he cleared his throat. And grinned at her wholeheartedly. "Awesome!"

They had carried one load into his house and come back for a second when he heard a vehicle pull into the drive and looked over the roof of Harper's SUV to see Max's truck. Behind it was Tasha's blue Jeep and behind that a car he didn't recognize. He gawked as everyone parked, and Max and his two brothers climbed out of his truck. Tasha, Jenny and Tiffany got out of Tash's Jeep and Peyton and her friend—a girl he'd seen in Bella T's but had never actually met—exited the third car.

For a second he was so surprised he could only stand rooted to the patch of asphalt in front of Harper's open hatch. Then he shook himself free of his momentary paralysis and went to meet everyone. "What are you all *doing* here? This is so frickin' *beast!*"

"And that's a good thing, I'm guessing," the new Bradshaw, Luc, said before he went around to the back of the truck to lower the tailgate.

"It is," Peyton replied in that snooty nose-in-the-air way she sometimes had when, Jeremy now understood, she was nervous. Her tone was completely different when she walked over to him, grabbed his arm and said warmly, "We came to help you move—and we brought stuff." She pulled him over to her friend, and he watched her face light up in the company of the other girl. "This is my best friend, Marni," she said, then turned to the dirty-blonde. "Mar, this is Jeremy, and over there is my boss, Tasha."

"It's great to meet you, Marni," Tasha said. "Peyton's said nice things about you."

Peyton colored and hastily told her friend, "And of course you know Tiffany."

"I do," Marni agreed, looking at the waitress. "And not only for the pizzas you've delivered. You gave me the tip on the MAC lipstick."

"And I see you took my advice," Tiffany replied. "I knew it would look great on you."

Peyton gave the men and two women she didn't know a regal wave. "I've sort of met you," she said to Luc, referring to the night the two of them had pitched in to help Tiff. "But for the rest of you, I'm Peyton, and this is my friend Marni."

Max's brothers and Harper and Jenny introduced themselves in return. Then everyone dug in and began carting all the things they'd brought into his new rental.

"Man, this is like my birthday and Christmas all rolled into one," Jeremy said as he opened a box and found a nearly complete set of dishes.

"The Myers, who gave those to me, said to warn you that they're old Corelle," Jenny said. "So they can't go in the microwave."

"That's okay." He laughed. "I don't have a microwave."

"Yeah, you do," Luc said from the door. "There's more stuff out here."

"My mom sent some food to get you started," Marni said, indicating the big grocery bag she'd just carried into the house. "It's mainly the basics—eggs and milk and bread and butter and some canned soups and stuff. I'll put the perishables in the fridge."

"This is so epic I don't even know how to begin thanking everyone. Or even who all."

"That's what we have Jenny for," Tasha said with a hip bump for her friend. "She's got a list for everything, so of course she made one for you *and* brought thank-you cards to fill out and the stamps to mail 'em. So a word to the wise—be sure you send them, or you'll have her to contend with."

"Oh, please," Jenny said. "I'm not as scary as all that."

"Yes, she is," Jake said and gave Jeremy a crooked smile. "Don't let the packaging fool ya, kid. She might look like a stiff breeze could blow her down the canal, but trust me, you do *not* want to run afoul of this woman. If she comes after you and has a steely glint in her eyes, you're toast."

Jenny blew a rude noise, then ignored them. "Marni, give me your address," she said. "I'll add you and your mom to the list."

"Oh, good, sheets," Harper said, digging through a box. "Hmm. I'm thinking either the white or the green. We'll save the pink floral ones for, um—"

"The day Jeremy bleeds out on his other ones and there's not a damn thing else to put on the bed," Max stated categorically.

Jeremy snorted his agreement.

"This from the guy who has ribbons on his bath towels," Jake said sadly.

"Keep it up, smart guy," Jenny told her fiancé. "I still have my eye on that set with lace for your bathroom. We've had this conversation before, but you seem to forget that men *and* women live in our houses, and we women? We don't think everything has to be industrial-gray." She shook her head. "Men. It's a good thing they're handy."

All the females hooted their agreement, and Jake strolled past Jenny, giving her a slap on the butt and a smoldering smile. "I'll show you handy later," Jeremy heard him promise in a low voice.

Harper and Marni made up the bed while Peyton carried in a little table he could use for a nightstand, then came back out into the living room and picked up a nice brass lamp with a beat-up shade. She looked over at him. "This okay for your bedroom?"

"Yeah, that's great." He couldn't believe all the stuff they'd gotten to make his house a home. He'd swallow a razor blade before he'd admit it to the other guys, but he'd have slept on the pink flowered sheets. They beat what he'd had, which was no sheets at all.

"Peyton," Tasha called from the other end of the room. "I have a new shade for that lamp in one of these boxes. I think it's— Ah, here it is!" She looked up as Peyton walked over to collect it. "I meant to put it on at home, but the lamp had already been packed into my car at least three layers deep."

"Oh, this is much nicer," Peyton said and sat down on the floor to remove the old one and put on the new.

"There are a couple more lamps around here somewhere. Jeremy can move things around later if he finds something works better in one place than another."

Overhearing, Jeremy smiled to himself. He hadn't even thought of lamps when he'd mentally compiled his list of the basics he'd need for day-to-day living—and here he had choices between more than one.

Max called his name, and he looked up to see him beckoning from the concrete stoop outside his front door. Turning away from the new box he'd been about to dive into, he went out to meet him.

Max led him to the truck and opened the jump-seat door. He reached in and dragged a big box closer, then lifted it out. "This is from Tasha, Mary-Margaret and Harper and me," he said, turning so Jeremy could see the front of the box. "You'll need a computer if you're going to college. We've prepaid a year of internet access for you, too. The installer's supposed to be here this afternoon between noon and three."

"Oh, man," Jeremy whispered, staring at the picture of a laptop. "Oh, *man,* Max." To his mortification, his voice cracked in the middle of the deputy's name, and he sucked in a deep breath and held it for as long as he could before he was forced to expel it. "*Thank* you. I've never had a gift this huge." Tears rose in his eyes and, horrified, he turned to furiously knuckle them away.

Max's big hand was a sudden heavy weight on the crown of his head, and he felt its rough stroke down to his nape, where the man gave a quick squeeze before dropping his hand. Something about the strength and warmth of that brief contact comforted Jeremy, and he sucked in another breath and hauled his emotions under control. "I don't know what to say," he admitted in a low voice. "This is just all so…great."

"You don't have to say anything. Just work hard when you go to school."

"I will. I swear it."

"I know you will. Tash is really pleased with your work, you know. And Bella T's is her baby, so she doesn't give praise lightly."

"I feel really lucky to be working for her," he said to the ground between his feet. "To have the help of *all* you guys." He turned back to Max. "I couldn't have done any of this on my own."

"Yes, you could have," a feminine voice said behind him, and he turned to see Tasha approaching. "I didn't mean to eavesdrop," she said, giving him a level look, "but since I did overhear your conversation, I have to tell you that while it would definitely be harder to do it all on your own, I know you could. You have a maturity about you, Jeremy, that's nothing short of amazing for an eighteen-year-old boy. I think probably Max had that kind of maturity as well when he left here to join the Marines when he was your age. And if he didn't, he sure came home with it. You have the drive and the work ethic to succeed. We just want to give you whatever boost we can to help you toward that success."

Luc strolled up, his hands in his jeans pockets. "I came to town with just a duffel bag, so I don't have anything concrete to contribute to your cause," he said. "But I want you to let me know if you need something that you didn't get today, and I'll help with that. I'm also good with my hands, so if you need anything fixed or maybe a lesson in fixing it yourself, I'm your man."

"Thanks," he said. He didn't really know Luc Bradshaw, but along with everyone else who had come out today, the guy had chipped in to haul in and set up Jeremy's amazing array of loot, so he resolved to take him up on his offer if the need arose. "I'm not bad with American car engines, 'cause my dad's a mechanic and I've done a couple of summers with him in the shop where he works. But I'm clueless about house repair, so I really like the teaching-me-to-fix-things idea."

A strange look flashed across Luc's face, but it was there and gone so fast that Jeremy couldn't get a fix on it. Then he figured he must have imagined it anyway because the new Bradshaw gave him an easy smile. "I'm serious about you letting me know if you need anything, as well. I'd like to contribute."

"Good, you can contribute lunch," Jenny said. "Usually we'd call Tash for pizzas, but clearly that's not gonna work today. Want to get some Vietnamese sandwiches or pho from Saigon Boat?"

"I can do that." He pulled his smartphone out of his pocket. "Give me your orders."

By three o'clock Jeremy's place looked like a home. It had just about everything he needed—as well as a lot of stuff he'd never even considered—like a rug on the floor and throw pillows and an afghan on the couch. In the almost-too-small-to-be-called-an-extra-bedroom he, Max and Luc had arranged a rickety desk that he planned to paint once the dust settled and under which Luc had shoved some shims to make it sturdy. Jeremy had grabbed one of the wooden chairs from the little kitchen set, then set up his new pride and joy: the laptop they'd given him, along with the smallest of the lamps he'd co-opted, which wasn't actually all that small. He planned to hit the General Store for a desk lamp since they tended to be both more compact in size and have brighter, directional lighting.

Tasha came up to him just as he was saying goodbye to the cable guy. "Come in to Bella's at five," she said. "I'll do the prep today."

"*Thank* you," he said fervently. He'd love to be all sophisticated, but everyone had done so much for him that it was simply beyond him. "For *every*thing."

"You're welcome, sweetie. You're a valuable employee. You know that, right?" She didn't wait for him to respond. "More importantly, Jeremy, you're one of the good guys."

Then, in what seemed like seconds, after tidying up the empty packaging and cardboard boxes that most of his goodies had arrived in, the adults climbed into their various vehicles and drove out, leaving him with Peyton, Tiffany and Marni. Tiffany ran out to her car for something, and the three teens took seats in the living room.

"This looks really nice," Marni said, and Peyton nodded her agreement.

"It does," she said. "Tasha and her friends sure have a knack for making a bunch of castoffs look cool."

"I heard her tell someone once that she and Jenny grew up on the wrong side of the tracks," he said. "So I guess they have experience making the most of stuff."

"Whatever their deal," she said, reaching out to touch the back of his hand, "you're pretty damn lucky to have them as friends."

He stilled and for a second just stared down at her fingers touching his knuckles. It wasn't until she slid them away that he remembered what they'd been talking about. "Yeah." He cleared his throat. "I really do get that, without that whole crew on my side, I'd probably be living hand to mouth." He looked around. "And it would definitely look a lot emptier in here."

Tiffany came back in with a little cooler. "Now, don't get the wrong idea and think that I plan to make a habit of contributing to the delinquency of minors," she said, pulling three bottles of beer out of the cooler. "But I thought this one time called for a celebration." She looked from the three beers to the four of them. "We better grab some glasses. Sorry, Marni," she said as Peyton hopped up to get them. "I didn't know you were coming or I'd have brought another."

The dishwater-blonde shrugged good-naturedly. "I can have a Coke. I don't really like the taste of most boozy drinks anyway."

"I'll get it, Mar," Peyton called from the kitchen and was back in an instant. She handed the can to her friend. "Sorry about the lack of ice. It hasn't frozen all the way through yet."

Tiffany handed out the beers and held her own aloft. "To Jeremy's new digs," she said.

"To new digs," they chimed in, clinked bottles and can and drank.

When everyone had gone, Jeremy walked around his

house, touching things and smiling to himself. Several times he walked past the pay-as-you-go cell phone he'd bought, then finally stopped, picked it up and punched in a number. It rang four times before a man answered, and the clangs and whirs of an automotive shop sounded in the background.

"Hey, Dad, it's me," Jeremy said. "I don't know what you're doin' at work on a Sunday, but I wanted to let you know I'm all moved in to the place I told you about—and to give you my new address and phone number."

CHAPTER FOURTEEN

"Wow. If I tried to do that, I'd probably hack off all my fingers."

Tasha looked up from her furious vegetable chopping to see Peyton entering the pizzeria's kitchen. She wasn't sure if she was irritated to have her exorcising-the-demons time interrupted or beyond relieved. But even if it was the former, she couldn't take it out on the teen, so she drew a deep breath and, exhaling it, changed her mind-set. "Hey, girl. What are you doing here early? I thought you kids would still be at Jeremy's."

Peyton executed an elegant little roll of her shoulders. "We thought we'd give him a little space to soak in his new place in peace." She flashed a smile that, to Tasha's surprise, seemed almost shy. "It looks awesome. You guys sure know how to decorate on a dime."

"Neither Jenny nor I had any money growing up, so we've had lots of practice." She gave the girl a wry smile. "And really, who doesn't watch HGTV these days?"

"Um…" The teen raised her hand. "Me?"

"Really? Well, maybe it's more the late-twenties-and-beyond crowd's thing."

"Must be." Peyton looked at the heaps of veggies on

Tasha's work space. "Are you expecting a huge crowd tonight?"

"What?" She stared down at them. "Well, crap." She'd allowed herself to get sucked into all the ways in which Luc was driving her insane when she'd gotten back from Jeremy's, but she hadn't realized how carried away she'd gotten with her food prep. "I have enough here for two days, easy." Mentally cursing herself for not paying attention, she reached for the storage containers.

"Daydreaming, huh? I do that sometimes—especially in the car. There've been times I've been so far in the zone that I've arrived at point B from point A without actually remembering the drive."

"I'm not sure which is scarier when your attention is elsewhere, piloting a ton of metal in motion—or speed-chopping with a precision-honed knife." But she was grateful to the girl for giving her an out. At least she didn't have to come up with an excuse for her aggression. Handy, that, considering she wasn't sure herself where it had come from.

She'd had a good time today fixing up Jeremy's place and getting to see his reaction to each new thing they set up. She'd managed to be around Luc for hours and survived just fine, being civil and pleasant whenever she had to interact with him, but mostly just sticking with the women.

In truth, he had seemed to avoid her as assiduously as she had him, so that had been a good thing.

Kind of.

No, no, it had been. It was exactly what she'd been

demanding. And she was…happy…that he'd finally listened.

But clearly she was still pissed at him for constantly making her act out of character. Okay, sure, at the end of the day her behavior was on her—but, dammit, he *drove* her to act in ways she ordinarily wouldn't dream of—had done so from the instant they'd met in the Bahamas. That had ended in disaster, and now here she was, acting like a crazy woman again.

That was what had driven her to blindly chopping onions and peppers—thinking of her every misstep since Luc Bradshaw had come to town. Not the fact that today he'd done what she'd asked and left her alone.

Because that would be idiotic.

She blew out a quiet breath. Idiotic was precisely how she'd been acting since he'd come to town. The man pushed buttons she hadn't even known she had, and she, a woman who would ordinarily take the time to think things through if anyone else tried that, turned into a damn reactionary with him.

Every. Single. Time.

Just look at what she had done to Axel. She'd been gently turning him away for years, but a couple of stupid kisses from Luc, and she had not only used a really decent guy but had hurt him, as well.

"So," Peyton said casually, "can I ask you something?"

Please do. Anything to get her mind off this crap. She looked up from scraping half the sliced peppers into a glass container. "Sure."

"How do you know when a guy likes you?"

Oh, God. Tiffany had recently clued her in to the fact that her teen employees thought she was cool. The poor deluded fools actually believed she had her shit together.

How sad was it that a month ago she would have agreed with them?

But now Peyton was looking to her for sage advice? On *romance?*

Oh, yeah, baby—I'm your girl. Because just look how well I've handled my own love life.

As she snapped the locking lid over the superfluous peppers, she had an almost-uncontrollable urge to yell, *"Run! Run like the wind!"* Or at least tell Peyton to go talk to Jenny. Or Harper. Now, there were a couple of women who had successful relationships.

But Peyton had asked her. And now that she thought about it, perhaps just a little too casually. The girl had come a long way since Tasha's first impression of her. When Peyton wasn't fiercely hiding her problems behind a snooty-girl facade, she was chatty and pretty darn sweet. And Tash didn't have a clue how to answer her question.

So she told the truth.

"You're asking the wrong person, kiddo." She set the onion container atop the one with the peppers and scraped the remainder into one of the stainless pots she used for the daily pizzas. "I'm the woman who, the only time I truly took a chance and opened myself up to a man—trusting him with everything I had—ended up embroiled in a disaster that included being slapped in cuffs and thrown in a Bahamian jail."

For a second the emotions of that night roiled in her

stomach. But shaking it off as best she could, she looked Peyton in the eye. "This is what I think it should be like, though—if he opens up to you, especially with personal details you've never heard him mention to anyone else, he probably likes you. If you can make him laugh when he's generally a pretty grave guy, and he seems to want to spend time with you, the same thing applies. And if you're talking about Jeremy, Peyton, and he looks at you the way I've seen him look... Well, I think it's pretty clear he's sweet on you already. So if you like him, too, then just be yourself with him. Treat him nice and be honest and you should have a good shot at building a real relationship with him."

Peyton studied her. "You're really big on honesty, aren't you?"

"Yes, I am."

"And the Bahamian-jail thing? I don't suppose you'd care to expand on that a little?"

"No. I wouldn't."

Peyton grinned. "Okay. But he really looks at me like he likes me?"

"He does." And she smiled gently because she remembered what it had felt like to discover the thrill of conquest with someone you were really, really attracted to. Unfortunately, since she hadn't had the time or social standing in high school for the usual crushes and experimentations, those feelings had been primarily with Luc. Before him, she'd had a couple of sexual encounters, but even with the boy she had given her virginity to she'd never felt a comparable rush of excitement and sheer joy.

So regardless that her heart had been dashed on the rocks of That Night, leaving her perhaps a little bit emotionally stunted, she still envied Peyton that everything-is-brand-new-and-glorious feeling. And she hoped like hell that it all worked out for her and Jeremy—for however long it lasted.

LATER THAT EVENING, she sat in Jenny's living room with her bestie. "You'll be happy to know," she said over tea and cookies, "that I've given up my plan to give Luc a taste of his own medicine. You were right. It was a stupid scheme."

"I don't believe the word *stupid* ever crossed my lips," Jenny said mildly.

"Still, you probably thought it, and rightfully so. It was a butt-brainless idea, but, dammit, Luc's to blame for the fact that I even came up with it." She grimaced. "Okay, saying that out loud makes me sound even dumber yet. I have free will. I'm in charge of my own destiny."

"You are woman," Jenny inserted dryly. "I know this because I've heard you roar."

"Mock me all you want, but, *man,* he brings out the worst in me." She filled Jenny in on her date with Axel. "I feel like crap over the way I used him."

"I agree it wasn't your finest hour, but you wanna know what I think you should do to take your mind off it?"

She hitched a shoulder. "Absolutely. It's gotta be better than anything I've come up with."

"I think you should have head-banging sex with Luc."

Yes! Yes! her body enthusiastically agreed, but her brain apparently wasn't as totally fried as she'd feared, because *that* had her gaping at her best friend. Tightening her jaw enough to keep from looking like the village idiot, she said sarcastically, "Annnnd I was wrong— it's pretty much on a par with what I can come up with. For God's sake," she snapped. "Did you trip and hit your head?"

"No. Think about it, Tash. You've tried avoiding him, right?"

She nodded. "For all the good it's done me when he's related to Jake and Max and lives in my own building. But I am trying not to think about him on those rare occasions when I'm not forced to be in his company."

"And how's that working for you?"

She grimaced. "Not great."

"Look, sweetie, you've been stuck for years—ever since your trip to the Bahamas, in fact—and it's past time you moved forward. The chemistry between you and Luc is off the charts—just ask anyone with eyes in their head. I've watched him pursue and you evade since he came to town, and I gotta tell you, girl, your avoidance doesn't appear to be making you happy. Instead of being your usual positive, goal-oriented self, you've been jumpy and cranky. And you said it yourself—your way of handling things isn't working all that well. Plus, how many times have I heard you complain that you're not getting any? So why not go for it with him? Screw the guy's brains out until you get him out of your system. At least you know he's good at it."

Oh. He is. Or at least he had been.

But that was not a direction in which she cared to have her mind wander, and she gave her head a little shake to cut loose the images that had started flashing across her mental screens. "Let me get this straight," she said slowly. "You're advocating that I dance with the devil?"

"Hell, yes, if it brings back the Tash I know and love."

She was tempted; she couldn't deny it. But the ugly truth was that, even knowing he was no good for her, it had taken only a couple of his kisses for her to start rationalizing à la Nola Riordan. And going to Stupidville for some man was simply not a trip she was willing to take.

Irritated that she had to spell that out to a woman who had been her best friend since she was sixteen years old, she rose to her feet and looked down at Jenny. "Yes, well, that's not gonna happen. I opened myself up to Luc Bradshaw once, and look where it got me. You're right. I was a wreck for a good long time. So you're crazy if you think I'm ever going to let him get close enough to wreck me again."

Then, unsure what to do with the feelings of betrayal that churned her stomach acids, she turned and strode out of Jenny's house.

JENNY BANGED THROUGH the front door of the Sand Dollar across the parking lot from her place and called Jake's name. Without waiting for him to answer, since she knew damn well he was packing for a six-day *National Explorer* photo shoot in the Ozarks, she raced up the stairs to the second floor.

"Up here," he called superfluously since the words were barely spoken when she barged into his bedroom.

She hung on the doorjamb to catch her breath. Then she stated categorically, "You and I are going to get Luc and Tasha together."

"What?" Jake paused in his packing to stare at her as if she'd lost her mind. Then his green eyes narrowed and his face went all stern. He glanced away to set a short stack of silk T-shirts in his suitcase, then straightened and gave her his undivided attention. "There is no way in hell we're getting involved in their love lives."

"Really," she said. "You're dictating what I can do now?"

He opened his mouth to say something, then shut it again. Blew out a gusty breath. And shook his head. "Shit. You're going to dig your heels in on this, aren't you?"

"Well, I could certainly use some help at the inn. You know Oktoberfest is about to start." She nodded. "Yep. I really should call Luc and Tasha."

"Yes, I'm sure she in particular would be thrilled to help you," he said neutrally. "Because it's not like she's busy running her own business or anything."

"Okay." Her shoulders slumped. "There is that. Business is really picking up for her this year. She hasn't had nearly the post–Labor Day drop she had the first two years." She shook her head. "Damn. I can't ask her."

"Hey, look on the bright side. This way she won't be taking Harper's job away from her."

"Yes, that's very helpful," she said flatly. "Thank you." She knew she sounded more sullen than Austin when they told him he couldn't play "Halo" until his homework was done, but she was embarrassed that, in the heat of the moment, it hadn't even occurred to her that she'd already hired Harper to handle Oktoberfest, since the girl could plan events better than anyone.

If she sounded stiff and insincere, however, she did mean every word when she added, "You have to agree, though, that Tash needs to hire more help. Even with Jeremy there shouldering part of the burden, she *still* hasn't taken an entire day off since Memorial Day weekend."

"I know, sweetheart. And, between months of nonstop work and Luc being in town, I'm sure the stress is getting to her." He picked her up, flopped down on the chair in his room and rearranged her across his lap. "But underhanded matchmaking isn't like you. You and Tash have one of the closest friendships I've ever seen, and the thing I admire most about it is your honesty with each other."

The truth of that struck to the marrow of her bones, and for an instant she could only stare at him. Then she blew out a long breath. "Dammit, Jake, I hate it when I'm wrong."

"Excuse me?" He stuck the tip of his little finger in his ear and wiggled it. Pulling it out, he examined its clean tip. "I could have sworn you said you were wrong. But that can't possibly be right."

"You're such a funny guy." She laid her head on his chest and blew out a sigh. "I just want her to be as happy as I am, you know?"

"I do." He stroked her hair. "But you have to let her

arrive at her relationship decisions on her own timetable." He pulled in his chin to look down at her, his eyes somber. "Has she ever told you the details of those days she spent in jail?"

"No. Not really, and I never pushed for them because it was clear she'd been traumatized."

"Luc's showing up here in town has probably brought everything she's buried to the surface."

She felt slightly sick to her stomach. "And I'm not helping by trying to push her into bed with him."

"No, you're not." There was no judgment in his voice, however, and he tipped his head to slide her a crooked smile. "But scheming to get her together with Luc wouldn't have flown even if they were a match made in heaven like you and me." He hooked a strand of her hair that had slipped forward behind her ear. "Think about how you would have felt if she'd tried to trick you into your relationship with me before we were ready to go there."

"I would have nailed her hide to the wall." She exhaled. "Annnd she's every bit as independent as I am. So I admit it, I miscalculated. Took a misstep. Still, I'll tell you what, smart guy. If I ruled the world, things would be one hell of a lot more efficiently run."

"Yes, they would," he agreed. "I don't doubt that for a second."

TASHA STEAMED DURING her march back to town. Luckily, she could maneuver the boardwalk blindfolded, because it was almost that dark out here tonight, low clouds obscuring the moon and a fine mist beginning to fall.

When she arrived at the pizzeria, she simply could not force herself to go upstairs. Not when she knew she'd only stew. Sure, she'd likely continue to do that anyway, but at least she could do so outside, where no walls hemmed her in. She crossed Harbor Street to the marina. *When in doubt, hang out on the water and look at the boats,* she always said. Well, okay, she'd never actually said that. Didn't mean it wasn't still a decent philosophy.

The floating dock off the main walkway rocked beneath her feet as she picked her way along its boards, the boats secured to it rising slightly with the gentle swell, then settling back down. Rising and settling.

She couldn't freaking believe Jenny. Had *she* involved herself in Jenny and Jake's relationship? She had not. So, what the hell was her so-called best friend doing trying to talk her into a sexual relationship that she didn't have the least desire to—

"You're really big on honesty, aren't you?"

"Yes, I am."

She stopped dead next to the stern of a huge wooden cabin cruiser. The name *Summer Samba* shone in the misty light of an overhead lamp, and she vaguely noted that it was out of Bellingham. "Crap," she whispered. "Crap, crap, *crap!*"

She wasn't mad at Jenny because her friend had interfered. She was mad at her because *she* had been tempted almost beyond enduring to do exactly what Jenny had suggested.

She hadn't, though. She had hung in there.

And she admitted that she was pissed at Jenny for that, as well.

She firmly believed what she'd told Peyton. She did think honesty was the most important element you could bring to a relationship. Being truthful, even when she'd known lying would ease her way in many situations, had been the cornerstone that she'd built her life view on. Too many people lied. God knew they had about her mother. And about her as well, plus so many other things both large and small. People lied all the time.

But she didn't.

Or she hadn't. But from the moment she'd first seen Luc sitting at Max's table, she'd been lying her fool head off. About the way she felt whenever he was around. About the want that was a banked fire in the pit of her stomach. And she knew what she had to do to rectify it.

She turned and picked her way along the floats back to the street.

CHAPTER FIFTEEN

LUC PACED AROUND the studio for a good forty-five minutes before finally plopping down on the couch. Swinging his feet up onto the coffee table, he stared at the dark mist pressing against the slider. It was rare for him to be bored. And maybe boredom wasn't the precise emotion he felt at this moment, but he couldn't say exactly what was. He was simultaneously enervated and restless—even as a part of him felt drained, he found it an effort to sit still.

Neither of the disparate conditions was enough to make him turn on the TV or go in search of one of his half brothers. Reaching for the book he'd tossed aside earlier, he hoped giving it another try would engage his attention better than it had before he'd impatiently abandoned it the first time around.

When a knock abruptly sounded on his front door, however, he tossed the paperback down on the coffee table without a second thought. Welcoming the distraction, he dropped his feet to the floor, climbed off the sofa and strode over to answer the summons.

Tasha stood on the other side of the door and pushed past him into the studio the moment he opened it. Her skin was dewy, and her orangey-red hair curled even more wildly than usual. Luc's weariness and minor dissatisfaction disappeared. He closed the door behind her.

"You got anything to drink?" she demanded, making herself at home on the wicker chair that faced the couch. "I have all kinds of wine in the restaurant, but of course I didn't think about grabbing any until I got up here—and I don't feel like going back down."

"I have a beer or two in the fridge."

"Nothing stronger?" She shot him a disgruntled *Well, you're useless* look. "I could really use something with a little more kick. Jet fuel is sounding good about now."

"All right, hang on. For you, I'll break out my special stock." He turned and went down to the kitchen end of the studio, where he retrieved a mostly full bottle of Buffalo Trace Straight Kentucky Bourbon from the top shelf of the little cupboard he mostly used to store his coffee paraphernalia and mugs. Snagging two smallish glasses that were short on fancy but would do the trick, he assembled them on the tray that had come with the studio—which was a damn good thing since he would never have thought to buy one. Adding the pint, he picked up the tray and carried it to the living area.

Tasha sat restlessly tapping a foot, but she stilled when she saw him. "Oh, good," she said and gave the little coffee table between her and the couch a pat.

"I don't have any kind of mixer." He set the tray where she indicated. "But if you want water—"

"Straight is good."

He wondered what was going on with her, but merely opened the bottle and poured a tot into each glass.

She twirled her hand in a *keep going* gesture, and he

obliged her with a couple more fingers of the fine whiskey. After returning the bottle to the tray, he passed her the fuller glass. "Mind telling me what's got you chasing the hard stuff?"

She tossed back her drink, coughed, then carefully set the empty glass on the tray. When she looked up at him, her pale eyes were somber. And for a moment she was silent.

Then, with a quiet exhalation, she sat back. She said something in a voice so soft he found himself leaning down to hear. "What?"

She cleared her throat. "The night I was arrested," she said a little more loudly, "the Bahamian police threw me in the back of a car and drove through the dark for what seemed like hours."

Feeling like a hunting dog going on point, he dropped onto the couch and sat at attention on its edge, his knees spread wide and his hands gripped together between them. Every atom of his being focused on her tense face. She had never discussed the particulars of that night—not with him, anyhow—and his heart drummed a ragged rhythm in his chest. This was something he'd wanted to know since discovering that night hadn't gone the way he'd always believed it had.

Yet a part of him didn't.

"There were three of them and me," she said. "At one point while we were in the car, somebody called Inspector Rolle—the man in charge—on his cell. I don't know if it had anything to do with my situation. I could only hear his side of the conversation, and that was mostly grunts and the occasional *yes, sir, no, sir.* But I got the impression he wasn't happy about what he was being told, and shortly after he disconnected they took me to this small building in the middle of nowhere. It didn't look like any police station I'd ever seen, but they fingerprinted me there and took photos and did some other police-type stuff.

"I kept trying to tell them they'd made a mistake and asked repeatedly to be allowed to call the American embassy, but while Inspector Rolle had answered my questions when we were in the hut, suddenly it was as if no one except me even heard my voice. I thought at the time, the way they ignored me was the worst part of the night, because how was I supposed to get out of the clusterfuck I found myself in if no one would even talk to me?"

She stared at the coffee table as if it fascinated her, then said with a wryness that struck him as forced, "It turns out I wasn't even close. Because when they finished the booking part or whatever you call it…" Her voice trailing away, she reached for the bottle and knocked back a swig directly from it. She lifted the bottom of her T-shirt to wipe the neck of the pint, exposing a pale slice of her stomach, then returned the bottle to the tray. Finally raising her eyes, she looked at him across the table, and a ragged sigh stuttered through her lips. "They escorted me to a room, pushed me in and closed the door."

Horror colored her expression as she stared at him, and, wrapping her arms around herself, she commenced a subtle rocking motion in her seat. "It wasn't even a room, really. It was more of a closet—about the size of the bathroom in my mama's trailer. And, God, it was so dark in there." Her eyes stared blindly ahead. "Why is it so dark? I've never *seen* a black so thick and dense. Shouldn't my eyes have adjusted by now?"

Her unseeing gaze and sudden lapse into present tense made Luc's gut ice over and the hair on his arms stand on end, and he scrambled for a way to pull her out of it.

Before he could come up with anything, she jerked. "Oh, shit, what is that?" Goose bumps flowed down her arms, and she batted the air. "Are those cobwebs? I can't *see*— Oh, God, they're *sticking* to me!" Muscles jumped under her skin, and her fingers went into a flurry of brushing and plucking at her head, her arms, her chest.

He surged up off the couch, stepped over the table between them and picked her up out of her chair. Turning, he dropped into her seat so abruptly that her long legs flopped over the arm of the chair and bounced back up before settling. He nestled her on his lap, wrapped her in his arms and held her tight. That was when he realized her clothes were damp and, pulling his chin back, he saw the fine mist that clung to her hair.

"It's okay," he said in a low, firm voice. "You're not there now. You're safe." He rubbed his hands down her arms, then used his fingers to firmly stroke her cheeks, her nose, her lips, her chin in hopes of dispelling those remembered cobwebs. He looked down at her, but her gray-blue eyes were blank, as if looking inward rather than out.

"Are they in my hair?" she demanded, thrusting her

head at him to inspect. "I hate spiders—*get them out of my hair!*"

The demand was whimpered, and he rubbed his palms over the richly textured mass from her hairline to the tips of her curls. "Shhh, *cariño,*" he murmured. Then, rethinking his strategy, he made his voice brisk and no-nonsense when he said, "No, forget that. Snap out of it! It was seven years ago, Tasha. There are no bugs in your hair now."

For a moment the studio was silent. Then…

"Shit." Her voice sounded more like her own, and as the tightly coiled tension left her in a rush, she sagged against him, her fingers uncurling their white-knuckled grip on his T-shirt. "I know that." She blew out a breath. "Holy crap. I sound more psychotic than Norman Bates during his mother-issues period. But, God, Luc, it was such a horrid experience."

Looking up, she gave him a fierce stare. "I don't go around reliving this every day, you know—I got past it a *long* time ago." Her faint shrug dug her left shoulder into his chest for a second before it relaxed. "Every now and then, though, something sparks a memory, and it might as well have been yesterday, because I can recall *every*thing. That my toilet was a bucket that a man, who never talked, emptied once a day. That it must have been over a hundred degrees in there and between the heat and that bucket it smelled like a sewer. That I didn't smell much better." She looked up, meeting his gaze. "And not just the spiders but the bugs. Jesus-God, I hate remembering those bugs. Do you know how many varieties there are in the Bahamas?" she asked wearily.

"There must be hundreds, if not thousands, and I swear I had at least half of them with me in that room, clicking and scurrying around and— Oh, God. It makes my skin crawl just thinking about it.

"But it was the not knowing that was the worst," she said. "If they'd told me I'd be in there for two nights it would have still been awful, but knowing I had a finite number of hours to tick off would've made getting through it a little more bearable. But I didn't know, and I was terrified I was going to be in that little hellhole of a room for the rest of my life. That I'd die in there screaming and clawing at my skin."

Suddenly, as if just now realizing where she was, she unfolded herself from his lap and climbed to her feet. Her usually unwavering gaze looked everywhere but at him, and the uncharacteristic uncertainty in a woman who always seemed to know just what she wanted left him feeling colder from more than just the body heat she'd taken with her.

He, too, rose to his feet. "You're always going to blame me for that night, aren't you?"

"What?" Her gaze snapped back to his, and she straightened. "No. That's actually what I came to tell you tonight. In order to understand why I've been so angry with you, I thought you needed to hear what I went through. And I wanted to tell you face-to-face that I've let it go."

"You have?"

He must have sounded as skeptical as he felt because she made an impatient movement. "I know, right? My behavior hasn't exactly telegraphed that message." She shrugged. "I don't deny a big part of me wanted to keep blaming you. Even learning that you weren't responsible for the drugs they found in the hut or hearing that you hadn't deliberately left me holding the bag or discovering that, not only had you not known about my arrest, you'd actually believed *I* had run out on *you,* I still wanted to hold you accountable. Because my arrest never should have happened, and seeing you again brought up too many memories that I thought were behind me. I guess I believed if I could just place the blame squarely on you, it would somehow make them more manageable."

She looked at him with devastating earnestness and gave her head an infinitesimal shake. "But I need to let it all go. Being angry is turning me into someone I don't recognize, and I don't want to be that woman. I wanna be me again." She straightened her shoulders. Blew out a breath. "So I officially absolve you, Luc Bradshaw." Her cheeks flushed—with embarrassment, he guessed at her next words. "And I promise to do a better job of not being such a bitch to you. In fact—"

A sudden calculation in those gray-blue eyes replaced the embarrassment, and she stepped up to him. Wrapping her arms around his neck, she came up onto the balls of her feet and kissed him.

His mind understood that this was her way of taking charge after displaying vulnerability in front of him.

His body didn't give a rat's ass. And for a moment he went with it, absorbing the thrill of her being the one to instigate a kiss for a change. Taking in the feel of her vibrant heat beneath his palms as he held her to him and the almost overwhelming urge he felt to carry her to the bed in the little alcove at the end of the room. He wanted to lay her out and reacquaint himself with the energy and selfless giving he had never been able to quite forget.

Instead, he reluctantly raised his head, breaking the kiss. Stroked his hands up her back and her raised arms until he could encircle her wrists. Pulling her arms from around his neck, he took a step back.

"You have no idea how hard it is for me to say no," he said and, hearing the embarrassing rasp in his voice, cleared his throat. "But you've been drinking, Tash, and you've had an emotional upheaval tonight, and I don't want to give you a new reason to hate me in the morning. So I gotta send you home."

She shrugged and stepped back. "Your loss," she said coolly.

"You're telling me, *bebe*. And anytime you're ready to take another go at this when you're clear-eyed and stone-cold sober, I'm your guy."

"I'll keep that in mind." She walked away, and a second later he watched as she closed the door behind her. He walked over to the nearest wall and thunked his head against it.

"Idiot," he said in time with each thump against the wood. "Idiot, idiot, idiot."

THE FOLLOWING WEDNESDAY, during the slowdown between the after-school rush and the dinner crowd, Tasha ran up to her apartment to change her T-shirt, because the one she'd started the day in had met with an unfortunate accident with an improperly sealed pizza-sauce container. Letting herself into the narrow hallway that ran the length of the building behind the apartments, she immediately spotted the manila envelope propped against her door. A moment later she bent to pick it up and saw that it was addressed to Luc.

For one blank moment, she stared down at it in her hand. She could hear music thumping faintly from his studio, so she wasn't sure why the mail hadn't been delivered to his door.

But as she straightened, she smiled.

She'd been much less impaired by Luc's bourbon Sunday night than he'd clearly believed. Yet she had to admit that the moves she'd slapped on him had been driven more by a need to eradicate her vulnerability and the less-than-stalwart mental stability she'd displayed when she'd told him what had happened That Night than they had been by a just-can't-leave-him-alone craving.

Not that she didn't ordinarily feel that in spades. It just hadn't been the primary force the other night.

So, yeah, he'd probably been right to call a halt to things before they'd gone too far.

And wasn't acknowledging that grown-up of her? Grinning, she brought the envelope into her apartment and tossed it onto the dresser in her bedroom. She pulled her soiled shirt off over her head as she walked into the adjoining bathroom and dropped it in the sink, which she filled with cold water. A week ago she likely would have viewed his actions as a rejection. And, all right, considering the way *he'd* kissed her several times, she no doubt would have used said rejection to add fuel to her mad-on at him.

Now, however…

She dug her phone out of her apron pocket and punched in a number. It rang three times on the other end before it was picked up with a cheerful "Bella T's Pizza."

"Hey, Tiff, it's me. Something's come up—do you and Jeremy think you can handle the dinner crowd?"

"Sure. So far it's looking a little dead, and midweek's usually not that busy anyhow. We've got it under control."

"Thanks. I'll see you tomorrow." She disconnected and filled the tub, throwing in a handful of bubble-bath crystals.

She took a relaxing if not particularly long bath and reached for her razor as she pulled the plug, shaving her underarms and legs as the water lowered. When she climbed out of the tub, she patted herself dry, then rubbed lotion all over her body. After brushing her teeth, she walked naked into her bedroom and pulled open her undies drawer, pawing through it in search of her better lingerie.

Her options in that category were pitifully limited, but she pulled out a ruby-wine unlined lace demi-bra and a matching pair of panties that she rarely wore because, frankly, she wasn't all that fond of thongs and didn't know what she'd been thinking when she'd purchased this pair. Okay, she did know—they were gorgeous, and she'd willfully disregarded the fact that they'd likely be uncomfortable. And at least they weren't all raggedy

like most of her underwear. She really needed to take
herself shopping one of these days.

For today's purposes, however, the thong would have
to do. She didn't plan to have it on for long anyway.

Not wanting to appear as if she'd fussed, she pulled
on a pair of worn skinny jeans and a royal-blue Henley
tee that was a couple of years old but still made her feel
attractive every time she wore it. Then she tugged the
coated rubber band from her braid, unplaited it and ran
her fingers through the crimped strands. Gathering it
loosely at the nape of her neck, she fastened it with the
rubber band she'd removed from her braid, but didn't
double- or triple-twist the band to make it tighter the
way she usually would. She pulled a few curls free for
a messyish just-tumbled-out-of-bed look. Then she applied a little berry-colored lip balm and stood back to
check herself out in the mirror.

"Good enough." She grabbed Luc's mail, then let
herself out of her apartment, traversed the short distance to his door and tapped on it.

There was no answer, and she sagged. "Oh, for God's
sake." All that buildup for nothing.

Then the door opened, and Luc stood on the other
side.

She straightened. Slapped the manila envelope against
his chest. "This is yours. It was delivered to my place."

He peeled it out from under her palm and looked
down at it. "Thanks. I've been waiting for this." He
raised his gaze to hers. "Is that all?"

"No. I'm clear-eyed and sober and ready to take another go at what you passed up," she said, repeating

what he'd told her she'd need to be in order to pick up where they'd left off Sunday night. "Did you mean it when you said you're the guy to see if I still want a shot under those conditions?"

"Oh, hell, yeah," he said. And reaching out, he snagged one of her wrists, pulled her into his studio and slammed the door.

CHAPTER SIXTEEN

ONE SECOND TASHA was out in the hall. The next she found herself inside Luc's studio, plastered to the door by a hundred and ninety pounds of hot-skinned, hard-bodied, turned-on man. Luc laced their fingers together and pinned her hands to the wooden panels on either side of her head.

She stared up at him, struggling to draw air into lungs suddenly unable to function. She didn't have time to catch her breath before he bent his head and kissed her. Which only guaranteed that she wouldn't be catching it anytime soon.

The man could kiss. Given the urgent full-body press and his rigid erection caught so hard between them it wouldn't surprise her to discover its imprint on her stomach, she'd expected a hot, wet, out-of-control kiss. The kind that ground the back of a woman's head against the hard wood she found herself pinned to.

Instead, he came at her openmouthed, only to pull his kiss centimeters from making contact. Then the dirty tease did it again. And yet again.

But just as she was about to wrest her hands free so she could wrap them around his skull to hold him in place and show him how they did things in Small Town,

U.S.A., he dipped his head and gave her bottom lip a quick bite. She jerked, and he lifted his head to look into her eyes. Then he transferred his attention to its mate.

Except this time he was anything but quick. Hot-eyed gaze watching her, he made love to her top-heavy upper lip leisurely, lazily. And, oh, God. So very, very thoroughly. The slickness of his inner lips massaged the fullness he'd caught between them. Her eyelids slid closed, but that only made the sensations all the more powerful.

And dragged a long, shuddering sigh from her.

He made a sound deep in his throat and gently bit the lip he held captive. He scraped his teeth over it, testing its tensility before allowing it to slip free. His warm exhalation set up a slight chill across the skin he'd left dampened, and he used the tip of his tongue to trace the sharp edge of her front teeth.

Then finally—finally!—he slid his mouth over hers and, slipping his tongue between her teeth, engaged hers in play.

Deep inside, she tightened, dampened, clenched—and she bucked against his hold. The fingernails with which she longed to anchor herself to him scraped impotently against the knuckles of the hands preventing her from doing so. "Inside me."

He ground against her for an instant, then brought himself up short. "Not yet."

"Yes. Now." She gave his tongue a strong, remonstrative suck.

And the tension that had strung between them like stretched-thin silver wires snapped.

Releasing her wrists, Luc speared his hands through her hair, his thumbs framing her cheekbones, his fingers gripping the base of her skull. He widened his mouth over hers and kissed her harder, deeper.

Wrapping her arms around his waist, she dug her fingers into his back. She rose onto her toes to bring them more directly in line and, hooking the back of her knee over his lean hip, yanked him even closer than before.

He ripped his mouth free on an explosive breath and slid his hands from her head. Reaching down, he curled his fingers around the curve of her butt and hauled her up.

Tasha grabbed for his shoulders. She brought her other leg up and crossed her ankles behind his waist, cocking her pelvis to align the seam of her skinny jeans to the fly of his Levis.

Eyes locking, they froze. Then Luc rocked his hips. The feel of his erection sliding against her, even through several layers of clothing, made Tasha's head thunk against the wooden panels at her back.

Swearing under his breath, he stepped away from the door.

She yelped in an embarrassingly Minnie Mouse–like voice as the surface supporting her disappeared. Tightening her arms and legs around him, she raised startled eyes—and found Luc looking down at her.

"We need to take this somewhere more in line with what I have in mind than a slam-bam-thank-you-ma'am fuck against the door," he said gruffly. And with her still clinging to his front, he headed with long-legged strides to the alcove at the end of the room that shared a wall with her apartment.

His every step shifted her in subtle configurations against his hard-on, and it elicited an involuntary, deep-throated moan.

His gaze snapped down, and she smiled sheepishly. "Um, take your time. Don't mind me."

"You moaned."

"Maybe."

"No maybe, *bebe.* That was definitely a moan. A *sexual* moan."

"Yes, well, this is a very…interesting mode of trans-portation."

"Yeah?" His sudden grin flashed white, bringing into play those soft slashing grooves on either side of his full mouth. "Want me to just keep pacing around the studio? See if that does it for you?"

"Nah." But she rolled her hips, then executed a mini bump and grind to show how on board she was with his method of locomotion. "Much as I appreciate the offer, I'd rather get naked with you."

"Ah, *Dios.*" He picked up his pace.

A moment later he tossed her lightly onto the bed and followed her down. Straddling her, he reached for the hem of her Henley T-shirt. She crunched up slightly and raised her arms over her head so he could pull it off.

He tossed it aside, then simply looked at her in her bra and jeans for a moment, apparently fascinated by the jiggle of her breasts when she sprawled back onto the pillow. Ultimately, he reached out to trace their rise from her bra cups, starting at the left strap and making his way to the right as if reading a road map written in Braille. Finally wrenching his gaze away from inspecting his dark fingers against her pale skin, he gave her a rueful smile and leaned forward to press a kiss into her cleavage. "Really nice," he murmured as he straightened back up.

No fooling. And she wasn't talking about her bra. She cleared her throat. "My turn." She reached up to slide her hands beneath the hem of his ultrasoft charcoal-colored tee. Rough-edged inside-out seams showcased his muscular shoulders and outlined the garment's arm holes, and she found herself captivated by the sight of the thin fabric pooling on her forearms as she slid her hands higher up the hot skin beneath it. Not to mention the glimpses of lower abs it exposed. "Lose the shirt."

Reaching over his back, he grasped a handful of fabric, tugged the T-shirt off over his head and dropped it over the same side of the bed where he'd disposed of her Henley.

She swallowed dryly at all that golden-brown skin stretched over beautifully formed muscle and sinew. She hadn't forgotten, exactly, what a gorgeous body he had. But she had done a bang-up job of deliberately burying her every recollection of him—the good as well as the bad—in a dark corner of her mind. Then she'd bricked it up, like a cadaver behind the cellar wall, for good measure.

Yet as it was revealed to her now, she realized she'd never truly forgotten it, no matter how deeply she'd hidden the memories from herself—or how assiduously she'd refused to check him out the day they'd swum together. His shoulders and tight abs and the long, hard legs that she didn't have to see in order to know they'd match the rest—they all added up to her favorite kind of male body. The kind that was built but not muscle-bound. The black hair that hazed his chest and arrowed down his torso to disappear beneath his waistband was just the lemon slice in her cosmo.

She sat up to reach for the metal button on the low-slung waistband of his Levis. The backs of her fingers pressed against the ridged heat of his lower abdomen as she pushed the fastener through its buttonhole, and she slowly lowered his zipper. She hunched to press a kiss into the opening she'd created.

Above her she heard him sharply inhale, and she looked up even as she reached into his open fly.

"Oh, no, you don't," he growled as her fingers grazed down his long length. "It's my turn again." He pulled her hand out of his pants and laid her back onto the bed. Leaning down, he slipped off her shoes and unfastened and unzipped her jeans.

Then he looked down at the denim's tight fit—and his dark brows drew together. "Man," he muttered, "these babies are narrow."

She shot him a smile and raised her hips to shove the jeans down to her thighs. "Grab 'em by the hems and pull."

He climbed to his feet and pulled her down to the end of the bed by her ankles. Then, as instructed, he grasped the hems. He worked them over her heels— then shook her free of the jeans so vigorously she had to fling a hand out to keep from flopping over onto her face. She ended up rolled onto one hip, facing in the opposite direction.

She sensed more than saw him freeze. "Aw, man," he said with a reverence that men usually reserved for their football teams. "*Great* panties." In the next second, he flipped her onto her stomach, came up behind her on his knees and tugged her up onto her own so her butt was in the air. He sat back on his heels, and she clenched the bed quilt in her fists as she felt his breath warm on her bare bum and the damp lace between her legs. He nipped her left cheek with his teeth—then gave the tiny sting a lick.

And who the hell knew that a muscle in her butt carried a direct line to the needy core between her legs? Well, she did now; it was hard to miss when hot sensation shot straight from the bite site to her vagina. She squeezed her thighs together and looked at him over her shoulder. "Enjoy them while you can," she managed to say with reasonable lightness, considering the tightness of her throat. "I'm usually more of a boy-shorts kinda girl, so the thong is pretty much a one-off deal."

"Then I'll just have to make the most of it, won't I?" Rising back up onto his knees, he inserted a thigh between hers and nudged her legs apart. She felt the backs of his fingers as he slid them under the thong where it rose out of the division of her buttocks, felt the motion as he stroked the lace above his fingers with his thumb. "Because this is one very fine view." With a wordless sound of appreciation, he glided his hand up and down the thong's fabric, his knuckles warm against her backside.

His fiddling with the narrow strip caused it to saw lightly between her cheeks and tug the increasingly wet crotch of her panties against her mons. Tasha's breath sped up. "Glad you like it," she choked out.

"Oh, I more than like it." His free hand smoothed over the curve of her rear, then reached between her legs to run two fingers along her wet lace-covered furrow until his fingertips nudged her erect clitoris. He spread his fingers on either side of it.

Then scissored them closed.

A sharp cry escaped her, and she pushed back into his touch. "Oh. Gawd. *Yessss*."

"Damn," he breathed. "That's exactly what I remember."

"Hmm?" Although she twisted to look over her shoulder, she couldn't quite focus. "Remember…what?" Her eyes drifted closed and she undulated on his fingers.

"How much you like sex and how generous and open you are in your enthusiasm. I fantasized about that more than once."

"Yeah?" She cracked an eye open to peek at him. She could have told him it was him—that there was just something about having sex with *him* that felt so natural and right. Yet the thought of saying anything of the sort made her feel uncharacteristically shy.

And they couldn't have that. So she gave him a sly smile instead. "Did you masturbate thinking about me?"

His own smile was wry. "Like I said—more than once."

"Nice." Reluctantly, she pulled away from his touch, moved up to the headboard and turned to face him. "Show me."

"I'm not gonna jerk off. I want to make love with you."

"That works, too." She eyed his erection behind heather-gray boxer-briefs, pushing at the open fly. "You should take your pants off, though. I don't see where we'll be doing much of anything as long as you're still wearing those."

"That I can do." He slid his fingers into the waist-band of the boxers and pushed both his shorts and his jeans down to his knees. She'd barely gotten a peek at the goods before he planted his hands on the bed and kicked his feet back to the floor in a modified squat-thrust, kicking clear of the garments that gravity had dropped around his ankles.

He jumped his legs back onto the mattress and knee-walked over to her.

Watching him, she swallowed dryly. He was so damn fine in the altogether, and she just wanted to get her hands on him. Especially that jutting—

Before she could make a move, he was reaching for her. "Let's get you naked, too."

She unfastened the hooks on her bra while he slipped her panties down her legs and tossed them aside. Once they'd stripped her out of the last of her clothing, they simply stared at each other.

Then grinned with mutual delight.

He dived on top of her, hot skin sliding against hot skin. Hands on either side of her shoulders, he levered his upper body above hers, an action that slid his erection along the damp furrow of her sex and sent them both sucking for breath.

Then, gently rocking his hips, he bent his head and kissed the side of her neck. "I remember this skin," he murmured, dragging openmouthed kisses down to where the curve of her neck flowed into her shoulder. He laved it with his tongue. "Remember the way you smell."

"Sweaty?" she inquired dryly.

"Sweet. Spicy." He breathed her in. *"Good."*

"I remember the ease of being with you." And she was unsure if she should be so pleased to be experiencing that ease again. Being with Luc had been unlike anything she'd ever had with anyone else. Superior to anything she'd had elsewhere, truth be told. And perhaps it would be smarter to be wary of the way she seemed to be falling right back into that rhythm.

Because look how well it had worked out for her the first time around.

Before she could start pointlessly obsessing over something she kept telling herself she'd moved beyond, he shifted fractionally, and the head of his penis bumped over her clitoris at the end of its shallow stroke. A sharp, wordless sound of approval exploded from her throat.

But he was already moving down her body, and that source of pleasure moved with him. He kissed her collarbones and the upper slope of her right breast, then shifted lower again, bringing his mouth closer to her nipple.

Yet didn't quite touch it.

"Seriously?" She pushed up on her elbows, thrusting it against his mouth. "Enough of the teasing—I'm not in the mood." Not when simply being around him these past weeks had felt like ongoing, overextended foreplay.

He grinned against her breast and opened his mouth over her nipple to lave it with his tongue, nip it with his teeth. Swallow it between full lips.

And all the while his black-brown eyes watched her.

"Gawwwwd." Her elbows melted out from under her, and, wrapping her arms around his head, she held him in place even as her own head arched back against the pillow.

As his mouth worked her over, however, she was bombarded by such sensory overload that she simply had to see what he was doing. She dipped her chin into her neck to look.

She couldn't see his eyes; they were downcast and heavy-lidded, his thick lashes casting pools of shade on the skin under them, spiky shadow tips dusting the sharply defined curves of his cheekbones. But she could stare at his lean cheeks as they hollowed, and she felt the lightning-strike zing from her nipple to the wet, restless heat between her legs.

It seemed all roads led there, and her hips instigated a slow bump and grind against the mattress. "Now," she panted. "Inside me now, now, now."

Her nipple slid from his mouth as he muttered, "Wait." He moved his hand down her torso with clear intent, and she tried to deflect it from its target.

"No, please. I want—"

But long warm fingers slicked down the lips of her cleft and two sank into her heat. The callused pads of his fingertips rubbed just the right spot inside her, and his thumb came up to feather a circle around her clit.

And she blew apart, breathy sounds of pleasure purling from her lips as her hips arched high, and her inner sheath clamped and unclamped around his fingers. Over and over again.

When the last frantic pulse of her orgasm faded, she sprawled back against the bedspread. And shook her head in denial. "Noooo," she panted. "No, no, no, no, no."

"Huh?" He slid his fingers free but kept them cupped over her sex as he pushed up on his free elbow. His dark brows gathered over the strong thrust of his nose. "You have an issue with getting off?"

"I do." Hooking an elbow around the back of his neck, she pulled him down so his chest was half over her and his chin tucked into the curve of her neck. "Well, not with the getting off so much as the delivery system." A ragged laugh escaped her. "And I know—very ungrateful. It's just…I wanted to come with you inside me."

She could feel his smile against the side of her throat. "That can be arranged," he said. And rolled fully atop her.

"Hold your horses." She shoved at his shoulder. "Not bareback it can't."

"Oh. Yeah. Don't go away." He pushed back to the end of the bed and swiveled to reach his pants on the floor. He came up with his wallet and fished a battered-looking condom from inside it.

She gave the worn foil packet a dubious once-over. "How long has that thing been in there?"

LUC GAVE THE CONDOM a suspicious look of his own and counted back in his head. "A pretty long time." He looked at her. "I don't suppose you're on the pill?" he asked hopefully. "The DEA docs gave me a clean bill of health when I left Colombia, and I haven't had any action since then that would put you in danger."

"I am on the pill," she said. "But it's a little too soon to expect that kind of trust. Luckily for you, I came prepared." Climbing from the bed, she went over to where he'd tossed her jeans. After rummaging through a pocket, she returned with several condoms. "They, at least, look to have been made in this millennium."

"Hey, I bought these this year." He hitched one shoulder. "It's just that where I've been, I haven't had a lot of opportunity to use them."

She rolled up onto her knees and straddled him, settling her butt on his upper thighs. "Looks like your luck's about to change." She handed him one of the prophylactics. "Here, put this on."

He did so by feel, as he couldn't seem to take his eyes off her. Her strawberry-blond hair was a wild nimbus around her head, her cheeks were flushed and her long eyes slumberous. "You're so damn pretty. You know that?"

"Aw." She flashed a megawatt smile between reddened, kiss-swollen lips. "Keep talking like that, Sweet Talker, and you just might get to second base."

"Only second?" He reached up and cupped his palms

beneath her breasts, vibrating them slightly to both see and feel the resultant jiggle. "I was kinda hoping for a home run." He swept the pads of his thumbs over her nipples and watched them bead. He did it again, and she wiggled atop him.

"That's a definite possibility."

She had sensitive nipples, so following the go-with-what-works theory, he captured them and lightly squeezed.

Her eyes went heavy, and she scooted forward, eliminating the couple of inches that had kept her from his dick. Holding his cock between her legs, she rubbed her sweet slit up and down his shaft. Then, her eyes fluttering closed, she licked her lips, held him in place with one hand and raised her hips to center herself over him.

Then slid down his length.

Seeing his dick disappear inside of her, coupled with the feel, all slippery, tight and furnace-hot, sent his hips thrusting up off the bed, driving him deeper. It lifted Tasha higher on her knees and her hands slapped down on his chest at the same time that he grabbed her hips.

"I didn't think I'd be ready again this soon, but I am," she said. Cupping her hand over her breast, she squeezed it, her fingers spreading wide, then closing with her nipple captured between two of them. She tugged on it as she rose and lowered her hips.

And looked down at him with slumberous eyes. "It's why I wanted to come with this—" she ground against him "—inside me. Because I remember that—I remember how good it was." She oscillated her hips.

Oh, God, so did he. But right now his need to get off was growing imperative, and the stroll down memory lane didn't encourage staying in command. He dug his fingers into her hips to keep her from moving too much. "You believe in simultaneous orgasms?" he asked between gritted teeth.

"Not particularly. At least, I've never experienced one. Do you?"

"I didn't. But if you could just please get off—" He looked up at her. "I'd be right there with ya."

"Yeah?" A speculative light entered her eyes. "Well, gee. It might take me a bit. You taking the edge off so nicely and all." She laughed. "I bet you're wishin' about now you'd paid attention to my requests for you to get your bad self in me."

He lost it for a moment and thrust up into her once, twice, three times before he regained control. But his balls were pulling up, and he was hanging on by his fingernails. "Or I could just leave you in the dust."

Tasha made his eyes cross when she clamped her inner muscles around him. She gave his chest a friendly pat. "You go ahead—you don't have to wait for me."

"Dammit, Tash, c'mon!" Then he shook his head. "Sorry. I'm sorry," he said in a more reasonable tone. "Yelling at you probably isn't the way to go about putting you in the mood." He hooked a hand around the back of her neck and pulled her down for a kiss. "I'm sorry," he said again when he let her up for air. "I've been thinking about this for a long time, and I'm losing my grip. Slide your legs around here." He helped her straighten them out from where they'd been bent under her and tugged them around his hips. "Yeah, like that. That puts these beauties in the perfect place." And bending his head, he lavished attention on her nipples.

He was almost immediately rewarded; her breath began to hitch, and she wiggled atop him. "Deeper. Please. I need you deeper."

That was the downside to this position; it didn't push him as deeply into her as some other ones would. But he tried his best.

Then she leaned back and braced her hands on the spread behind her. The action popped her nipple from his mouth but it made their sexes fuse.

"Oh, God, that's it," she panted as she ground against him. "That's it, that's-it-that's-it."

Yes! Thank you, Jesus. He was holding his shit together with everything he had, but feared it wasn't going to be enough. Hearing her firmly back with the program, however, gave him hope, and delving with his finger and thumb, he pinched her clitoris and gave it a gentle roll.

And felt his mouth pull back in a feral grin when it blew her right over the cliff. Her inner muscles went berserk around his cock.

And that was all she wrote. Letting go of his rigid control, he hauled her tighter to him and thrust hard upward, driving him deep. And he finally came.

And came.

And came.

Until he slumped onto his back, pulling Tasha down atop him. Wrapping her in his arms as she rearranged her legs and made herself comfortable on him, he felt her heartbeat begin to slow in concert with his own. And something deep inside of him seemed to shift.

He tried to tell himself that this was just sex like it had been with any number of other women. But it wouldn't gel in his mind. As he buried his nose in Tasha's fragrant hair and stroked his hands down her long body, he had a sudden uneasy feeling. He'd like to think he was wrong about this.

But he very much feared she'd just rocked his world. Irreparably.

CHAPTER SEVENTEEN

LUC WOKE UP the next morning to find himself wrapped around Tasha. She was warm and soft, and recalling the feelings that he'd fallen asleep with last night, he searched inside himself, expecting to be squarely back to his usual lone-wolf love-'em-and-get-back-to-work self.

That didn't happen.

Of course, he'd also expected to wake up alone as he always did—and things hadn't worked out on that front, either. Usually he was out the door after the sex as soon as he could manage without bruising any feelings. Or in cases like this, where the woman came to his place—

Okay, there hadn't actually been a case like this, not since he'd joined the DEA out of college. But if there had been, he fully expected he would have gently eased any other woman on her way long before dawn.

Instead, he was snugged up, spoon-style, behind his softly scented long, tall redhead. Her very nice butt was firmly nestled against his morning hard-on as she lay wrapped in his arms, and it felt right to have her there. He couldn't fool himself; his world was every bit as rocked by her as it had been last night. He actually felt... happy.

That made him nervous.

Because this was not like him. Why wasn't he his usual self, itching to get back to the seamy, electrifying living-by-his-wits world of cartel busting? God knew the minute an agent committed to a woman, he could kiss all that goodbye. It was no life for a family man.

But there was just something about Tasha. He'd felt it seven years ago, and he felt it now. She possessed this weird power to—

"Buyer's remorse?" Her voice was morning rough, and she raised a hand to rub at her eyes. Then she tunneled her fingers into a wide swath of curls that had fallen forward and flipped it back. "I smell circuits frying."

"No," he said. A little panicky, maybe. But otherwise surprisingly good. He brushed her hair off her shoulder and, pushing up onto one elbow, bent his head to kiss her neck. "Thinking too hard, maybe. But no remorse."

And he rolled her onto her back, the better to demonstrate just how happy he was to see her this morning.

TASHA HAD BEEN gone a good two hours before he remembered the incident report she'd brought over last night. He went looking for it, but didn't find it right away. Then he spotted a corner of the manila envelope peeking out from beneath one of the wicker chairs.

Christ. He didn't even remember dropping it. Yet not only had he patently done so, from the envelope's placement it looked as if he'd winged the damn thing with some force before going at Tash against the door.

His mouth ticked up for a second as he got sidetracked by the vision *that* memory evoked. Then, giving his head a sharp shake to get it back in the game, he ripped open the envelope and plopped down on the couch to read.

He snapped upright a few minutes later. "Son of a *bitch!*" Hauling his cell phone out of his pocket, he punched in a number.

His call was picked up on the second ring. "Special Agent Paulson's office."

"Jackie," he barked at his SAC's personal admin. "It's Luc Bradshaw. Put me through to Paulson."

"I'm sorry, Agent Bradshaw," she said, sounding genuinely regretful. But her tone was firm when she added, "He's still on vacation."

"Then give me his number. This can't wait."

"Again I apologize. But I can't do that, either."

He swore creatively. Then he realized who he was talking to. "I'm sorry, Jackie. I don't mean to take my frustration out on you." Snapping and snarling might be his first inclination, but it wasn't likely to get him anywhere. He and Jackie had flirted harmlessly the few times he'd been in his SAC's office, however, so he made his voice go silky when he said, "I received the report you sent me, darlin'. But when I read it, it said that on the night in question, SAC Paulson had knowledge that the Bahamian police arrested Ta—that is, Ms. Riordan."

"I can't speak to that, sir."

Sir? Except for maybe the first day they'd met, he couldn't recall another time that she'd ever called him sir. And Jackie was linked in to damn near everything that went through Paulson's office—what she didn't know simply wasn't worth knowing. He dropped all pretense of friendliness. "Can't? Or won't?"

She hesitated, then said regretfully, "Won't."

"Fuck. It's true, then. Paulson let Tasha languish in jail for something she hadn't done, then deliberately lied to me about it."

"I'm sorry—"

"Yeah. Me, too," he said, cutting her off. Dropping all signs of friendliness, he added with icy crispness, "I know you know how to get hold of him. Tell him I expect a call ASAP."

He thumbed the End button and blew out a frustrated breath as he let the phone fall onto the cushion next to his hip. Digging his elbows into his knees, he dropped his head into his hands.

"Fuck." It had all been in the report he'd read, right there in black and white. But he hadn't wanted to believe it. Dammit, he'd dropped everything that last night with Tasha in the Bahamas—had been yanked away from his only personal time in over a year. And worse, from the only woman to grab his undivided attention in, well, *ever*—because Paulson had demanded he come in. He'd done that…and the guy had lied to his face.

Looking back, he realized it hadn't been the first time. Well, maybe not the lying so much, although now that that door had been opened, who the hell knew, really? But he'd lost track of the number of incidences where Paulson had insisted he was needed on a job that only he could do. It had made a serious dent in his personal time, including the big one—all the irreplaceable time he'd missed with his dad before he'd died.

Suddenly his every assignment was suspect. His SAC had damn well better get back to him, and soon, if he expected Luc to continue working for him.

Because, he was *this* close to throwing in the towel.

"Don't even try to kid a kidder, Riordan," Jenny advised flatly the minute the waitress who'd interrupted Tasha's abbreviated recap of her time with Luc the other night walked away. "You're not going to make me believe it's only sex."

"I don't see why not," Tash disagreed, picking up her beer. "Since that's precisely what it is." She shoved down the little voice in her head that murmured, *Liar, liar!*

Clearly Jenny could read her mind. She shot her a glance that all but shouted *bullshit* and said dryly, "Don't look now, but your pants are on fire." She slapped her hands down on the tabletop, making Tasha jump. "But on the off chance I misunderstood, let me make sure I've got this straight. You had head-banging sex with the only guy who's ever really and truly floated your boat. Sex that you refuse to give details about but which you will admit blew you away. Yet you think it's just because you have good chemistry with the man? Emotions don't enter the equation?"

"Well, of course they do." *Maybe too much,* she thought privately, but brushed the notion aside. "I like Luc, obviously, or I wouldn't be having sex with him at all." She reached across the table to touch her best friend's fingertips with her own. "But you've known me since we were teens, Jen—you *know* my thoughts on romantic love."

Jenny pulled her hand back and wrapped it around her beer mug. "And my and Harper's experiences these past few months haven't changed that one iota? Because—what?—you think we're just fooling ourselves? Or maybe you fancy that you know better than we do how we feel?"

Tasha hated the unaccustomed coolness in her best friend's voice. But she wouldn't be coerced into saying something she wasn't ready to say, just because Jenny wanted her to. "Think you can dial back that melodrama a tad? I'm not blind, Jenny. I can see that this True Love thing is working for you and Harper. That doesn't mean it's in the cards for me. Even if I wanted to see this whatever-I-have with Luc as some grand, enduring love, I'm a Riordan woman. Just look at my mom, for God's sake—do you remember her *ever* meeting a new man that she didn't immediately label as the love of her life?"

"Nope, can't say that I do. And it really is a damn shame that *you,* of all people, are so hell-bent on tromping along in her footsteps. You really need to take a big step back from all that lusting after love you insist on doing. Not to mention quit hooking up with loser after loser. It's not healthy."

"Huh?" She simply stared at her friend, because Jenny might as well have been speaking Mandarin. "What the hell are you babbling about? I've *never*—"

"No, you never have," Jenny agreed flatly. "That's your mama's shtick. Your. *Mama's,* Tash. Not yours.

And you might want to consider that before you throw away what just might be a good thing."

She blinked. Having to look at it from that angle radically diverged from her long-established way of thinking. She'd always bent over backward to stay as far away from her mom's M.O. as possible. But maybe Jenny had a point. Maybe making poor choices wasn't what she had to fear. Perhaps the true concern in the back of her mind was more that if she did give her heart she would do so with no filter. That she'd honor no boundaries.

"All right." She gave Jenny a terse nod. "I'll think about that." Meeting her friend's eyes, she promised, "*Really* think about it. I'll even go so far as to admit that I may have more feelings for Luc than are safe." Enough that she'd been trying desperately to hold some small part of herself aloof ever since they'd made love.

"Safe?" Jenny repeated. "That's an odd word to use."

"You think so? Because say that I do go crazy here and fall in love, which appears to be your goal for me. What then, Jenny? Where do you see my happily ever after coming from? You do understand that Luc is an undercover agent for the DEA, right?"

Jenny nodded.

"That means that, sooner rather than later, he's going to leave, and I won't know where he is or how much danger he's in or even how long he'll be gone—never mind if he's ever coming back."

Good God, girl, shut up, shut up, shut up. Yet she couldn't seem to. Clearly she'd thought about this way more than she'd realized and now had a burning need to get it off her chest. "I'm not willing to put my heart

on the line under those conditions. You know me, Jen—
there's no way in hell I'd ever be able to live with that
sort of uncertainty." She exhaled a mournful sigh. "So
just let me enjoy this for what it is while it lasts." She
met Jenny's pretty brown-eyed gaze levelly. "Can you
do that for me, please?"

To her mortification, tears rose in her own eyes. An-
grily, she knuckled them away.

"Oh, crap, Tash." Jenny reached across the table and
gripped her free hand. "I'm sorry. I have no business
trying to run your love life. And you're right. His job
is an obstacle. A huge one, and I didn't really stop to
consider it. I just thought, 'Yes! Big step up from drug
dealer,' and that was as far as I got."

Before she could respond—not that she had any idea
what she might say—a male voice called from a short
distance away, "Hey, look who's here." Glancing out
into the room, Tasha saw all three Bradshaw brothers
weaving through the tables. They were still a couple
of yards away but were clearly headed toward her and
Jenny's booth.

She shot them a hopefully carefree smile, then looked
across the table at Jenny, who shrugged at her as she
turned back from craning partway around in her seat,
clearly unable to see with the high back of the booth
blocking the men's approach.

"The Bradshaw boys," she murmured and wiggled
her fingers at her face. "Am I okay?"

"Yes. You only have a little smidge of mascara here."
Jenny touched a spot beneath her own eye.

Tasha swiped the corresponding place beneath hers, then raised her eyebrows inquiringly.

"Got it." Jenny turned to watch the men as they came within her line of sight. And her face lit up. "Jake!" She scrambled out of the booth and threw herself into his arms. "Hey, I didn't expect you home until Saturday night."

"I know. But I was, as always, a very efficient boy." He grinned, then gave her a thorough kiss. When he came up for air, he hooked a slippery strand of dark hair behind her ear. "I called the inn to let you know I was home, and Abby told me you were here."

"So—what?—your first thought was to call your brothers for a get-together?" Her slender eyebrows furrowed over her nose. "You obviously didn't pine for me during your stay in the Ozarks."

"Much as I'd love to leave Jake twisting in the wind," Max said before his brother could respond, "it was actually more a matter of the Bradshaw Brothers' magic timing. Luc hailed me from his balcony when I was over on Harbor Street contemplating taking a break before heading back to my desk to plow through a mile-high stack of paperwork. Then your boy here damn near ran us down turning into the parking lot." He shrugged. "Clearly we're related, since talent this great isn't assigned to just anyone."

"Yeah," Luc agreed. "Great minds think alike." Then he met Tasha's gaze. "Hey," he said softly.

Her heart, which had begun to bang against the wall of her chest at the sight of him, steadied under the warm look in those almost-black eyes. It was kind of amazing how the man could be the most exciting thing in her life, yet at the same time, the most soothing.

Coming to terms with the two disparate traits was a bit unnerving, and after a quick "Hi, yourself," she tore her gaze away with more effort than she cared to admit and turned her attention back to Max. "Why not just take your paperwork home?"

"No point. Harper's putting in extra time at the Village this evening, so I thought I'd grab a burger here and catch up on my backlogged paperwork while the catchin' is good. Move over," he ordered.

She did, and he dropped down onto the seat beside her.

WELL, SHIT. LUC DEBATED for about three seconds the odds of hauling his larger brother out of the booth so he could take Max's place next to Tasha. Then he shrugged and slid onto the bench across from her.

And cheered right up when she gave him a little one-sided smile and a barely-there shrug of her own. What the hell. The view from over here couldn't be beat. Plus, he'd be the one to walk her home anyhow, not Max. His smile grew.

There were definite advantages to living next door to the woman you loved.

Whoa. For several seconds, every muscle in his body went tight. Who said anything about love? Sure, she was smart and funny and a good friend to those she cared about, but it wasn't like she'd shown *him* a lot of that since he'd come to Razor Bay.

But Tasha had pulled at him from the moment he'd

met her on that dawn-lit beach all those years ago. It was as if everything was brighter, more sharply focused with her around. She was more fascinating than any other woman he'd ever known—outspoken and genuine in a way that grabbed him by the throat. From the moment he'd first met her he'd felt as if he'd known her forever.

But that didn't necessarily equate to love.

He made himself relax. This wasn't the time or the place to carry on an internal *Did he or Didn't he.* Sliding over to make room for Jenny and Jake on the bench, he gave thanks for the next several minutes that were spent deciding on then ordering their drinks and a burger for Max.

"I think I'll have one of those, too," Tasha said. "Sometimes it feels as though the only thing I ever eat anymore is my own food."

As if a big gong had gone off in his head, Luc straightened in his seat. "How about I take you to dinner in Silverdale one of these nights? Get you away from the pizzeria entirely." He'd made love to her in two countries, for crissake, but he'd never taken her on a date? For a guy who was reputed to be reasonably charming, he'd sure shown her damn little of that side.

Her pale eyes lit up. "That would be really, really nice. We might have to make it lunch instead, but let me check my schedule." Then she made an erasing gesture. "No, you know what? Even if Bella's is busy, dinner is probably doable."

Max studied them. "So I take it the war's over between you two, huh?"

"Yes," Tasha agreed with a little smile that made

Luc's heart pick up its beat. "We've reached a definite détente. And now that I've got my fabulous staff, I can go on a dinner date guilt-free. I have to tell you, hiring Jeremy was the smartest thing I've done since signing on Tiffany. He's been such a boon." She dug an elbow into Max's side. "And I have you and Harper to thank for it. The kid has such a good head on his shoulders and he's one hell of a hard worker."

"Hey, you gave him a chance when a lot of people in town wouldn't have," Max replied. "Plus, I've seen you with your employees, so I think your management skills probably have more to do with his progress than our recommendation."

"That's true," Luc agreed. "You have a real easy way with teens. Every time I've been in there during the after-school rush, I've caught more than a few bits of the talk going around. And, *cariño,* those kids *luv* your ass." Tilting his head as if he had X-ray vision capable of checking out the body part under discussion, he wagged his brows at her. "I gotta admit, I do, too."

"Yes, well…" She huffed on her nails, buffed them against her top, then curled them toward her palm to inspect their nice glossy surface. "What's not to love, when it comes right to it? My booty *is* very nice."

"She said modestly," Jenny said dryly.

"Oh, look who decided to join the conversation." Tasha grinned. "I thought for a while there, we were gonna have to tell you two to get a room."

Jake gave her a satisfied look from across the table. "Jealous, Tash?" he asked.

She flashed a glance at Luc that had him shifting

in his seat, then gave Jake a satisfied look of her own. "Can't say that I am."

Jake blinked, then slowly turned his head to look at Luc. "Seriously?"

He returned his well-honed drug-dealer hundred-yard stare.

"Well, shit." Jake shook his head. "I leave town for a few lousy days and miss out on all the action."

"What, you were planning on joining him?" Max asked. "With our Tasha? That's perverted, man."

"What?" Jake's expression lost its usual urbane amusement, and for a second he looked downright shocked. "No, that's not what I meant at— Ahh." He nodded wisely. "You're being your usual asshole self. Very funny."

Luc knew it was a dumb thing to covet, and maybe it was because he'd grown up an only child, but he really envied his half brothers their bickering.

And he must have been losing his edge because Max studied him for a moment, then said, "What's that look?"

"Huh?" He looked at his half bro as if he didn't have a clue what he meant, then pointed at his face. "Normal expression, man."

"No, for a second you got a look on your face. What were you thinking?"

His first inclination was to cling to his claim of ignorance. Then he shrugged. What the hell. He might as well come clean. "I was just thinking that I actually envy the way you give each other shit. I didn't have any brothers or sisters growing up, and you two were obviously very close. That must have been nice."

Jake and Max exchanged looks. Then they laughed their asses off.

Struggling not to feel left out of what was clearly an inside joke, he looked from one to the other. "What?"

"We grew up hating each other's guts," Max said.

"What?" he said again. He made an abrupt gesture with his hand. "I mean, I heard you. I just can't process it."

Jake leaned forward. "Do you remember me telling you the night you came to town how our mutual father left Max's mom for mine?"

He nodded.

"And that once Charlie switched his allegiance to me and Mom, Max ceased to exist in his eyes?"

"Yeah, it's pretty tough to forget, since that goes against everything I've ever known about my dad." He looked at Max. "It doesn't mean I don't believe you. It's just…hard to hear."

"I can understand that since you and Charlie had a long, really good relationship," Max said. "And the truth is, by the time he moved out on us he'd already been traveling a lot for work. And I was really little, so under ordinary circumstances I probably wouldn't even have missed him all that much.

"But my mom couldn't let it go, so I grew up hearing ad nauseam how Jake's mom had stolen Charlie away and how her little shit of a son—" he shot Jake a lopsided smile "—that would be you, bro—had gotten everything that rightfully should have been mine. I'm not proud of what an angry kid that made me. But as soon as Jake was old enough to graduate to the fourth-fifth-and-sixth-graders' playground at our elementary school, which put us together for the first time, I took great pleasure in taking it out on him."

"That was the beginning of the two of us trying to beat the crap out of each other every opportunity we got," Jake said. "It continued right up until Max left Razor Bay to join the Marines. It wasn't until I came back to town last spring that we managed to cobble together a relationship." He shoved a shoulder into Luc's. "So, you, too, can feel free to bicker with us."

"Yeah," Max agreed. "You even have an advantage. We started out actually liking you."

Every time he was together with these guys he learned something new about them. And this...

Well, for the first time he realized he probably wasn't as far outside the friendship/brotherhood loop as he'd thought. Both Jake and Max had just basically agreed that there was a place for him in the family dynamic.

Something about their acceptance vanquished once and for all the low-grade nervousness he'd been experiencing off and on since the other morning when he'd realized how happy he was with Tasha. It was possible that he had nothing to be nervous about.

Hell, he'd been given a family when he thought the last of his was gone and that he was well and truly, once and for all, alone in life. Plus, look how successfully his brothers balanced the various aspects of their lives. Both of them were making their jobs work even as they made lives with the women they loved. And they were forging a real brotherhood with each other.

There was no reason he couldn't do the same.

The idea stopped him in his tracks. Where the hell had *that* come from? He wasn't Mr. Impulse; he didn't just one day suddenly think, *Hey, why don't I dump the job I love and start all over again because I have the hots for some woman I've known for a total of, what? A month and a half?*

Even if it was a woman he'd never been able to entirely scrub from his memory—and for a lot more reasons than the stellar sex they shared. Not to mention that the job was developing cracks.

Deep into contemplating that, and the randomness with which it had popped into his head, he couldn't say how much time had elapsed when Max suddenly snapped his fingers in his face.

"Dude, you okay?" his half brother demanded, leaning over the table to peer into his face. "You look like someone dropped an anvil on your head."

"I'm fine," he muttered, even as he thought that was exactly the way he felt. Hell, if this were a cartoon he'd probably have little x's in his eyes and chirping birds circling his head. *Oh, my God,* he thought dazedly, ignoring Max to stare at Tash across the table from him. *Oh. My. God.*

I love her.

CHAPTER EIGHTEEN

JEREMY HEARD THE CAR in his driveway and was at the door before the driver could even shut off the engine. Yanking it open, he stared out at the beater car. Then at his dad, Ben, who was climbing out of it.

He could feel the grin that split his face. "Hey!" he called. "What happened to your truck? You coming down in the world?"

For a second he thought his dad looked uncertain. But he must have been mistaken, for the old man shrugged. "Nah, I still got it. I brought this one for you."

He froze. "For *me?*"

"Yeah. I know she's not much to look at," his father said, "but—"

"You punkin' me?" he interrupted. "If you've had a hand in tuning her up, I bet she runs better than the most precision-engineered engine in the world. Holy *shit,* Dad!" He cleared the stoop in one leap and strode over. Slinging his arms around his father, he hauled him in for a bear hug so enthusiastic it lifted his dad's feet clear off the ground—and never mind that they were the same height. Then he set him loose to inspect the car.

It was a Ford Escape SUV from probably the first year they were made. It looked as if it had started out black, but was now faded to kind of a dull charcoal and generously spotted with lighter gray primer in several places. It wasn't the prettiest ride in the world, but he turned back to his dad with a huge smile on his face.

"This is the greatest gift *ever!* I bought myself a thirdhand bike to get to work, and it's been way faster than walking. But I sure wasn't looking forward to the rainy season. So far, on the coupla days it has rained, I've been lucky to be picked up by the busgirl at work." Who, okay, he'd grab any excuse to see. He managed to stay on point, however. "But having my own wheels is gonna rock!" He'd had so many mad gifts lately he could hardly process it all.

His father grinned back. "I hammered out the dents and was going to paint it for you but ran out of time. I figured you'd probably rather have it as is than wait, but maybe we can carve out a block of time when we both have a coupla days off. If you can bring it into town, we'll paint it together at the garage. Harry said he's got a nice forest-green that some customer decided didn't have the exact right shade of 'spruce,' whatever the hell that means. His boss told him he could take it, so he'll donate it to the cause."

Harry was their next-door neighbor who worked at an auto-body shop—and the mention of his name had Jeremy shifting uneasily. "That's really nice, considering the last time I saw him I kicked in his basement window and called him an asshole."

"Let's not sugarcoat it, kid. You called him a *fucking* asshole." But his old man's muscular shoulders hitched.

"You were going through a rough patch, and he's just happy you're in a better place."

"I am, Dad. I'm in a really good place. I love my job, and I've made some friends you'd actually like. I'm sorry I let you down so many times."

His father reached out a callused hand and gave the back of Jeremy's neck a squeeze. "You *never* let me down," he said fiercely. "If anything, it was the other way around. Your mama let you down over and over again and so did I for not cutting her loose sooner instead of letting you put up with her craziness."

"So you're really going through with the divorce?"

"Yes. Screw for better or worse—I shoulda done it years ago when I saw how her refusal to take her meds was affecting you. I'm sorry I didn't, son. I thought for way too long that she would put your needs first. It wasn't until the judge sent you to Cedar Village that I realized that was never gonna happen. It was the final straw for me. I told her she could choose to stay well for us by taking her medicine or she could get out." He made a face. "She chose to take a walk."

Jeremy gave his father a brief hug, then, ending it with a manly slap to the old man's shoulder, pulled back. "Don't regret my time at the Village, Dad. I think maybe I was meant to go there. My counselor made me understand the patterns I'd fallen into."

"Like what?" With a final gentle squeeze, Ben dropped his hand and stepped back, giving him his full attention.

"Like the way I kept responding to Mom's choosing her illness over you and me with my own destructive behavior. I thought my counselor was full of it when he first suggested that's what I'd been doing. But little by little I came to see he was right, because the truth is I did keep doing the same things over and over again. I blew up instead of trying to communicate how Mom's choices left me feeling like a second-class citizen who was less important than what she considered her right to be an erratic maniac one moment and too depressed to get out of bed the next. I hated her when she was in a rage but seemed to think it was okay to do the same myself. And I picked friends I knew damn well would get me in trouble.

"But now, instead of just getting mad and acting out, I'm a lot better at stepping back to assess." He gave his father a crooked smile. "Or at least at assessing the best I can. I still need some work there. But I'm taking the time to think more, so I react less."

"And that's a real good thing," Ben said.

"Yeah." Jeremy grinned. "Plus, my time at the Village got me the job at Bella T's. I love this cooking shit, Dad. Tasha says I have a knack for it. And I really think I do. I can't tell you how good that feels."

"I actually know how good." His dad hooked an elbow around his neck and pulled him in for a knuckle scrub to the skull before turning him loose. "Discovering your skills is one of the best feelings in the world. For me, when I work on an engine, I just feel kind of, I dunno know...strong, I guess. And happy."

"Yeah." He felt lit up inside. "That's it exactly. That's how I feel when I'm in the kitchen at work. Hey, while you're here I should take you in and introduce you to the people I work with. Make you a slice."

"I'd like that," Ben agreed. "But you think I could see your place first?"

"Oh, man, I can't believe I haven't even invited you in. Sorry about that." Then he laughed, gave his dad's shoulder a slap and headed for his new car. "But you still gotta wait, because right now you and me are gonna take this baby out for a spin!"

PEYTON HAD HAD a crappy day and was in a foul mood as she drove into work. At the best of times, hanging around her house these days was like being caught in the middle of the Cold War. This morning hadn't even been close to the best. The so-called adults had been going at it with more aggression than the Western and Eastern Blocs she'd been studying in history class. She'd spilled orange juice on her favorite top in her hurry to get the hell out of there, then had been late to school.

She wished she had missed it entirely. Because when she finally did get there, she'd discovered that word was out on the state of her parents' marriage. Several of her erstwhile friends had walked right past her as if she were invisible. Others had given her a load of crap.

Not that this was a massive surprise. She'd been waiting for that particular shoe to drop for some time now.

But suspecting a storm was approaching and being caught in the eye of one were about as similar as eggplant and eyelashes.

Still, she had Marni, who was worth all the other small-minded, big-fish-little-town girls put together. And she had a great job. She loved being around Tasha and Tiffany. And Jeremy, of course.

She swallowed a snort. *Who do you think you're kidding, girlfriend?* It was Jeremy who made her job particularly great.

He was practically all she could think about. Just being in the same building with him was the highlight of every day they were on the schedule together. Days like today when they didn't share a shift seemed dull and gray by comparison.

Luckily, they were usually both on at the same time. He worked long hours, and God knew she'd been grabbing every available shift so she could save money for college next fall.

They'd also hung out at his place a few times, but while it was fun and felt grown-up to be in a place that wasn't ruled by adults, it was never just the two of them. Either Marni or Tiffany—and sometimes both—were always there, as well.

That was why she loved the times when she gave him a ride to or from work. For the space of that too-short drive, she had him all to herself, and she lived for the moments she caught him looking at her as if he might want more than a simple friendship from her every bit as much as she wanted more from him.

If that was the case, though, he was doing a good job of concealing it. He never invited her in when she pulled into his dark yard to drop him off. Neither had he ever actually said anything that might indicate he had feelings that went beyond those of friendly coworkers.

And yet...

Ferrying him to and fro gave her hope. Who knew? The possibility existed that *this* time he would invite her in. Or maybe he'd ask her if she wanted to go into Silverdale with him sometime to catch a movie.

She swung wide in the alleyway behind Bella T's in order to squeeze into the parking space she usually occupied next to Tiffany's car.

And had to slam on the brakes. What the hell?

An old beater SUV was in her spot. God, could this day *get* any worse?

Forcing herself to shake it off, she parked on the next block, walked back to the pizzeria and let herself in through the kitchen door.

And was just in time to hear Tasha exclaim, "Oh, how nice to finally meet you! I'm glad to have an opportunity to tell you in person what an invaluable addition Jeremy is to Bella T's."

Peyton perked up. Was he here? Moving slightly to the right, she spotted him out in the dining area with Tasha and a man who was an older, beefier version of him.

She made a beeline for the most direct route out there.

"I'm gonna give him the grand tour," she heard Jeremy say. "Would it be okay if I made us a couple of slices? I'll pay, of course, but I want to give Dad a peek at what I do."

"Of course it's okay! And your money's no good here, kid. That's one of the perks of being a Bella T employee—you eat free and so do your special guests." She turned to his father. "Would you like a glass of wine, Mr. Newhall?"

"Please. Call me Ben. And I'm afraid I never developed a taste for wine. I'd love a Pepsi or a Coke, though."

"Coke it is. Tiff!" She raised her voice to call the waitress who was swabbing down a table at the end of the dining room. "Come meet Jeremy's dad. Is Peyton in yet?"

"I'm here." She walked up to the older Newhall and stuck out her hand. "You must be Jeremy's father. You look just like him." She laughed. "Or I guess he looks like you."

He gave her a firm, warm-handed shake. "You think?"

"It's true." Jeremy treated them all to a rare huge smile. "I got my good looks from Dad."

It didn't take a genius to see he was happy to be with his father, and Peyton had to battle twinges of jealousy that she couldn't claim a similar relationship. Her black mood reemerged.

But for only a moment. Because stronger than her envy was a fierce desire to make a favorable impression on Mr. Newhall.

And wasn't that a kick in the pants? Because she could hear her stepdad's voice in her head pointing out that Jeremy's father was from a far lower socioeconomic stratum than their own. That even though he was neat and clean, he was dressed in cheap clothing. And even though the man's hands looked well scrubbed, they nevertheless held vestiges of black beneath his nails.

Except that was just…bull crap, she realized. As if she or her dad or anyone else was somehow better than Mr. Newhall simply because they were rich. That kind of thinking was every bit as bad as the kids at school who felt free to give her shit now that they'd learned her social standing was about to be ripped out from under her.

Raising her chin, it dawned on her how much she was changing this fall. She was trying really hard to think for herself these days, and she knew Tasha would be ashamed of her if she thought for a second that *Peyton* thought she was superior to Jeremy's dad.

And since her new mantra this fall was WWTD— What Would Tasha Do?—she set out to make him feel welcome.

It worked like a charm, too. Right up to the moment she remembered the beat-up car out back.

"Oh," she said, turning to Tasha. "Did you know there's an SUV parked in one of our spots? It's a POS, so I wonder if someone abandoned it."

She didn't know what she'd said wrong, but Jeremy's dad's face went carefully neutral, and all the warmth she was accustomed to seeing from Jeremy himself dissipated like morning fog under the sun's rays.

"That piece of shit is mine," he said coolly. "My dad fixed it up and brought it for me."

Noooooo! She knew she should apologize, but all she could think was that crappy, crappy car meant Jeremy had no reason to ever catch another ride with her. A sick-making combination of despair and embarrassment settled in her stomach. Yet, even *knowing* this was coming out all wrong, she couldn't seem to stop herself from saying with her old hauteur, "*That's* fixed up?"

Oh, God. As if she were looking down her nose at him.

"Yes." He studied her as if she were one of the asshole snobs at school. "Not all of us get a brand-new ride from our daddies. But *my* father is one of the best mechanics around, so while the POS, as you called her, may not be as pretty as your car, she runs sweeter than a BMW."

"How…nice for you." Her tone suggested how "nice" for someone who didn't know any better. And she wanted to shut up. She really *needed* to shut up. But something inside of her just screamed and screamed in pain. Trying to drown it out, she said coolly, "I guess you won't be needing any more rides from me, then."

"No," he agreed flatly. "I guess I won't." He turned to Mr. Newhall. "C'mon, Dad. Let me show you the kitchen. You can watch me make us a slice."

"Sounds great." The older man gave her a thoughtful glance before he followed his son into the kitchen.

Peyton watched until they disappeared around the far side of the storage closet, then blew out a breath. And turned away.

"Nice going there, Ace," Tiffany murmured, but gave her hand a pat before heading back to wait on three women who had just come in.

Bracing herself to face Tasha's condemnation, she turned.

But the woman she admired so fiercely merely said, "You could have handled that better."

Tears rose in her eyes. Because she could have; she could have handled it so much better than she had. She nodded jerkily. "Anything would have been an improvement over what I actually said," she admitted.

"Do you know why you acted out?"

She looked at the floor. "Yes."

"You want to talk about it?"

Her head jerked up, and she carefully studied Tasha's gray-blue-eyed gaze. It was plain to see the offer was genuine. And yet… "No."

"Okay. I'm always here if you change your mind. And I know you didn't ask, but my standard advice covers every situation. You should be honest with Jeremy, if no one else. Because by dissing that car, you dissed his dad. And it doesn't take especially brilliant powers of observation to see he's crazy about him."

"I know." She glanced into the kitchen again and watched as the guys examined the wood-burning pizza oven. "Would it be okay if I gave Mr. Newhall his pop?"

"Sure. That would be a nice gesture." Tasha gently bumped her hip against hers. "Particularly if it's accompanied by an apology."

She pulled herself up. "Yes, ma'am. I plan to give him one of those, as well."

"Oh, now you're just trying to piss me off."

Peyton looked at her in surprise, and Tash pointed an authoritarian finger at her. "Do not call me *ma'am*."

She didn't know why, but that lightened her mood and she snapped off a salute. "Yes, sir!"

The strawberry blonde sighed. "Go get that drink for Mr. N., smart-ass. Then get to work."

JEREMY DIDN'T KNOW what to think when he turned back from retrieving dough from the refrigerator to see Peyton handing his dad a jumbo cup of Coke and leaning in to talk to him in a low voice.

He was so mad at her. And he hated to cop to this, but he was *maybe* a little bit hurt, too. He'd begun to think she was a real sweetheart in addition to being pretty and fun to talk to. He'd thought that maybe there was potential for them. So for her to turn around and turn up her nose at his father's offering…

Well, that was a shitty thing to do.

He waited for her to return to the dining room before he stomped over to his dad. "What did she want?"

"To give me this pop—and apologize for disrespecting my gift."

Damn. He could *feel* his dad studying his reaction and had to work like hell to keep his expression bland. "Good. That's…good. She *should* apologize."

Although he noticed she hadn't bothered doing so to *him*.

"I suppose," Ben agreed. "Still, it was classy that she did so." He tipped his head to study him some more. "She a rich girl?"

"Yeah. Or at least she used to be. Her folks are divorcing, though, and her stepdad's pretty much cut her off. He said if she wants to go to college, she can pay for it herself."

"What a douche." Ben shook his head. "Man, I'd give a bundle to have the means to put you through school."

"I know you'd do it in a minute if you could. And Peyton's stepdad *is* a douche, from everything I've heard. Which sucks. No two ways about it." He squared his shoulders. "Doesn't mean that she gets a free pass to act like one herself."

"You like her, don't you?"

"What?" He blew a gusty *pfttt! "Noo."* He spotted her cleaning a table in the other room and watched for a second as she leaned over to grab a couple of plates on the far side. A small slice of skin appeared between her top and the low waistband of her pants.

Then, catching himself, he pulled his gaze away to meet his father's. "You saw for yourself she's a spoiled brat."

"I'm not sure I think she is, entirely."

"Are you *kidding* me?"

"No. Oh, I don't doubt that she has her bratty moments. But her willingness to face me on her own and apologize made me think maybe she's trying to move past that spoiled-girl attitude. Plus, she said something that—"

"What?" he demanded. "What did she say?"

"I think she'd probably want me to keep it to myself. But maybe you oughtta cut her a little slack."

"It was *my* fault that she was so bitchy?"

"Of course not. But you've been known to dig in your heels when just flowing past a problem would be a lot more productive."

That was true. It was one of the things Ryan, his counselor, had worked with him on. So he blew out a breath. "Okay," he said. "I'll think about that." When his dad raised a skeptical brow, Jeremy looked him straight in the eye.

"I mean it, Dad. I really will consider what you said. But not today, okay? Right now, I'd just like to wow you with my mad cooking skills."

CHAPTER NINETEEN

"THIS ISN'T EXACTLY what I had in mind when I invited you out to dinner," Luc muttered as he held open the door to Wok On Fire for Tasha.

"Not fancy enough for you?" She grinned up at him as they entered the restaurant. "Silverdale tends to be on the slim side when it comes to upscale. Next time, though, you can take me to Silver City, buy me a Woo Woo and an order of their panko-encrusted fish and chips and have your wicked way with me after. But tonight—well, I've had a jones for veggies for what seems like forever, and I love the Mongolian grill here."

"I'm sorry, did you say something after 'have my wicked way with you'?" He gave her a wry one-sided smile. A second later his dark eyebrows pleated. "What the hell is a Woo Woo?"

"A cocktail made with vodka, peach schnapps and cranberry juice."

"Seriously?"

She laughed and headed for a table. "No need to look so horrified. I don't expect you to drink it. The Silver City Brewery is down by the mall, and it has several award-winning beers. Well, the production facility actually moved to Bremerton, but I'm talking about the flagship restaurant anyway. Annnd I'm rambling." She drew in a breath, then blew it out. "All of this is a long way of saying it's the company that makes that Ridgetop Red Ale Max likes so much. And I'm pretty sure we could find you something you'd enjoy, as well."

"So, if I eat my vegetables without whining, will you let me buy you a drink at the brewery after dinner?"

"You bet." She dropped her sweater on a table and held up two fingers for the cashier to see.

"You've got a deal, then. Hey! Where are you going?"

"To assemble my bowl."

He followed in her footsteps. "Say what?"

She stopped to look back at him. "Haven't you ever eaten at a Mongolian grill?"

"I've spent a good part of my adult life in South America, *cariño,* so, no, I can honestly say I've never been to one. I have had corn tortillas every way known to man, though."

"Ooh, what we have here is a teaching moment." She rubbed her hands together. "Follow me." After leading him to the food bar, she handed him an empty bowl. "Fill it with whatever catches your fancy—veggies, noodles. Tofu is at the end, so I'm sure you'll wanna leave room for that."

The look on his face was priceless, and, laughing, she bumped her shoulder against his upper arm. "Kidding. There's also beef, pork, chicken and I think shrimp to choose from."

They filled their bowls and ladled sauces that appealed to their individual palates atop their selections. Then they handed off their bowls to the cook manning the grill. Moments later they were delivered plates fragrant with rice and their freshly grilled stir-fry.

Luc took a few bites—then smiled at her across the table. "Damn," he said. "This is really good."

"Toldja."

"Oh, good, gloating. That's such an attractive trait."

She grinned unrepentantly. "And yet, the truth is what the truth is," she replied. And dived into her meal.

CONVERSATION GREW DESULTORY as they ate, but eventually they pushed back their plates. Luc had a tough time keeping his eyes off of Tash, which seemed to be an ongoing condition these days. But, hell, her hair was down, which was a rare treat, and it was a wild, bright tangle of curls that tumbled down her back. Errant corkscrews had escaped from where she'd pushed them back to tease an ivory collarbone here, to pile atop a shoulder there. And several swayed upon her breasts with every breath she took. She wore a short, light brown corduroy skirt over darker brown tights, cordovan boots that came up to her calf and a thin, rich amber-brown scoop-necked tunic-length sweater that looked soft as a cloud. The pullover wasn't one of those skintight numbers, which at first he considered a crying shame. Then he found himself seduced by the way it clung to the upper slopes of her breasts and skimmed the rest of her upper torso as it flowed to her hips.

Her looks, however, weren't the primary ingredient holding him mesmerized. One thing he'd begun to realize was that, while the girl he'd met in the Bahamas had been compelling, today's Tasha was exponentially more so. She'd always had killer confidence, but now she was even easier in her skin than she'd been back then. There was something gripping about her sense of humor, her competence and resourcefulness—and he was pretty sure he wasn't the only one who'd noted and appreciated all of those things. Damn near every person he'd come across in Razor Bay liked and admired her. *Respected* her.

Which was saying something, from what he understood of small towns and her particular position in this one when she was growing up.

He planted his chin in his hand. "So, tell me how you got Bella T's up and running. Who are your investors?"

She blinked, and he clarified, "You know—who staked you?"

"Staked me?" She looked at him with a furrowed brow. "No one." She waved an erasing hand. "That is, no individuals—I didn't have friends in high places. I took my business plan to the bank and showed them that I had almost a third of the start-up money, thanks to an investment guy I met in Tacoma who'd taken the savings I'd started putting together when I was a kid and doubled it." She laughed aloud, her face alight with pride and delight. "And they decided I was an acceptable risk and floated me a loan for the rest."

"And you were how old?"

"Twenty-six."

"Man." He looked at her in pure admiration, and his own already sky-high respect did the impossible and soared even higher. "It's pretty damn amazing to accomplish a business start-up—particularly in the restaurant industry, which I understand has a high failure rate—without investors, let alone under the age of thirty. How does a girl manage to save money in her teens? Babysitting?"

"I did babysit from the time I was just under twelve years old until I turned sixteen. Then I waited tables at the Sunset café. And watched and learned everything I could about running a restaurant."

"You own the building, too, right?"

"I do," she agreed. "Well, me and the bank. But someday it'll be all mine. Of course, I included the projection for its rental income in my business plan, as well."

"Of course you did," he agreed dryly. "I admire the hell out of you, you know. You've accomplished a helluva lot on your own."

She shot him a pleased smile even as she shook her head, making several more curls fall forward. "Well, not completely on my own. Old Mr. Jacobs, who owned the building before me, wanted me to buy it, so that undoubtedly went a long way in persuading the bankers. Plus, Jenny has supported me from practically the moment we met—and that's worth more than a bucketful of rubies." She made a face. "Well, okay, the rubies would have come in real handy more than once. But she's believed in me since the first pizza I made her in my mama's single-wide when we were sixteen, and she's offered support and encouragement over the years that I can never repay."

"Why? Didn't you support or encourage her in return?"

"Of course I di— Oh. Very clever. My point is, though, that she's very special to me."

Watching the look on her face as she talked about her friend, he suddenly realized that for all his acknowledgment of his feelings for her the other day, he'd still half believed that maybe they didn't go nearly as deep as he'd believed at that moment. Because, face it, what the hell did he know about love? Hell, he'd believed in his parents' epic love story—only to find out his dad had been kind of a hound and a crappy father before he'd settled down with Luc's mom.

And as for him… Well, since joining the DEA, his so-called relationships had generally lasted a week, max.

And yet…

He couldn't pretend any longer that this overwhelming surge of emotion inside of him was anything *other* than love. God knew that nothing he'd ever felt before came close to the things that stirred his soul when he was near Tasha. He wanted her. Not just for today and not just for tomorrow or next week. He suddenly couldn't conceive of a time when he wouldn't want to be with her.

So, what the hell. He was going for it. He leaned into the table, ready and willing to make this happen. Step One: charm her pants off.

But before he could even open his mouth, she focused her attention on him. "Enough about me. How did a big strong man like you—" she batted her lashes at him "—end up a super–secret agent?"

He smiled at the label. "It started in college when a girl I knew was slipped a roofie and date-raped."

Her expression lost every speck of flirtatiousness.

"That's horrible! What did you do—beat the rapist to a pulp?" She leaned into the table. "Please, tell me you beat him to a pulp."

"I wish I could, *mi* bloodthirsty *princesa,* but I'm afraid I can't. What I did do was pretend to be his new best friend. Then I arranged to have the campus police there to arrest his ass the next time he tried to pull that shit on another girl."

"Okay." She gave him a sharp, satisfied nod. "That works, too."

"What I learned from the experience was that I was good at role-playing. And that I got off on the adrenaline rush of it. So I changed my major to criminal justice, and two and a half weeks after I graduated, I joined the DEA."

"So, I'm guessing you must…love it, huh?"

"Yeah," he said, but discovered his answer was like that old screeching-needle-across-a-record sound effect from an old television series a bunch of the girls in his dorm loved when he was in college. Because did he? Did he, really?

"I love the rush, anyhow," he amended. "But it's sure as hell isolating." He stared at his hand when it made an involuntary, jerky I-take-that-back gesture. "Don't get me wrong. I manage to make connections. I spend my time with lowlifes and killers, yet it's been my experience that people are rarely all good or all bad. So, during those periods when I'm undercover, I can generally find one or two I enjoy being around.

"But the truth is, it never pays to get close to anyone on more than a superficial level. Because, face it, they are lowlifes and killers, and I'm lying my ass off all the time, so it's not like they're real friends." He met her gaze squarely. "I'm constantly aware of that, even if they aren't."

Saying so out loud made him understand how much he'd been enjoying the company of regular, decent people like Tasha and his brothers since he'd come to town. He opened his mouth to tell her so.

Except...

He got a kick out of her viewing him as some kind of kick-ass super–secret agent. So, what was the point in reiterating that, before coming to Razor Bay, he hadn't had a real friend to his name for more years than he liked to admit?

No, he was better off keeping his trap shut unless he had something to say that might charm or entertain her. At least that gave him a shot at making her feel something for him.

Even if it was only a fraction of what he felt for her.

THEIR DATE HAD jumped the rails, and Tasha wasn't sure what had happened.

Okay, that wasn't true. It had been after he'd talked about his undercover work and how it had isolated him. Even then it wasn't as if the date had suddenly crashed and burned. But it had lost the earlier intimacy that made it feel special.

Silver City Brewery, when they moved their date down the road, hadn't helped. The place was jam-packed with the after-work crowd, making the space crazy loud and more hectic than she'd ever seen it during the few previous times she'd been there. The high noise levels took away from the ambience and definitely contributed to the growing no-man's-land between them. But the real problem, she couldn't help but believe, stemmed back to him admitting that because he lied, he didn't have any real friends.

Hello, lowlifes and killers. Okay, so she couldn't even imagine how exhausting that must be, never being able to just be yourself. Always having to monitor every word that came out of your mouth. Yet now that he'd put it out there, at the same time she couldn't help but wonder…had he lied to her? To his brothers?

Oh, God. To *all* of them?

Get a grip, girl! Her suspicion was no doubt unwarranted and not only unworthy of her, but unfair to him. She tried her damnedest to shake it off.

But his sudden facile charm following that brief moment of opening up to her had sunk deep claws of a doubt she'd love to deny.

Until she couldn't stand it any longer and leaned into the table. "Let's go," she yelled. "I'm tired of shouting."

He nodded, and she gathered her purse and stood. With his hand warm on the small of her back, he steered her toward the door.

"God, my ears are ringing," she said when they stepped out of the brewery. "Sorry about that. I've been here before but not at this time of day, I guess."

"Do you want to try another place? Or go to a movie or something?"

"No. I've got a headache. I think I'd just as soon call it a night."

They were quiet on the drive back to Razor Bay. She felt him look over at her several times, but he clearly didn't feel compelled to fill the silence, for it continued to stretch out between them.

When they reached her apartment a short while later, however, he took the key she'd pulled out of her purse and unlocked her door. He ushered her in and kicked the door shut behind them. "So," he said in a flat, inflectionless voice. "I thought you were a big proponent of honesty."

"I am!"

"Yet the minute I gave it to you, you clammed up." He narrowed his eyes at her until they were the barely-there glints of black between dense, dark lashes. But she didn't doubt for a moment that those all-seeing eyes observed her every reaction.

"So, what's the deal?" he demanded. "I tell you the truth and you start wondering if I've been lying to you—and, oh, wait, let me guess—everyone else since I landed in town?"

"No!" she said indignantly. Then, "Well, yes. Maybe." She shook her head. "I don't know, okay?"

"Okay, fair enough. C'mere." He cupped a hand around her elbow and escorted her to her couch. "Sit."

"Stay!" she snapped. "What am I, a disobedient dog?"

His teeth flashed white in his golden-skinned face. "You are kinda bitchy right now."

She shrugged petulantly, then straightened her posture. "All right, I'll give you that. If you'll admit that you went from telling me probably the first from-the-heart honest thing you've ever said about your work to Mr. I'm-too-smooth-for-my-shoes."

He blew out a sigh and rubbed a long, lean hand across his face. Dropping it to his side, he looked at her. "Can we sit down and talk about this?"

She shrugged, but took a seat on the couch. And gave him a pointed look. "Talk."

He dropped onto a cushion a couple of feet away from where she sat hugging the sofa's corner. "I admit I was maybe a little superficial," he said. "But I couldn't help it. I kind of panicked."

She blinked. Mr. Tough and Ready, panicking? "Why on earth would you do that?"

"Jesus, Tash." He thrust his fingers through his hair. "I've seen things, *done* things, that would straighten your hair. Hell, who am I kidding? That would turn your stomach. I'd just admitted that I hadn't had any real friends since I graduated college. And you went quiet on me, developed a headache and wanted to go home."

"Because you started talking like a snake-oil salesman, it was too damn loud in there and... Well, I wasn't having fun anymore."

He scooted a little closer. "But you were having fun before that?"

"Yes. I was having a great time. It felt both effortless and exciting, the way I remember it being when I first met you in the Bahamas. Aha!" She pointed at him. "You lied to me then." She couldn't believe it hadn't been the first thing she'd thought of when she'd started in what-ifing—

"I lied to you back then because I was on a job and

had had it drummed into my head that you never, but *never,* broke cover. It didn't matter that I was a thousand miles from the job at the time—those were, and still remain, the rules for covert operatives."

He moved closer yet and held her eyes with a steady, level gaze. "But I swear on my mother's grave that I have not lied to you since I found you again. Nor have I lied to my brothers or their wives or Austin or—hell, anyone in this town when it comes right down to it."

"Okay. I guess I just needed to hear it said aloud."

"So, you believe me?"

She paused to take an internal reading, then said honestly, "Yes."

"Good." Twisting around, he picked her up and hauled her onto his lap facing him. "Now, about that having my wicked way with you…"

Her mouth dropped open, a strangled laugh escaped her, and she gave him a straight shot to the shoulder. "You're such a pig!"

"Hey, I'm a guy, and we just had our first— Hell, I'm not even sure what you'd call this—a fight? A misunderstanding?" He tugged at the leg that was partly caught on his pelvic bone until she straddled him head-on. Then, looking up at her, he shrugged. "I haven't been in a real relationship for so long I'm pretty sketchy on the terminology. I do know, though, that either one of those situations calls for makeup sex."

Her heartbeat picked up its pace. "Is that what we're in, you and I? A relationship?" *OGod, OGod, OGod, I thought it was no strings attached.*

"Hell, yeah. At least…that's what *I'm* thinking it is."

A slight wrinkle developed across his forehead. "Why? Do you disagree?"

She wanted to ask how long he intended this so-called relationship to last, but somewhere along the way, when she hadn't been paying attention, she'd turned into a raging wuss. It was the only explanation she could come up with for the fact that where she ordinarily wouldn't have hesitated to outright ask, she instead kept her mouth shut except to say, "No. I don't disagree." Then she bent her head to kiss him. Strictly because she wanted to, dammit.

Not because it provided her a legitimate reason not to have to examine her own feelings. Or discuss where—if anywhere—this thing between them was going.

CHAPTER TWENTY

WHEN LUC ARRIVED at Max's house the following Wednesday evening, he found the front door cracked open to the chilly night air, music pouring out of the living room and his brother dancing with Harper. For a minute or two he simply stood on their porch, watching them. Max had some moves. He was a better dancer than Luc, that was for sure.

He rapped on the door frame just as Max was in the midst of dipping his woman—and looking as though he were seconds away from laying a hot one on her, as well. "Did I get the wrong night?"

Max pulled Harper upright and turned to grin at him. "No, come on in. Harper and I were just passing the time until everyone arrives."

"Can I grab you a beer, Luc?" the pretty biracial woman asked, shooting him an easy smile as she extricated herself from Max's hold. "Or maybe a cup of coffee or a glass of wine?"

"A cup of coffee sounds good."

"One coffee, coming up. How do you take it?"

"If you have milk, that would be great. If not, black is fine."

"Oh, sugar, you name it, we've got it."

"We do," Max agreed. "Tonight, anyhow. You all have been good enough to offer your help on my campaign, so we laid in some serious provisions. The least we can do is see that you're fed and watered. Speaking of which, will skim milk do ya, or you want to go crazy with half-and-half?"

"Crazy is my middle name," he said dryly.

"Half-and-half it is," Harper said and left for their not-quite-finished kitchen.

Max turned down the music. "Let's go grab a seat."

"Jesus, Max," Jake's voice said before they'd moved two feet, and they turned to watch the youngest Bradshaw brother usher his soon-to-be-wife into the house. "Is there a reason you're heating the great outdoors?"

Austin dashed past his dad and Jenny and headed straight for the two of them.

"Hey, Uncle Max, Uncle Luc! I'm gonna help tonight, too. Dad said you might let me use the staple gun."

"You know what? A staplin' guy is *exactly* what I need," Max said. "Come with me—I'll show you the station I set up for the campaign signs we're going to put in people's yards and along the highway."

Harper came over with Luc's coffee and he accepted it with thanks. Taking a sip, he followed Max as he led Austin over to a table made from an old barn-type door and two heavy-duty sawhorses. On its working surface was an industrial-sized stapler and a stack of big glossy signs reading Max Bradshaw for Sheriff that featured both a head shot of a sober-faced Max in his black uniform sweater with its cotton epaulets and another of a laughing Max casually dressed in a white T-shirt, a bandanna tied around his head. Smaller letters along the bottom read There's a New Sheriff in Town. A pile of flat wooden stakes resided next to the signs.

He looked from the sign to Max. "I've never seen two portraits on one of these."

His brother grimaced. "Tell me about it. And I look like a crack-happy Hell's Angel in the informal picture. My vote was for the one of me in my uniform, but the women shot me down. Harper said the casual photo shows my approachable side."

"She's not wrong," he said, staring at the open joy on Max's face in the laid-back photograph. "Where was this taken?"

"Rebecca Damoth took that on her smartphone at the Cedar Village Pancake Breakfast fundraiser a few months ago. I was the chief flapjack flipper that morning."

Jenny joined them. "It's brilliant marketing, Max. You look all official in the professional one. But the other shot is more approachable and reminds people that on top of keeping Razor Bay safe and orderly, you've given a lot of your free time to the community."

"That's true," Tasha said from the doorway, and Luc's head snapped around as she let herself in and closed the door behind her. It had been only two days since their date, but she'd been busy since then, and it felt a lot longer.

She unwound a long, fringy scarf from around her neck and shed her coat, draping both items over the arm of a chair before coming deeper into the room where the rest of them had assembled. "That snapshot reinforces your ties to your neighbors, and that's something your opponent seriously lacks. He's never lived or worked here, and even if I didn't love you dearly, I can't see myself ever voting for him. He just strikes me as too rigid and inflexible—which I guess are the same thing, aren't they?" She made a dismissive face. "But would he know how to handle Wade Nelson when he starts in on Curt and Mindy?" she demanded, referring to a local who couldn't accept that his ex-wife had moved on—even though she'd been with her second husband for nearly a decade. "I don't think so."

"Hell, *I'm* not sure what to do about Wade," Max said. "It's not like anything I try ever sticks."

"Well, yeah, Wade's an idiot. But he's Razor Bay's idiot."

"He is," Jenny agreed. "He's one of ours, and Swanson would probably have him doing hard time alongside my father if he had to deal with the guy."

"Even Curt and Mindy don't want that," Tasha said. She came over and patted Max's arm. "You're going to blow him away in the election."

"From your lips to the voters' ballots."

"Wait," Luc said, looking at Jenny. "Your father's in prison?"

"He is. When I was a teen, he was convicted of defrauding a lot of people in a Ponzi scheme and has been in Monroe Penitentiary ever since. Or maybe he's out now." She shrugged. "We haven't talked much since last spring, when I refused to tell the parole board he had a job waiting when he got out in the inn's—wait for it—accounting department." She shook her head. "He was insulted when I offered him a position with the grounds crew, but it will be a cold day in hell before I trust him anywhere near Austin's inheritance."

Holy shit. The things he learned every time he was sure his brothers and their women lived a Mayberry, U.S.A.–type life.

"Could you guys stay on track?" Austin demanded impatiently. "Getting back to the election stuff, we all know Uncle Max is gonna be sheriff. Let's staple!"

Max hooked an elbow around the teen's neck and gave him a noogie. "We know that, do we?"

Twisting in his hold, Austin grinned up at him. "Sure."

"Sounds like a campaign motto to me," Luc said. "Maybe we should replace *There's a new sheriff in town* with *We all know he's the man for the job*."

"See?" Austin demanded, as if Luc's agreement sealed the deal. "*Now* can we make those signs? After all," he added piously, "that *is* why we're all here, isn't it? To work on your campaign?"

"That we are." Max turned him loose.

"And since you're such a conscientious, altruistic little go-getter," Jake said, "maybe we should give you a stack of the smaller signs and send you into town on your bike so you can ask all the merchants and restaurant owners if they'd display one in their window. I bet you'd make a great ambassador for your uncle."

"Uh—" Austin was clearly thrown off balance for a moment, but quickly rallied. "I would, Dad, but this is Razor Bay. Except for Tasha's pizzeria, the streets have already rolled up. And by the time I could make it there, Bella T's will prob'ly be closed, too. Tash is right here anyhow, so she can take 'em herself."

Max grinned at Jake. "He thinks as fast on his feet as you do," he said dryly. Then he turned back to Austin. "Let me show you how I want these done." Selecting a stake, he laid it out on the cleared middle of the table and placed a sign atop it. "See how the center of the stake lines up behind this star? Plus, how much I left free at the bottom so we can push it in the ground and still have it be tall enough to see?"

Austin nodded, and Max picked up the stapler. "The only trick here is to not staple over any of the pertinent information. So, put one here." He positioned the stapler just above the star.

"Let me do it!"

Max handed the tool over, and Austin pressed its business end against the poster in the spot his uncle had shown him and pulled the trigger. "Booyah!" He looked down at the poster. "And here?" he asked, lining up the staple gun in a clear spot near the top of the stake.

"Perfect. I see my signs are in good hands."

"Yeah, it ain't rocket science." He stapled it and picked the sign up to admire his work. Then he gave the contents a closer look. "These are pretty cool."

"They oughtta be," Max said. "Your dad designed them."

Austin grinned at his father farther down the room. "Good work, Dad."

"Thanks, son," Jake replied from where he was doing something on his laptop, Harper watching over his shoulder. "Glad you approve."

Luc had already discovered he liked Austin. The kid had the same offbeat sense of humor as the rest of this group, and for a teenager, he was surprisingly free of angst. His unquestioning, openhearted acceptance of Luc had caught him by surprise and filled him with gratitude. Austin treated him as if Luc being his uncle was just an ordinary, everyday given.

And now, after watching the byplay between him, Jake and Max, he realized he'd kind of like to stick around to watch Austin grow up.

So, why don't you?

Everything inside of him stilled. Because, seriously, what was there to stop him? Not his fucking career, clearly. It had been days since he'd demanded Paulson's admin have the special agent in charge call him back—but had his SAC bothered to do so?

That would be a great big *Hell, no.* So why not think about changing careers? Working in an area that would keep him closer to his brothers and their families? To Tasha?

He went and took a seat on the couch to think about that.

A short while later, Tasha's voice cut into his thoughts. "You're kind of quiet tonight," she said, and he looked up to find her standing over him.

"Yeah." He moved over on the couch and patted the freed space on the cushion for her to sit down. "I've got some stuff on my mind." Then he sat taller in his seat. "But that's not why we're here. So, I'll put it out of my head for now so I can do my part for Max."

"That can wait a sec," Jake said and took the spot

Luc had expected Tasha to occupy. "I've got something to ask you."

"Sure. Shoot."

"You know that Jenny and I are getting married in January, right?"

He nodded. "Yeah. Or I knew you were engaged, anyhow. I can't say I was real clear on the when."

"The when is January seventeenth. It's going to be a small wedding, only family and a few friends—but a big-ass reception. Austin's my best man and Max is my usher." He looked Luc in the eye. "I'd like it if you'd be my other usher."

"You want me to be your usher?"

"His other usher," Max called from the far end of the room.

Jake laughed. "Right. My one of two. Not that there'll be many people to usher, since, like I said, the wedding itself is going to be small and private. But you're my brother and I'd like you to be part of it." He studied him for a moment. "Tuxes will be involved, if that helps persuade you. That's what sucked Max in." He shook his head. "The guy loves his dress-up."

"In *guy* clothes," Max said, then muttered to Harper, "The way he says it, you'd think I had a closet full of women's underwear I liked to strut around in."

Austin shot him a horrified look. "Gross!"

"I know, right?" He shook his head. "Your dad's weird."

Luc laughed. But inside his heart was pounding, and an emotion so large he could barely contain it swelled in his chest. Jake wanted him to be part of his and Jenny's wedding. Because they were brothers. Brothers in the same way that Jake and Max were. He met Jake's steady, good-humored gaze and nodded. "I'd like that," he said gruffly. "I'd like it a lot."

"Score! The wedding party is now complete." He looked over at Harper. "Okay, then, we're here to work," he said. "What do you want us to do first?"

PEYTON DUMPED THE bussing tub next to Bella T's industrial-sized dishwasher and turned to Jeremy, propping her hands on her hips. "Do you *ever* plan on talking to me again?"

He had been giving her the silent treatment since last Friday. On the occasions when Tasha had been in the pizzeria kitchen with them and he couldn't get away with ignoring Peyton entirely, he'd kept communication between them curt and chillingly polite.

But Peyton had apologized more than once. Tonight she'd reached her limit and was ready for a throw-down. Tasha was at Deputy Bradshaw's place doing…whatever it was that people did on campaign stuff. Tiffany was out in the restaurant, chivying the last stragglers on their way, and would be busy after that for a bit wiping down their tables. So, while Peyton had a few moments when it was just her and Jeremy in the kitchen, she planned to find out once and for all if they had any relationship left to reclaim.

She stared at him, taking in his shuttered eyes and rigid jaw. She hated the frigid silences he'd been treating her to, but if she'd secretly hoped that tonight he would finally relent and start chatting her up—or, crap, even acknowledge her—she was clearly in for another disappointment. And, heart thudding with frustrated misery, she turned her attention to doing what Tasha paid her to do. Presenting him with her back, she unloaded the tub's contents into the dishwasher.

For a while, the only sounds he made that let her know he was still in the kitchen with her were those of filling containers with the leftovers and depositing them in the fridge. During the seconds of silence that stretched between the clatter she generated transferring cutlery and dishes into the machine, she also heard him scraping dough off the work top. Finally she fit in the last of the soiled pans, put detergent in the dispenser, closed it up and started the washer.

Then she turned to look at him again and caught him gazing at her. His eyes immediately looked elsewhere.

"I'm sorry I insulted your car," she said in a low voice. "But when I found out it was yours, I was... wrecked."

His head came up. "Why?" he snapped. "Afraid someone might expect you to actually ride in that— How did you so eloquently put it? Oh. Yeah. Piece of shit?"

She should just let it go. Cut her losses. Because she could tell him the truth and still have him be pissed at her—only this time she'd have handed him even more ammunition than the kids at school who were giving her a bunch of crap had.

But, dammit, she remembered how Tasha had given her this job against her original better judgment. Peyton admired her fiercely—more than any other adult she'd ever known.

And every time Tash had given her advice, she'd advocated honesty.

So she drew in a breath, then shakily exhaled it. "No," she answered. "Because giving you rides to and from work was the highlight of my days. And I knew that you having your own car meant an end to them."

Once again Jeremy's silence beat against her eardrums and she made up her mind that this was her last attempt at a reconciliation. She liked him better than any boy she'd ever met, but she couldn't do this anymore. Shoulders tight, the base of her skull beginning to telegraph the beginnings of a stress headache, she stared down at the kitchen floor.

More than anything she'd love to meet this defeat with insouciance. Because, hey, you won some, you lost some.

But all she could think was: losing sucked.

"What?" he croaked, and her head came up.

He was actually looking at her instead of looking through her the way he'd been doing for the past five days. Fragile hope made her heartbeat stumble, and she squared her shoulders. "I said I hated that you have a car now and won't be needing rides from me anymore."

He stepped closer. "And it never occurred to you that you might ride with me occasionally instead?" He narrowed his eyes at her. "But then you probably don't wanna be seen in a piece-of-shit car."

"Oh, for God's sake, Jeremy, would you let it *go,* already? I said that when I thought the car had been abandoned out back. I never would have said it if I'd known it was yours—and I sure as hell wouldn't have insulted your father. I'm green with envy that you've *got* a dad who made a special trip from Seattle to give you a car. I keep waiting every day for my stepdad to repo the one he gave me back when he still loved me." Her lower lip trembled, but she bit it hard to stop it.

Because damned if she'd let herself cry in front of him.

WATCHING PEYTON'S WHITE teeth clamp down on her full, pink lip broke Jeremy's paralysis, and he closed the space between them. She'd been shooting him glances from the corners of her eyes, and he watched them go wide when she found herself suddenly nose to collarbone with him. He hauled her into his arms and drew in a deep breath, savoring the never-forgotten scent of her shampoo even as he demanded, "Is that what you said to my dad?"

Tipping her head back, she looked up at him. "What?" She scowled at him. "I haven't seen your dad since last Friday."

"He asks about you when he calls," he said. "And he told me that night that you'd said something that made him question my less-than-flattering assessment of you."

Her eyes narrowed, and he grimaced apologetically, but then shrugged. "Hey, you'd dissed his present to me and I was pissed. So…did you say something that compared my dad to yours like you did just now?"

"I don't remem— Oh. Yes. I guess I did. I said you were lucky to have him, and that I'd give a bundle for a father who cared half as much as he did."

"I think that meant a lot to him."

She stepped back, and he dropped his hands to his sides. "Yes, *he* accepted my apology right away. Why did you stay mad at me for so long?"

"Dad says I have a problem getting out of my own way even when just going with the flow would make my life so much easier." His shoulders twitched. "He's not wrong, and I have been working on that. But when I thought you were looking down on me and mine, it—I don't know—just hit kind of hard. So I did my usual and shut down."

She stepped close again. "Because I have the power to hurt you?"

He pulled himself up to his full height, and the stubborn look he slanted on her said, "Hell, no—real men don't admit to that shit." Yet when he opened his mouth, what came out was "Maybe."

"You have the power to hurt me, too, you know. So, maybe we should try real hard not to do that to each other."

"Yeah." He took a step closer to her, as well. "Maybe that's exactly what we should do." And slowly, slowly, he lowered his head.

Clearly, he was going to kiss her. But just as clearly he was giving her ample time to stop him.

As if! She rose up on her toes, wrapped her arms around his neck and pressed her lips to his.

And, oh, God, it was heaven. Jeremy's fingers, a little dry-skinned from the constant washing that was required in a kitchen, framed her face with a tenderness that made her ache. And his mouth was warm and soft-lipped, but firm. Wow. So, so firm. She opened her own and sighed when his tongue slid in.

Simultaneously, they tightened their hold on each other and clung, exchanging soft sounds of appreciation as they explored the other's taste and textures. Peyton couldn't say how much time passed before he finally lifted his head.

He touched his fingertips to the fringe of black hair feathering her temple. "So," he said, gazing down at her.

Her eyes soft, she returned his look. "So."

"Want to take a ride in my new car?"

"Yes." She smiled at him. "I'd like that a lot. I thought you'd never ask."

CHAPTER TWENTY-ONE

CLAD IN RAGGEDY jeans and a threadbare sweatshirt, an old faded bandanna tied over her hair to keep it out of her way, Tasha charged into cleaning her apartment as though a horde of white-gloved cleanliness-is-next-to-godliness mavens was about to descend on her home and swipe their pristine fingertips across her furniture to judge her efforts. Her stupid crew down in the pizzeria had insisted they had things under control and sent her home.

Okay, not stupid—that was a crappy thing to even think. In fact, she oughtta be happy about their thoughtfulness, right? Grateful, even. Because how many times had she *dreamed* of having free time? Of getting so much as an hour devoid of responsibility, time in which she could maybe read a magazine or run errands without her mental clock infernally tick-tocking away the minutes taken from the work she felt she *should* be doing?

But this was different. It was Friday, for God's sake—she truly shouldn't be away from Bella T's on a Friday! The kids had said it was a test—that they could always call her if something came up that they couldn't handle. But then Jeremy had flashed her a cocky *trust*-me smile and assured her that wouldn't happen, because he had it covered.

Huh. He'd probably wanted her out of there so he and Peyton could mess around in her kitchen. It hadn't escaped her attention that they'd made up.

She really ought to go down and supervise.

"Oh, for God's sake, girl, get a grip." And really, she needed to do just that. Yet feeling grouchy for no good reason, she slammed the few dirty dishes scattered across the countertop into her dishwasher without consideration for their chipability.

Dammit, she was happy for them—and maybe even happier for herself, since both had been moping around all teenager-angsty for the past week. Plus, she knew perfectly well that Jeremy would always act professionally on the job. The truth was, her mood had nothing to do with the teens' love lives and everything to do with the fact that her big talk about wanting occasional downtime was obviously just that: nothing but talk. Because without all the usual restaurant tasks to keep her occupied, she was climbing the damn walls. Feeling itchy and jumpy and thinking that a nice cathartic screaming meltdown would feel good about now.

There was such a thing as *too* much time to mull things over, dammit. Sometimes a woman just wanted to do and not have to think, think, think. Thus the manic clean-athon. She needed something to combat this hamster-on-a-wheel brain spin she was in.

All because a week ago yesterday Jenny had assured her—no, flat-out *told* her—that Tasha was not her mother. That she was, in fact, *nothing* like Nola. And never would be.

She'd thought about it a great deal since then. In her head, she knew her best friend was right. For as long as she could remember she'd worked like a demon to avoid following in Nola's footsteps.

Yet here she was, falling for Luc all over again. Only this time it was worse than the first time around, because this wasn't a few fantastical days out of time in a faraway exotic locale. She'd seen exactly how well he fit into her mundane daily life. Had garnered new scraps every time they were together that helped her understand what made him *him*.

And apparently she believed she was in *loooove*.

The mug that had been in her hand suddenly crashed against the wall, and she barely blinked when it shattered into a billion shards. She merely stood there, chest heaving with each labored breath as she stared blindly inward. Because...

If jumping from getting to know someone better to believing herself in love wasn't Nola-like, she didn't know what was.

Tasha couldn't deny the way she felt. What she damn sure could do, however, was not erect a bunch of pie-in-the-sky dreams around it. Because Luc had never promised her anything. He'd told her outright, in fact, that he loved his job. And in truth, she expected any day to discover him packing his bags to disappear once again into his dark and dangerous world.

She just didn't know what the hell she'd do when that happened.

Luc had been listening to Tasha bang around in her apartment since arriving back at his place twenty minutes ago. And as much as he'd wanted to go over to see what she was doing, he'd decided maybe she needed some space. She was generally pretty quiet, and the noise she was making today sounded a little on the pissed-off side. No man wanted a piece of that, so the prudent thing, he decided, was to give her a wide berth.

Until something crashed inside her place. Then he was out the door and in front of hers before he even thought about it. He pounded his fist against the solid panel. "Tasha," he called authoritatively, "let me in!"

There were several seconds of silence. He was getting ready to bang on the door again when her voice, from the other side, said flatly, "Go away, Luc."

"Not gonna happen. Open the door or I'll—"

It whipped open. "What, big shot?" she demanded. She faced him in the doorway, her skin flushed and her hands on her hips. "Bust it down, kick it in? Not if you want to stay out of your brother's jail, you won't. Because I will have him arrest you so fast it will make your head explode."

He stared down at her, puzzled as to why she was mad at *him.* Yet there she stood, combatively blocking him from entering her apartment, and everything about her said No Trespassing in hard-to-miss neon.

"What the fuck is up with you?" he demanded. Then his eyebrows relaxed above his nose as he realized what the likely answer was. "Ahh." He nodded sagely. "Is it that time of the—?"

"Oh!" A you-did-not-just-*say*-that look on her face,

she slapped her hands against his chest and gave him a shove that actually stopped the word he was about to speak and moved him back a step. "You do *not* want to finish that sentence, buster. Not if you know what's good for you. I know this might be difficult for your tiny male brain to comprehend, but sometimes a woman has actual moods that have nothing to do with her menstrual cycle."

"Okay, I'll give you that. But why is it all right for you to make a point of insulting the size of my brain when you're all up in my grill for thinking you might be on the—that is, having your period?"

She simply stared at him for a moment before muttering, "Crap." Then she turned and stalked on fleece flower-power-patterned sock-clad feet back into her apartment.

He took the fact that she didn't slam the door in his face as an invitation to come in and did so, quietly closing the door behind him.

"I have no good answer for that," she said and blew out a breath. "Not a single comeback in sight, because as much as I hate to admit it, you're right—I can't have it both ways." Shaking her head, she flopped down on her couch and looked up at him. "I really am in a mood, and when you turned up with your commands and demands, you became a handy target for my general pissiness. I'm sorry."

He sat down next to her. "You want to talk about it?"

"No." She slid down on her spine and rested her head against the back of the couch, staring at the thick white fog on the other side of the French doors. "It's just stupid stuff."

He should have been relieved not to have to listen to shit about *feelings*. So why did he have to bite his tongue against demanding she tell him all about it instead? God knew he'd ordinarily be trying to break land-speed records in the opposite direction. But he was coming to realize that he wanted to know everything about Tash. He wanted to know what made her tick. What had happened to set her off.

But she was clearly in no mood for a heart-to-heart, so he let it go. Instead, something his mom used to say when he was down or out of sorts popped into his head, and he asked, "Want a hug?"

Slowly, she turned her head against the couch back to look at him—and for a second he thought she was going to cry. The mere idea scared the shit out of him.

Luckily, however, she lost the tears-are-imminent look and nodded. "Yeah," she said in a low voice. "I'd like that a lot."

He picked her up and carefully arranged her on his lap. Tucking her head beneath his jaw, he rubbed his chin against her crown as he wrapped his arms around her. They were quiet for several long moments.

Then he tipped his chin in to look down at her. "It's been a long time since I've given a back rub, but I used to have seriously mad skills in that department. I might be a little rusty, but for you I'd break out my best moves."

She sighed. "That would be really nice."

He climbed to his feet and set her gently on hers.

"You wanna lie on your stomach on the sofa? I'll sit astride you." When she looked doubtful, he added, "Don't worry. I won't crush you."

"Why don't we take it to the bedroom instead?" she counter-suggested. "There's more room to spread out."

His dick loved the idea, but he mentally issued it a stern *Down, boy.* "The bedroom it is," he said casually and followed her there. "Get comfortable," he advised and walked over to the window to close the blinds to dim the room. There was a charger with several half-burned vanilla-scented candles on her dresser, and he dug out a book of matches he carried in his change pocket and lit them.

When he turned back, his heart slammed up against the wall of his chest to find her pulling her rag of a sweatshirt off over her head. She unhooked her bra, tossed it aside, then flopped face-first onto the mattress.

The corners of his mouth ticked up. "So, you're on board with this idea, I'm guessing."

"I *so* am." Pushing up slightly, she smiled at him over her shoulder. "I don't remember the last time I had a good back rub." Then she turned back to lie on her stomach once again, her arms crossed on the mattress and her right cheek turned to rest upon her uppermost forearm.

He knee-walked across the bed, slung a leg over her thighs and settled, making minute corrections until he bore most of his own weight. For a moment he simply gazed down at her long, creamy back. Then, leaning forward, he curled his fingers over her shoulders and kneaded them while massaging the heels of his hands rhythmically into the muscles on the opposite side and digging his thumbs into the tightness she carried in her neck.

She groaned long and low, and his cock nearly gave itself a concussion ramming its head against the zipper of his fly. Biting back a groan of his own, he tried to concentrate strictly on the back rub. This was supposed to be just for her, to chill her out and loosen her knotted muscles, but she kept making little noises that did nothing to help his hard-on subside.

He did, however, get the satisfaction of feeling her start to relax.

"You do have mad skills," she sighed, turning her head to the other side.

Once her neck and shoulders lost their rigidity, he moved down her back. At one point, his fingers curved over her sides, their tips brushing the crease where her breasts rose away from her rib cage. Every time he pressed and rotated the heels of his hands, his fingers tugged her breasts against the comforter.

He was so busy keeping his own body in check that it took him several moments to realize she was beginning to lift her upper body a bit with every tug. "Tasha?"

She undulated beneath him, and the low sound in her throat this time had a definite sexual component to it.

Leaning over her, he pressed a kiss against the side of her throat, then moved to lip her earlobe into his mouth and give it a gentle nip.

She shivered.

"Tell me what you want," he ordered in a voice made hoarse with need.

"Touch me," she whispered roughly.

"Isn't that what I'm doing?" he asked, but even as he put the question to her, he slid his fingers more fully onto the side curves of her breasts. "Or did you have something more along the lines of this in mind?"

She twisted her shoulder to rotate her left breast closer to his palm.

Oh, yeah. A rough noise sounded deep in his own throat, and he slid his hand forward to cup the offered breast. And, oh, Jesus. It was full and soft, and he massaged its jiggly weight before capturing her nipple between his thumb and index finger to give it a tug.

"Oh, God, Luc," she breathed—and you would've thought she was spouting the dirtiest words in the universe, so hard did it hit him. His gut twisted, and his heart pounded, and if his dick grew any harder he was afraid one inadvertent knock would splinter it to dust.

Climbing off her, he rolled her onto her back and reached for her jeans. He had them unfastened and around her ankles in seconds flat.

Then simply stared for the next several seconds.

Finally he got his power of speech back. "Look at you, all commando," he murmured—and damned if he didn't sound easy. As if the sight of that neatly groomed little patch of ginger curls at the base of her smooth torso and the jewel crowning the glory of those long, shapely legs hadn't damn near pushed him right over the edge.

Surging up onto his knees, he fell over her, catching himself on his palms and bending his head to kiss her. She lifted her hands to cup his neck and kissed him back.

And he was lost.

He had no concept of time and lost track of how much had passed when he finally raised his head. Knowing it was time well spent, however, he smiled down at her. "God, Tasha. Everything about you just knocks my socks off." And because that was true and he was still uncomfortable exposing how vulnerable it made him, he forced a little wryness into his smile. "It doesn't suck that you're so damn beautiful."

"I know, right?" she agreed dryly. "I am quite the beauty. That's because I'm so great at dressing to accentuate my best features."

The wryness he'd been half faking turned real as he thought of the cleaning duds she'd worn.

She'd been poking fun at herself, but her hands suddenly flew up to pat her head. "Good grief, I still have my bandanna on." Her crooked smile exuded a wealth of self-deprecation. "I really am one helluva fashion plate." Reaching behind her to untie the knot at her nape, she pulled the bandanna off, then shoved her fingers in her curls to fluff them up. She gazed up at him. "You obviously go for the Seattle Grunge look in a big way."

"Yeah, I like my chicks a little rough. I just love a woman who can keep me in line."

"With what, a whip and a chair?" She grinned at him, however, slung her arms around his neck and hauled herself up to kiss him.

And just like that, he was fired up again. He kissed her in return for several long, heated moments before pushing away to slide down her body. Pausing when he reached her navel, he paid homage to it for a moment before moving lower still to stroke her thighs and study her up close and personal.

He raised his gaze to meet hers. "I love the contradictions in your body," he said. "Love that your legs, your arms, are strong as an athlete's. Yet over all that fine muscle is this sweet, sweet, girlie-soft skin."

She'd pushed up on her elbows to stare down at him, and Luc felt the heat of embarrassment climb his throat and onto his cheeks. *What the hell, man?* Undercover agents didn't talk all mushy. Partly to counteract the fact that he'd just done precisely that and partly because it was exactly what he wanted, he thumbed her labial lips apart and dipped his head.

For a second he merely looked. At the sweet, wet, flushed-pink lips, the frilly inner ones and the tiny pearl of Tasha's clit. Then he lowered his head and gently lapped the flat of his tongue from her opening to the top of her slit.

"Ohhhhhh," she breathed, spreading her legs. And he got lost in her sweet-and-salty slickness, in her complex textures. Long moments passed before he became aware of her fingers tangling in the emergent curls he hadn't gotten around to buzz-cutting since his arrival in Razor Bay. And he heard the hitch in her breathing as her grip on him tightened.

"Oh, God, Luc," she panted, "that feels so—" She inhaled sharply as he used the tip of his tongue to feather just above her clitoris, and her thighs tightened around his ears. "Oh, God, I'm going to com—"

"Not yet, *bebe,* not quite yet." He pulled back. "I want to feel you come all around me." He looked for his pants.

Then looked again. "Where the hell did they go?"

She rolled away but came right back. "Here," she panted. "Condoms. Hurry." Then, shaking her head, she scrambled to her knees and closed the distance between them.

"Yes." He watched as she tore the wrapping off and rolled it down his length. "God. Yes. I need inside you. *Now.*" And he turned her away from him.

She fell onto her hands and knees and looked at him over one pale, smooth shoulder. "I want you in me, in me, in me."

"Ah, Jesus, Tash." He smoothed a dark hand over the pale curve of her ass at the same time he inserted his knee between hers and nudged her legs farther apart. Then, thumbing down his erection, he aligned it with her opening and pressed his hips forward, watching as his cock disappeared into her hot depths, inch by inch. Seeing it, feeling her inner sheath wrap all around him like a lubricious rubber band, had him gritting his teeth to keep from going off like a fourteen-year-old. He whispered to her in gutter Spanish he was grateful she couldn't understand and pulled out almost all the way before giving her ass a slap and thrusting back in.

She made a sound both high-pitched and guttural and pushed back against his dick. He pulled almost out again, slammed in and swiveled his hips.

Reaching back, she gripped his wrists to hold him

deep inside her, arched her back, and with a series of long breathy moans, came with cyclone force.

He hissed through his teeth as her interior muscles clamped down around him. When he felt her start to come down, he recommenced a strong, steady thrusting. And grinned with feral satisfaction as she started in once again.

This orgasm was shorter and sharper and, as the last contraction faded, her upper body slid in a boneless heap against the mattress, her arms stretched out toward the headboard. Luc grasped her still-upthrust rear and lasted six, seven, eight more strokes. Then, her name spilling from his lips, he pushed deep one last time and ground against her as he came as if he'd been saving it up for years instead of a couple of days. When the last pulsation faded, he, too, collapsed like a sack of bricks.

Directly on top of her.

THIS IS YOUR IDEA of keeping your distance? Tasha's inner survivor demanded. She was feeling way too good at the moment to give the question the consideration it deserved—but she knew it was a valid one. Because she'd gone and done it now.

She'd fallen moon-faced in love with Luc Bradshaw. It was no doubt the dumbest thing she could have done, but if she truly valued honesty so much, she had to admit it to herself at least.

Because the truth was, she had never felt this way with anyone else, and love was the only explanation. It went so far beyond the physical it wasn't even funny, although she certainly didn't sneer at that part. But he was intelligent and patient and had a great sense of humor, the latter of which she'd discovered in the Bahamas but had buried when everything turned to shit. He was just…a good man, and she loved him. Part of her thrilled right down to her toes at the knowledge.

But her pragmatic side knew if she didn't start holding a part of herself aloof from him and all this out-of-control feeling—and fast—she was going to end up hurt in a way from which it could take her forever to recover. She just had to find a happy medium, a way to enjoy him and the special way he made her feel.

Yet hold enough of herself in reserve that she wouldn't be destroyed when the day came that he went back to his job.

CHAPTER TWENTY-TWO

LUC LIFTED HIMSELF off Tasha, rolled onto the mattress next to her and turned to pull her into his arms for a little after-the-lovin' snuggle. Before he had a chance to reach for her, however, she turned away and climbed from the bed, shooting him a smile over her shoulder.

He didn't miss the fact, however, that her gaze focused on something over his own shoulder. "Gotta use the loo," she said.

That could very well be true. But he noticed she paused to sweep her discarded clothing off the floor, and he knew damn well she wouldn't climb back in bed with him when she returned. She'd be dressed and have something that needed doing elsewhere.

In the week since they'd first made love, he'd felt her pulling away. She was a wildcat in the sack, but everywhere else she'd been growing a little more distant with each passing day. And he didn't know what to do about it.

Okay, that wasn't entirely true. It wasn't outside the realm of possibility that he was partly at fault here. He'd had a helluva lot of opportunities to verbalize how he felt about her.

He hadn't taken advantage of one of them.

Defensiveness caused his shoulders to tighten. Hey, he'd grown accustomed to keeping his own counsel, and in his line of work it wasn't smart to break a habit like that. Not to mention that telling someone you loved them was a big-ass step—and one he had never taken in all of his thirty-five years. Well, if you didn't count his parents, at any rate, which he didn't. So, yes, he'd put it off.

But he sure as hell had done everything except perform gymnastic back bends in an attempt to *show* her his feelings. Weren't actions supposed to speak louder than words?

Apparently not, since they had gotten him goddamn nowhere. Because while she'd shown evidence of appreciating his gestures, the more he tried to demonstrate how he felt, the more tightly she seemed to hang on to the status quo of this lovers-for-however-long arrangement they seemed to have.

The really stupid part was he didn't even remember making such an arrangement. But he supposed it had been implied between them, at least in the beginning. And it likely hadn't helped that he'd never actually *told* her about his almost-cemented decision to give up undercover work. Women seemed to need the words when it came to that sort of thing.

Thinking of all the stuff he'd recently discovered about that night on Andros Island, he realized there were a whole hell of a lot of things he should have put in words.

He got out of bed and reached for his jeans. So, big deal, this was an easy fix. He'd tell her now. Yeah, yeah,

so he should have already done it. But what the hell.
Better late than—

She came out of the bathroom and, as he'd suspected,
she had dressed in the jeans she'd arrived in an hour
ago, along with the lightweight orange sweater that
should have clashed with her hair, yet somehow worked
instead. Seeing him, she paused in the doorway. "Oh.
You're up. I've gotta go back to my place and grab some
stuff for work. I need to get the fire started in my oven
and do up a batch of sauce."

"Spare me ten minutes before you go," he said. "Or
if you're pressed for time, I'll come down with you, because what I have to say may take a while."

"Is that so?" She'd started for the door to the hallway, but his words stopped her in her tracks. Slowly,
she turned back to carefully study his expression. "Care
to give me a hint what this is all about?"

"Sure." Yet, given the opportunity, he suddenly wasn't
sure where to start. So he simply went with the truth.
"First off, I need to tell you I love you."

TASHA GAPED AT HIM for several silent moments, her heart
thundering furiously in her chest. With desperate, joy-
ous hope. With scared-right-down-to-the-bone terror.

The fear won—and that made her furious. So she did
what any self-respecting red-blooded woman would do:
she kicked defensive mode into high gear. "Don't tell
me that," she snapped. "You do *not* get to tell a woman
you love her when you plan to just turn around and take
off any day now for some god-awful life-risking job in

South America. One, I might add, that will keep you gone for God alone knows how long."

He stepped close. "Maybe I will have to take off. But maybe I'm staying."

Maybe. She looked up into his tough-eyed face. *Dear God, Tasha*—this *is what you want to hang your hopes on—a flipping* maybe? How many Good Time Charlies had she watched over the years giving her mother the same kind of weak so-called incentives to fall face-first in love? "Wow," she said coolly. "What an amazingly definitive statement. It must be a real treat to have all your bases so thoroughly covered."

"Hey!" His blacker-than-a-crow's-feather eyebrows met over his nose. "Who the hell said I planned to take off in the first place?"

"*You* did." When he gave her an infuriatingly incredulous look, she qualified, "Maybe not in those exact words, but you told me you love your work."

"And I do."

"Well, we both know what your job involves! So, I rest my case."

"Oh, no. Not quite yet." He stepped even closer yet. "Yes, I love my work. I freely admit that. But maybe I love you more."

"Quit saying that!" *Note again the* maybe, she warned herself fiercely. *When a man qualifies his feelings like that, you do not get your hopes up. Do. Not—you hear me?* She tried to shove him away, but all that accomplished was to knock a curl loose from her braid. Luc, she didn't budge an inch.

"Why not tell you?" he demanded. "I do love you

more than I love my job." Brushing the curl back, he tucked it through a more well-anchored strand. "Think about it, Tash. You and me? We're good together. *Dynamite* good. So, what if I did stay?"

The hope she kept warning herself not to feel bloomed as lush and extravagant as a cactus flower in the dead of winter. It was so sweet and so damn scary—and it sent her into a full-blown panic.

She had, however, learned her lesson about trying to move him and this time took a huge step back herself. "And do what? I built a *life*, you know! All by myself, I did that—you can't just come waltzing in here and decide on your own to turn it upside down without even consulting me. We had a deal. This is a fling and that's all it is. You don't get to go and change all the rules."

He stepped up and lowered his head until they were nose to nose, making her aware of the heat pumping off his still-naked chest. She had to inhale through her mouth to keep from smelling the devastating soap and water and warm, male skin scent of him. She jerked her chin up to show him he wasn't getting to her.

And looked straight into his angry, hot-eyed stare.

"You and I have *never* been just a fling," he said flatly. "We weren't seven years ago, and we sure as shit aren't now. I freely admit I tried to convince myself that's all it was, but I was full of it. It wasn't just sex for me—and, *bebe,* it wasn't for you, either."

"You don't talk for me," she snapped. "Because *I'm* in it strictly for the sex." *Oh, God, Tasha, so much for your Honesty is the Best Policy credo.* Even as she abhorred the fact that she was lying through her teeth, however, she stiffened her spine, looked him squarely in the eye and did it all over again. "And that is all I'm in it for."

His head reared back, and he slowly straightened. He looked her up and down. Inch by thorough inch.

Then it was his turn to pin her in the infrared beam of an assessing gaze. "Well, I'll be damned," he said. "You're scared."

"What?" She took a large step back. Made a rude noise. "The hell you say."

He nodded sagely. "I know—blows me away, too. After everything I've learned about the way you built your pizzeria, from the ground up all by yourself, after watching you show your employees how to run a business with honesty and integrity and seeing what a kick-ass friend you are to the people you care for—damn, Tasha." He shook his head. Looked at her as if she'd sorely disappointed him. "I gotta say, I never expected this. Because the last thing I ever thought I'd hear myself say about you is that you're a coward."

She felt the condemnation like an electric current right down to the soles of her feet. But before she could assure herself that it was for the best, that it was better to let him find her a big disappointment, better to just let him *go,* for God's sake, now rather than after he'd upended her entire life and she was in so deep that she would never recover, a loud knock sounded at the door.

Tasha latched on to the interruption like a woman tossed a line as the cliff's edge she stood on crumbled beneath her feet. But she kept her heartfelt gratitude to herself. Outwardly, she merely raised her eyebrows. "Are you expecting company?"

"No." He shook his head. "I suppose it could be Max or Jake, since neither is big on calling before they come over. But I don't have plans to get together with them. So ignore it—whoever it is can go away. You and I aren't done."

"Oh, we are definitely done." Dear God, they so were—she didn't think she could do this one moment longer without imploding.

No. That type of thinking was for the pampered girls who'd grown up on the town's mountain-and-water-view cliffs. Women like her sucked it up. *No man brings me to my knees.*

Hiding her pain and confusion, she raised her eyebrows at him. "Go put on a shirt. I'll let in whoever it is, then get out of your hair." And without awaiting his response, she strode, head held high, to answer the door.

Damn glad, she assured herself, for any excuse to call a halt to this whole frigging fiasco.

STEWING, LUC STALKED down to the bedroom end of the studio.

But as his gaze swept the area in search of his ivory crewneck sweater, he had to admit that maybe Tasha had a legitimate reason for not trusting his declaration of love. Because, *Jesus, Bradshaw, really? Maybe* he'd be willing to stay?

Not five minutes before they'd gotten into it, he had planned to tell her he was 99 percent sure he intended to stay in Razor Bay. But her reaction to his *I love you* had slapped him back a step. Had made him wonder: Did he want to stay if she didn't want him?

His immediate knee-jerk reaction had been a re-sounding *hell, no!* So, sue him, he'd backpedaled. Covered his ass—and in the process protected his pride.

He located his sweater where he'd tossed it on the floor when Tash had dropped to her knees in front of him earlier. Swiftly erasing the image from his mind—particularly what she'd done in the wake of it—he swept the garment up, gave it a brisk snap to knock off the evergreen needles and leaf bits he must have tracked in from the deck, then pulled it on over his head and thrust his arms through the armholes.

He'd straightened its fit and was pushing his sleeves up his forearms when he heard Tasha's perplexed "Mr. Paulson?"

He froze, then double-timed it back to the main part of the studio.

"How did you know where to find me?" she asked the man in the doorway.

"I wasn't looking for you," his SAC said with his usual impatient get-with-the-program delivery. "I'm looking for Agent Bradshaw." He pushed past her into the apartment.

Luc watched Tasha blink, then turn to look at the man she clearly knew in a different context. "How do you know Luc?"

"He's not a mister, Tash," Luc informed her, coming up to stand by her side. "This is Special Agent in Charge Jeff Paulson. My SAC."

"Your...boss?" She looked between the two men,

then concentrated her attention on him. "Not an embassy worker?" Her eyes narrowed. "Because he's sure as hell the same man who bailed me out of jail seven years ago." Getting right up in Luc's face, she snapped, "You want to tell me how your relationship with this man relates to what happened to me in the Bahamas back then?"

"Do you mind?" Paulson interrupted with brusque annoyance, clearly irritated at having his agenda usurped. But before he could add anything, she whirled to face him.

"Yes," she snapped. "I do—I very much mind. So why don't you just shut up and sit down?"

Delighted with her, Luc almost grinned. The girl had serious cojones; in the entire testosterone-driven DEA, he didn't know a single person who talked to his SAC in that tone of voice.

Paulson wasn't similarly amused, if the way he bristled and drew himself militarily erect was anything to go by. "Do you have any idea who you're dealing with, young lady?"

"A goddamn liar, for starters, *Mr.* Paulson of the United States embassy. I'm going to go out on a limb here and guess that you knew I was in jail all along. That you could have prevented that or, at the very least, gotten me out a helluva lot sooner than you did." She whirled back on Luc. "How about you, hotshot? Did you know, too, that I was being held on trumped-up charges in that damn dark cell?"

He opened his mouth to say, "Dammit, Tasha, we've been over this—you *know* I didn't!" But Paulson, who wasn't known for his forbearance at the best of times, stepped in front of him, facing her.

"Look, lady," he said. "Forget about that—it's immaterial."

"Immaterial to whom?" she snapped. "It happens to be pretty damn relevant to me."

"To the United States government!" he roared. "It is unimportant and of no goddamn consequence to the government. We don't have time for your little hissy fit. The important thing here is the job that needs to be done. And the fact that your government requires Agent Bradshaw's expertise *now*."

Then, as though she had ceased to exist, he looked past her to Luc. "I need you. Wheels up in ten."

Luc watched the color drain from Tasha's face, but before he could tell Paulson where he could stuff his wheels up, she tore her gaze from his SAC's face and gave him a look that nailed his feet to the floor.

It held not one iota of the warmth he associated with her.

"Well," she said. "This sounds painfully familiar. Second verse, same as the first."

Then, dismissing him with an about-face that would have done a soldier proud, she strode out into the hall through his still-open front door. She didn't bother to close it behind her. A second later, before he could so much as draw breath to set his feet in gear, the exterior door opened, then clicked shut behind her.

Softly, he closed the door to the now-empty hallway. He sucked in a deep breath and exhaled it…then turned back to his SAC.

And saw red when he saw the older man tapping his foot and consulting his watch. He closed the distance between them. "You lied to me."

Paulson shot another irritated glance at his watch. "We don't have time for this."

"Make time." If his voice was flat…well, it merely reflected the way he felt at this moment. Angry. Bitter. *Betrayed.* This was a conversation that was long overdue, and he was in no damn mood to allow the other man to continue dodging it. "You lied to me, and when I discovered that and wanted an explanation, you avoided me."

"Avoided you? Hell," Paulson snapped, his voice frigid, "I was on a much-needed vacation."

"Excuse me if I don't show you a whole lot of sympathy. Remember my last real vacation, sir? It was seven years ago—and you didn't hesitate to interrupt it."

"You were needed. Just as you're needed now."

When Luc merely looked at him, Paulson gave him an arrogant-eyed stare. "I'm here, aren't I? I have many talents, but being a mind reader isn't one of them. I had no way of knowing you wanted to talk to me until I got back."

"Oh, bullshit!" He was sick and tired of his SAC's prevarications. It had become painfully evident that when it came to this man, the truth was an extremely stretchable commodity. "I told your admin I needed to talk to you, and I made it clear that it was urgent. You and I both know that Jackie is nothing if not efficient. So cut the crap."

The SAC blew out a put-upon breath. "I wanted to avoid this very conversation."

"Yeah? And which one is that, exactly? The one where I want to know why you lied to me back then and why you're still lying to me now?"

"No," the older man snapped. "The one where you blow up a spotless thirteen-year career in the DEA over a goddamn piece of as—"

Luc took the giant step forward that put him squarely in his SAC's face. "You better think long and hard before you finish that thought, sir. I have never hit a member of my team in that spotless thirteen-year career you think I should be so proud of. But that's damn well going to change if you keep going down this track."

He stepped back. "Tasha is not a piece of ass to me, and she never was," he said flatly, then gave the special agent in charge a searching look. "But you knew that, didn't you? You could tell by something in my manner when I tried to get back to her that night, and you didn't like it, so you arranged to have her thrown in jail while you got me out of the country and back to the job that you deemed more important."

"It *was* more important!"

"You don't get to decide what's important to me!" he snarled, losing his cool completely for the first, the only, time in his entire so-called unblemished career. "It's my fucking life, not yours!"

He might not have spoken, so thoroughly did Paulson ignore his statement. Instead his superior went back to the charge Luc had leveled at him. "I didn't arrange for Riordan's arrest," he said dismissively. "That was the Bahamians' decision. I simply took advantage of it for a day or two before I arranged for her release." As if that settled the matter, he looked at his watch again. "Now, grab your bag. You're needed in Juárez, Mexico." He headed for the door.

"No."

The other man halted, then slowly turned to face Luc, his eyes colder than an Arctic night. "What did you say?"

"I said no. I'm not going to Juárez."

"You are treading a very fine line here, Bradshaw. You might want to think a moment before you tank your career. Because I'm about five minutes from firing your ass. I'd hate to do it, but—"

Luc considered it for about twenty seconds. *Did* he want to shit-can up his career? For thirteen years he had loved the hell out of this job.

He sure didn't love the way he'd been lied to, though, or the dishonorable way that Tasha had been treated at the hands of his department. It made him question what other times he'd been given false intel. And looking deep inside himself, he realized that, when it came to this job, the thrill was gone.

"I'm serious." Paulson interrupted his lightning-fast rumination. "Like I said, I would really hate to fire you."

You can't hate it all that much if you're not even willing to give me a full minute to think about it.

Luc smiled at the older man and guessed by the way Paulson took a step back that it didn't come across real friendly. But his voice was mild when he said, "Then let me save you the trouble of having to do something you'd hate."

A satisfied smile began to spread across the SAC's face, and Luc was more than happy to dispel it. "I tender my resignation, sir. My letter will be emailed to your office this afternoon."

"What? You can't just quit!"

"Yeah. I can." Stepping past his heretofore special agent in charge, he opened the door—then looked Paulson in the eye.

"I recommend you don't let this hit you in the ass on your way out."

CHAPTER TWENTY-THREE

"COWARD, MY ASS," Tasha snapped. Rain lashed the windows out in the restaurant, but she'd started the fire in the pizza oven with apple wood from the stack in the built-in on the south wall, and it was beginning to take the chill off the kitchen. Or maybe, considering she was hauling her final load of wood back to the oven to fill the small space beneath its floor, she was warming up because she hadn't stopped moving since she'd come downstairs.

But that wasn't the point. "When a woman hears a whole lot of maybes regarding something that can affect her future," she muttered, "she's *smart* to show a little caution."

But you do understand that he never knew you were in that Bahamian jail until you told him, right?

"Oh, shut up," she mumbled to her mouthy conscience. But, yes, fine, she did know that. She might have questioned it in the heat of discovering that Luc's boss had known damn well she'd been incarcerated. But the truth was, she knew Luc wasn't the kind of man who would tell her one thing when something entirely different had actually taken place.

She gave herself an impatient shake. Dammit, she

didn't have time to think about that right now. She needed to sauté the onions and garlic, then dice the fire-roasted tomatoes and pull together her spices so she could get her sauce on. She liked to simmer it for a nice long while before the lunch crowd arrived.

Because while that trade tended to be light this time of year, Fridays were always busier than the other week-days. And of course the kids would start pouring into Bella T's as soon as the school bus rolled into town.

Thoughts of the teens almost made her smile. The kids that frequented Bella T's were generally interest-ing, and Tiffany had been sharing the after-school-rush talk in the dining room with her. These days it was all about who was going to wear what for Halloween next week. She'd gotten a kick all this week out of hearing about the various costumes they were putting together. Teenagers could be wicked inventive.

Today, however—well, she wished she could feel more enthused, but she simply couldn't drum up the interest. She just felt…numb inside. Or maybe sad. Or pissed off.

She preferred the latter to the neediness of the first two options. But regardless what specific emotion was chewing at her craw, she'd get over it. Hell, she'd get over *herself.* Just give her a few hours. Or a day or so.

Or a millennium.

The sauce, Riordan. Forget everything else and just focus on the sauce.

She was adding kosher salt, basil and oregano to her stockpot when Jeremy let himself in the back door a short while later.

"Hey," he said and shook like a wet dog before shedding his coat and tossing it on a hook above the wood box. "It smells great in here." He flashed her a big grin. "Okay, it always smells good in here. But your sauce when it's just made? That's extra killer on a day like today."

The smile she mustered up was several kilowatts shy of her usual wattage, and to direct the teen's attention away from that fact, she tilted her chin toward the work table Jeremy had co-opted as his own. She'd piled vegetables on it next to the precariously stacked lidded pots they used to keep the toppings fresh between use. "You wanna get started on the slice and dice?"

A slight frown puckered his brow as he studied her, but all he said was "Sure."

"Excellent." Seeing the sauce finally begin to produce bubbles that popped on the surface, she gave it a good stir, eased down the gas flame beneath the stockpot and went back to thinking about Luc as she reached for a lid. Her fingers had barely touched its cool stainless curve when her hand made a weird spasmodic movement.

And instead of picking it up to seat the lid atop the pot, she knocked it to the floor.

"Son of a fucking bitch!" She stared at it as it clanged off the leg of her workstation and skittered across the floor. It was all she could do not to chase the damn thing down to give it an enraged kick.

"Whoa!" Jeremy gave her a concerned look, and she wanted to kick him, too.

No! No, of course she didn't want to harm a great kid whose only crime was to look at her sideways.

"Are you okay?" he asked.

"Yes," she lied between clenched teeth. "I'm dandy."

He simply stared at her, and she shifted uncomfortably. "Okay, I'm not sure what I am, exactly," she admitted. "But I do know that I don't wanna talk about it right now, all right?"

"Sure. But if you change your mind…" Despite trailing off without completing his sentence, the way he studied her for another interminable moment said loud and clear that he would listen. When she didn't reply, however, he finally turned back to his chore.

She picked up the lid, washed it off and placed it carefully atop the pot. Then, after looking around to see what needed doing next and realizing it was the sausage, she decided she didn't trust herself to cook something that would produce hot grease. Face it, her head wasn't 100 percent in the game today.

She turned back to Jeremy. "Here, let me take some of your veggies." She crossed over to his table, tossed the green peppers into one of the storage pans and the fresh pineapple into another and packed them back to her space. "Finish up the onions. Then you can start frying up the sausage, okay?"

"You bet."

The only sound for the next little while was the rapid chop of their knife blades against the solid butcher-block wood tops. Tasha was aware when Jeremy finished, for he scrubbed down his work surface, carried his containers over to the industrial-sized refrigerator to store until the lunch orders started coming in, then returned with four packages of raw sausage. Soon, the scent of cooking pork blended with that of her sauce.

She tried to concentrate only on things that would make her pizzeria run smoothly today, and for a while she even succeeded—and quite admirably, too, if she did say so herself. So it was with considerable surprise that, apropos of nothing, she heard herself abruptly say, "Some people just aren't cut out for love."

Jeremy's head jerked up, and he stared at her. Then he nodded. "That's true. I've never really talked to you about my mom, but she has severe bipolar disease with IED."

That yanked her right out of her pity party. "Oh, Jeremy, I'm sorry."

He shrugged. "It is what it is, ya know? I'm sure that when she and Dad got married, she thought she was cut out for family life—and I know she loved me when I was little. But more and more her bipolar disorder stepped smack in the way of her ability to show us affection—and the worse the disease became, the meaner she got, which is where the Intermittent Explosive Disorder, or IED, comes in. She did better with Dad than me, and he loved her like crazy. But because of the way it started affecting me, he felt he had to cut her loose."

"Is that what brought you to Cedar Village?"

"Yeah. I got that she was sick, but it was really hard to remember when she was going off on me or hitting me—and I started acting out. I took up with a sketchy crowd and just generally got myself in a lot of trouble." He shook his head. "That wasn't my point, though. *That* is I know from firsthand experience that some people aren't cut out for love. But, Tash?" He looked her in the eye. "You aren't one of them."

She jolted as if she'd brushed up against an exposed electrical wire. "We weren't talking about me."

"Sure we were." He looked at her with eyes that had seen far more than any eighteen-year-old should.

And she paid him the respect of dropping her pretense. "Okay." She gave him a small, self-deprecatory smile. "I guess we were. But you don't know my history."

He laughed. "You're kiddin' me, right? This is, like, a postage-stamp-sized town. I might not have grown up here, but I know that *you* grew up in a trailer and your mama has a reputation."

Well…shit. Of course he knew. As he said, Razor Bay was a small town. A freaking itty-bitty burg that loved its gossip.

"But even if I hadn't known," he forged on, "I'd know that you're packed to the eyeballs with all the right stuff, like that empathy shit. Look at the people you hire. Well, Tiff comes from a functional family and has her act together, but you took on Peyton and me and, admit it, the two of us have had our share of issues."

His praise made her want to squirm in place like a toddler in need of a bathroom, so she raised her eyebrows at him and said with commendable dryness, "You do know that Max and Harper asked me to take you on, right?"

"Yeah, I do. But did they ask you to hire Peyton, too? Or find me a place to live or rope your friend Jenny into teaching me how to research grants and scholarships so I can go to college?"

She simply stared at him.

"See, I do know you," he said. Then he squared his shoulders. "What I don't know is what Luc did."

He told me he loved me, the bastard. He called me a coward.

"But I understand being pissed when someone you care about screws things up. I was hacked off big-time when Peyton dissed my dad. But, I gotta tell you, I'm sure glad I decided to forgive her. Because she messed up when she reverted back to Snotty Peyton, but it was one mistake. And I would have missed out on a whole lotta good stuff if I'd held on to my mad-on."

She opened her mouth to tell him it wasn't that simple with her and Luc.

But then she closed it again, her protest unspoken. Because it was.

It was exactly that simple.

Suddenly feeling a little light-headed, she gripped the butcher block with both hands while she hooked her stool with a foot and dragged it close enough to collapse upon.

So her mother flitted from one relationship to the next and couldn't maintain a lasting one to save her soul. That had nothing to do with her. Jenny had told her and *told* her that she wasn't Nola. She had assured herself of the same thing—and had even thought she believed it.

Clearly she hadn't. And that was pretty damn dumb on her part. Because in reality? She released a breath she hadn't even realized she was holding. In reality she knew a thing or two about lasting relationships. Maybe not so much of the man/woman variety, but she'd had a best friend in Jenny since shortly before she'd turned seventeen. She had other friends, as well—*good* friends. And as Luc had reminded her, she had built a pizzeria from the ground up, and she'd done it on her own terms. She had employees and would have even more if business kept accelerating at the same rate it had been growing since summer.

That's *who I am. I'm not like Mom in any other way, so why on earth have I clung to the belief that I'm her clone when it comes to love?*

Luc was right about something else. She *was* a coward.

But that could change. She pulled off her apron and turned to Jeremy. "Can you hold down the fort?"

"Sure."

"I'm not sure how long I'll be gone."

"Doesn't matter. I can do it. Tiff will be in for lunch, and Peyton is on the after-school to closing shift. We can handle things—and if something comes up that we can't figure out, we have your number on speed dial."

Tasha looked at the pool of pineapple juice on her work surface and the scatter of rinds and the fruit's exotic top that she hadn't yet disposed of. "I haven't even finished this up."

"Go," Jeremy said. "I'm almost done with the sausage—I'll finish that after I clean up here."

"Okay. Thank you." Standing, she crossed to the sink and washed her hands, then dried them on the discarded apron and tossed it in the standing laundry bag. About to head for the door, she wheeled around and crossed to Jeremy. Wrapping a hand around the back of his neck, she pulled his head down to press a kiss to his forehead. Then, releasing him, she stepped back.

"Hiring you was one of the smartest things I ever did," she told him. "Don't ever doubt it."

Then she ran for the dining room. As she let herself out the front door and dashed through the downpour to the side staircase, she was suddenly awash in fear that she might be too late, that Luc had already gone. Paulson had said wheels up in ten minutes and it had been a lot longer than that. And if she'd let him leave without telling him that she loved him?

Oh, God. She'd never forgive herself.

SOAKED TO THE SKIN, Luc hauled ass for the stairs leading to the living quarters above Bella T's. Not that getting indoors in the next few minutes made a helluva lot of difference at this point. He couldn't get any wetter.

So, okay, probably not my most genius move, going out in a downpour without a jacket.

But then again, when his SAC had slammed out of his place forty minutes ago muttering threats about Luc never working for the DEA or Department of Justice again, the weather hadn't been a consideration. Not that the intimidation tactic had particularly worried Luc. He—and more important, Tasha—had a legitimate grievance against his SAC, and Paulson knew it. So, chances were slim that the guy would start a war with him. Not when the fallout was more likely to harm the special agent in charge than it would Luc.

But whether Paulson tried to make things difficult or let their differences slide wasn't even a blip on Luc's radar at this point. Right this moment he had zilch interest in ever working for either organization again.

What *had* struck him like a thunderbolt to the chest was the depth of the bond he'd developed with his brothers over the past seven weeks. He'd realized at Max's campaign party that he no longer felt he had to play an eternal game of catch-up with the existing connection that Jake and Max shared, that they treated him exactly like they did each other. But until this moment, it hadn't truly sunk in how much that meant to him.

Thrilled wasn't a word any self-respecting guy would ever voluntarily utter—yet it was a secret he'd take to the grave that he felt precisely that knowing he had them. That he had *brothers*. He'd never shared a relationship with siblings before.

He liked it. And contrary to his knee-jerk *hell, no* when he'd questioned whether he could stay in Razor Bay if he and Tasha were no longer together, he didn't think he could simply walk away from this family he'd found. He wanted to see Jake and Jenny get married. He wanted to watch Austin grow up and have a front-row seat at the kid's boy-to-man process. He wanted to be the same brother to Jake and Max that they were willing to be to him.

Tasha or no Tasha.

Yet—Jesus—if she cut him out of her life, he didn't know how he could be around her without going crazy.

His mind had bounced from pro to con and back

again until the walls had started closing in on him and he'd just had to get out where he could stretch his legs.

Where he could *breathe*.

So he'd taken off down the beach and hadn't given two thoughts to the fact that it was pouring so hard you couldn't see the mountains across the canal. By the time it sank in, it had literally *sunk in*—his jeans and sweatshirt were saturated, and he could say with authority that that wasn't fun. If he stayed in Razor Bay, which his march halfway down to The Brothers Inn and back had pretty much clarified he intended to do, he'd have to invest in some rain gear. His blood was still thin from years in the Southern Hemisphere, and he was cold to the fucking bone.

When he arrived at the bottom of the exterior stairway, he heard the door above slam shut, and his heartbeat revved into gear like a NASCAR contender. Even knowing Tasha was more likely to make a break for her apartment than run into his arms if she found him coming up behind her, he loped up the steps, taking them two and sometimes three at a time to the small landing at the top. He yanked the door open.

And was just in time to see Tasha down by his doorway. She whirled to face him.

For a few fraught moments, they simply stared at each other. He was still grappling with his thundering heart rate when she broke the silence.

"I wasn't sure you'd still be here," she said, then shook her head. Her cloud of curls swayed, the only bright spot in the gloomy hallway. "Forget that. It's not the main thing I wanted to say to you."

"No?" He strode down the hallway to her. "What would the main thing be?" He wasn't sure whether to brace himself or go for the gusto and embrace a little hope.

"That I'm an idiot." She looked up at him when he stopped a few feet away from her. "You told me you love me and I gave you the brush-off." She took a step toward him. "What I should have said is that I love you, too. And you were right, Luc. I was a coward."

He didn't hear anything beyond her declaration of love. Relief, elation—soul-deep happiness—speared through him. Threading their fingers together, he crowded her against the wall with a full-body press, pinning her hands to the plaster on either side of her shoulders. He looked down into her pretty gray-blue eyes for an endless moment. Then he stamped his mouth over hers and kissed her with everything he had.

He groaned deep in his throat when she wrenched her hands free, wrapped her arms around his neck and kissed him back.

He could have made love to her mouth for an eternity, but he wanted to hear her tell him again that she loved him. So, half reluctantly and half eagerly, he raised his head and stepped back.

She shivered and patted down her clothing. "Holy crap. You got me all wet."

He flashed her a cocky smile. "Then my work here is done."

Tasha gave him a shot to the shoulder with the flat of her hand. "Not that kind of wet, you tool!" Then she laughed, that full, rich from-the-belly laugh of hers.

"Well, maybe that, too, but I was talking about my close, personal relationship with your soaked clothing. What did you do, take a dip in the bay?"

"I walked the shoreline while I thought some things through," he said, then shook his head impatiently, because like her, that wasn't the main thing he wanted to talk about, either. Licking his bottom lip, he stared down at her. "Tell me again, Tash."

She didn't pretend she didn't understand what he was asking. But then Tasha had never been one to play that kind of game.

"I love you," she said, and her heart was in her eyes as she stared up at him. "God, Luc, I love you more than I knew it was possible *to* love a man."

She sucked in a shaky breath, but maintained eye contact with her usual straightforwardness. "You were right, you know—I was being a total chickenshit. I've always considered myself fairly fearless, and in every other aspect of my life I like to think I mostly am. But this romance stuff throws me off my game, and my first impulse is always to run like the wind in the opposite direction. What I finally realized, though, is that I'm not doing myself any favors by attempting to evade future hurt. Not if it only means breaking my heart now. So—"

She squared her shoulders. "I'd really rather you didn't go back to South America, and in all honesty, I can't quite wrap my mind around how this relationship is going to work if you're off putting yourself in danger for huge chunks of time. But if you think we can make a go of it, I'm willing to listen."

Luc felt as if he'd just knocked back a shot of pure

sunshine, and he gazed down at her in wonder. "So you'd try to make it work if I had to leave?"

"Yeah."

"Oh, man, Tasha. I love you so much. But—"

"Oh, God, there's a *but?*"

"Yes, but you'll like this one, I swear. I'm not going anywhere, *bebe*. After you left this morning, I quit."

"You quit what?" Then she gaped at him. "Your *job?* You quit your job?"

"I don't want to work for someone who's done the things Paulson has or told the lies he's told. So, I quit. You need to understand something, though." He bent his knees to bring their eyes to a more equal level. "I'm probably always going to be in law enforcement, and I can't change the fact that I like a little danger in my job. So if you need a deskbound nine-to-five kind of guy, I don't think I'll be able to make you happy."

She leaped on him, wrapping her arms around his neck and her long legs around his hips. "Oh, you just have. You've made me so very, *very* happy. I don't want to change you, Luc, and I can't promise that I won't worry about the risks you take. But I know what you do is part and parcel of who you are, that it's as large a part as Bella's is of me. And I can't see you taking risks just for the sake of taking them, so just come home to me every night." She faltered for a second, then got her verbal feet back under her. "Or I guess I should say as often as you can if you have to go undercover."

"Now, that I can promise you I won't do. Undercover work is just an all-around bad idea for a man with a family."

Her face lit up. "Is that what we're going to be, you and me? A family?"

"Yeah. I plan to tie you to me with everything I've got." Knowing her mile-wide independent streak, however, he held his breath.

But she merely smiled and pressed her cheek against his. He breathed in the faint scent of homemade pizza sauce that wafted from her hair.

Then she pulled back to look into his eyes. "Ordinarily I'd tell you I'd love to see you try."

Giving her a wry smile, he moved a curl out of her face with a gentle finger. "Don't I know it."

"Smart man." She kissed his chin, then tilted her face up to his again. "Not this time, though—I'm giving you a pass. Because that being-tied-to-you-with-everything-you've-got thing?

"It sounds like my idea of heaven."

EPILOGUE

January 17. The Brothers Inn

"I HATE THIS TIE! Bow ties are for losers."

Luc looked over to where Austin was struggling to tie the accessory and grimaced sympathetically. He wasn't all that great at tying his own.

But Max stepped up to the teen with a quiet "Here, let me get that" and untangled the mess Austin had made. He deftly retied the bow, stepped back to straighten two of the black studs in the kid's pleated shirt, then handed him his satin-lapeled jacket.

And all the while the quiet burst-shot on Jake's camera sounded as he captured the moment.

Austin shrugged on his jacket, and Max adjusted it for a better fit on the teen's skinny, but wide-shouldered, frame. Then he stepped back. "There," he said in satisfaction and nodded at the mirror. "Check yourself out. You look like the handsome stud you are." When the boy turned to comply, Max said, "See? Bow ties might be for losers in some situations. But they rock a tux."

"And Max should know," Jake said with a fond smile. "He loves to dress up."

"But not in girls' underwear," Austin said with a huge grin.

Max laughed. "You got that right." He nudged Austin. "But this—well, chicks love a guy in a tux." He grinned over at Luc. "Right, bro?"

"So I've been told." He gestured to his own tie. "Wanna give me a hand, too?"

"You bet." Max came over to stand in front of him and reached for the dangling ends.

Luc heard the camera shutter once again as he raised his chin so his brother could work his magic unimpeded.

When Max was done, he stepped back, brushed a piece of lint from Luc's shoulder and looked over at Jake. "How 'bout you, groom?" he inquired. "You need any help with yours?" Then he immediately answered himself. "Nah, you look your usual *GQ* self."

Luc studied Jake, as well. His youngest brother was impeccable from his sun-streaked brown hair to his sleek black wing tips. Yet, although Jake looked every inch the groom, Luc still found it incredible that he was actually getting married today. "Are you nervous?"

"No," Jake said and looked at Austin. "We're beyond ready for this, aren't we, buddy?"

"Yeah," the boy agreed. "To spare my impressionable mind, Jenny wouldn't let Dad live with us until they were married. She snuck over to his house, like, every night for you-know-what, but God forbid he should move in with us." He grinned when his uncles and dad laughed their appreciation. "So, hell, yeah. We're way ready for this."

IN THE INN'S bridal suite down the hall from the room the men were using, Tasha and Harper carefully lifted

Jenny's wedding dress over her head and helped her arrange the two layers that comprised it. After Jenny wrestled the formfitting strapless satin under-dress into position, Harper zipped it up, then did up the row of tiny pearl buttons on the sleeveless illusion sheath that began at the base of Jenny's neck and skimmed over the under-dress in a slim silhouette.

Tasha carefully fitted the two vintage-look crystal-embellished hair clips into Jenny's updo and placed her friend's silver high heels in front of her. Raising the skirt of her gown, Jenny stepped into them, and both Tasha and Harper stepped back so all three could get the full bride effect in the closet's mirrored slider.

Tasha was the first to speak. "Oh," she said in a little voice. She cleared her throat. "Oh, my God, don't let me cry and screw up my mascara. But, Jenny—" Reaching out to brush her fingertips down Jenny's bare arm, she met her best friend's gaze in the mirror. "You look so, *so* beautiful!" She fanned her fingers at her welling eyes. "Damn." Tearing her gaze from Jenny's reflection, she glanced at Harper. "Did you play bride when you were a kid?"

When Harper shook her head, Tasha shook hers along with her. "Neither did we. That wasn't even a consideration when we were growing up—we were more about how we were going to get our careers off the ground and our butts out of poverty." Then she stepped around to gaze at Jenny face-to-face. "But you, my dear, dear sister of the heart, are the most gorgeous bride that ever was."

Jenny's smile was radiant, and she leaned a bit to the

side to see around Tasha, gazing at her reflection and taking in her wedding gown with its delicately appliquéd lace curving in a beautiful India-inspired design down the front. "I *feel* beautiful. And, God, Tash, I'm so damn happy."

Then her dark eyes and rosy mouth went comically round. "Oh! I almost forgot. I have something for you two." And turning away, she went over to the dresser, where she picked up two gold boxes with elaborate wired-ribbon bows.

Tasha watched as Jenny brought them back and handed one to her and the other to Harper.

"I thought these would look pretty in your hair," Jen said. "But if they don't work with your 'dos, don't sweat it. We'll just have to go somewhere that calls for jazzin' up our hair another time."

Tasha exchanged a glance with Harper. Then they both grinned, tore into the ribbons and pulled the box lids off. "Oh, Jenny," Tasha breathed, staring at the gift within. "This is so pretty." Reaching into the box, she lifted from the cotton batting a dainty double-band silver headband that shimmered with round-cut crystals amid myriad tiny crystal-set leaves and stems.

Harper's exclamation mirrored her own, and the two of them took their gifts over to the mirror to carefully arrange the bands in their hair. Tasha admired the way the ornament looked among her curls. "Sweetie, *thank* you! I feel like a fairy princess." Glancing over at Harper, she found her friend doing the same thing that she was: turning side to side to catch the flashes of crystals among—

in Harper's case—her inky curls. "And, oh, my gawd, you *look* like one!"

They both rushed Jenny to give her hugs of thanks. All three of them were howling with laughter as they mugged for the camera Jake had set up on a tripod and put on timer mode when there was a rap on the door. "Jenny?"

"Hey, Austin!" Jenny crossed to the suite door and pulled it open. "C'mon in! Oh, my, don't you look handsome!"

The teen seemed rooted in place as he stared back at her. "Wow," he said. "*Wow.* You look just like…" Voice trailing off, he shook his head and simply gaped at her in awe. "Like a movie star or something."

Tasha watched Jenny's expression melt. "Awww," she said, reaching out to cup her hand around the jaw of this boy she'd long thought of as her brother. "*Thank* you. That's exactly how I feel today. Do you want to come in and hang out with us? We just put the finishing touches on all this beauty."

He grinned at all of them. "And you did a dynamite job," he replied, exhibiting an early proclivity toward the Bradshaw way with the ladies. "But no. I'm here to get the flower things for our lapels."

"The boutonnieres are in the fridge down in the restaurant kitchen. But get in here for a minute first. We need a photo with you."

"Not another picture," Austin groaned. "Dad's been taking those nonstop."

"All the more reason to be in one with us. Team Estrogen clearly needs to catch up."

Austin gave in and soon fell in with the women's silliness, letting them all kiss him in one shot and cockily posing with his thumbs tucked behind his satin lapels in another. When they finally cut him loose, Jenny gave him an affectionate hug. "Will you bring our bouquets up here, too?"

"Sure."

"Better take the guys theirs first, though, because the guests will be showing up soon, and Max and Luc need to be downstairs to greet them."

"I'm on it," Austin assured her. Catching sight of himself in the mirror, he stopped, reenacted his cocky pose and beamed from ear to ear. "Man, wait until Bailey and Nolan get a load of me in my tux!"

He was still grinning when he left the suite and raced off down the hall.

TIME SEEMED TO GO into hyperdrive after Austin left, and in what felt like mere moments, the women heard the opening strains of Pachelbel's "Canon in D." The next thing Tasha knew, they were down in the hallway that led into the lobby. She and Harper arranged Jenny's short train, then took their places in front of her for the processional.

Through the opening, she could see Jake, Austin, Max and Luc in front of the fireplace, the handful of friends Jenny had invited ranged in chairs facing them. She waited for the right beat in the music, then touched Harper's arm to cue her and watched as newly elected sheriff Max's head came up. He stared at Harper with single-minded focus as she crossed the threshold into the room and commenced the slow step-touch-step march down the room. The guests turned in their seats to watch.

Then it was Tasha's turn, and she realized in that moment that all the Bradshaw brothers shared the same trait. Each had eyes only for his woman. She saw Jake look past her to Jenny still standing in the hallway opening, and when she turned her attention to Luc, it was to find him looking hotter than sin in his tux—and staring at her with possessive eyes.

The ceremony was short, simple and heartfelt. But it seemed to Tasha as though the groom had barely kissed the bride before the entire town was crowding into the inn for the reception. For the next hour she circulated through the crowd, greeting and visiting with whomever stopped her. Which felt like everyone.

Luc materialized in front of her and handed her a glass of wine. "Want to get out of the crush for a minute?"

"God, yes." She let him take her free hand and lead her to the staircase that Jenny had closed off with a velvet rope to keep the reception contained to the first floor. Moving one of the stanchions it was fastened to, he ushered her through, then set the pole back in place. With a warm hand on the small of her back, he escorted her up the stairs.

She dropped onto a settee in the upper corridor. "I don't know why I'm suddenly so tired—it's not like I've been stacking wood all day."

"Have you eaten anything?"

"Sure. I had a slice for— Oh. Breakfast." She gave

him a self-deprecating smile. "Well, that explains why this wine is going to my head. And especially why I was beginning to feel so claustrophobic down there. I usually get energy from being around people, not feel crowded."

"Here, this might help." Luc reached in his jacket pocket and pulled out a square of aluminum foil. He unfolded it and extended it to her.

"Chocolates!" She selected one and popped it in her mouth. "Oh, God," she moaned around the confection. "And not just any chocolates, either, but salted caramels. No wonder I love you so much."

"Right back atcha, beautiful. Which reminds me—I haven't had the chance to tell you how gorgeous you look tonight." He reached out a golden-skinned finger to skim its tip along the curving strapless top of her deep plum-colored gown. "This is hot. I spent most of the wedding wondering what you had on under it."

"God, you're such a perv." She laughed in delight. "I really appreciate that about you, but I wonder what the Kitsap County Drug Task Force would think if they knew. It'd sure be a shame to get fired from the job you've only been on for eight weeks."

"Yeah, I really like this job," he agreed. "But I'm not working tonight, and right now I'm more interested in knowing what you're wearing under that thing. So, tell me. Is it a strapless bra? Or—oh, man—a *thong?*"

"Yes and no. I prefer going commando to a thong." Not that she'd gone so, but she'd let him discover the transparent little pair of panties later.

"Sweet Jesus. This I've got to see."